THE
BROTHERS
PENDRAGON

JOHN CONLEE

Pale Horse Books

Coypright © 2016 by Pale Horse Books

Library of Congress Control Number: 2016911797

ISBN: 978-1-939917-16-4

Cover Design: Sally Stiles

www.PaleHorseBooks.com

Also by John Conlee:

> *THE DRAGON STONE*
> *A CUP OF KINDNESS*
> *THE KING OF MUD & GRASS*
> *IN THE SUMMER COUNTRY*
> *THE HEATER*
> *ROUNDING THIRD*
> *THE VOYAGE OF MAELDUN*

THE

BROTHERS

PENDRAGON

THE CITY

CHAPTER 1

The youth brought his old horse to a halt in a small clearing just beyond the brow of the hill. From there he looked out across a wide valley and had his first view of the gleaming city, its whitewashed walls glowing in the morning sun. After five days of hard traveling, he was saddle-sore and his ancient gelding, a stalwart and uncomplaining beast, was surely footsore. Now, with his destination no more than an hour away, there was no good reason why the two of them shouldn't enjoy a moment's respite.

The lad, whose name was Lute, slid from the saddle and wrapped the horse's reins about a low branch. Snatching up a fistful of grass, he held it up toward the old roan's mouth. He rubbed the horse's neck affectionately before slinging his knapsack down upon a large rock where he soon hunkered down himself. He uncorked his water pouch and swallowed several large mouthfuls. After re-corking the pouch, he directed his eyes once more toward the distant high hill and the sights it offered.

The city he gazed upon was larger than any he'd ever seen. It rose, tier upon tier, majestically up the hillside. On its highest level loomed a many-towered citadel. In the sky floating a short distance above the citadel's soaring tower he could see a small dark shimmering object. He knew it must be the king's famous banner. While he couldn't make out its design, he knew what it depicted—a fierce red dragon upon a field of green.

No longer in any special hurry, Lute remained on the rock for several minutes as he studied the city. He observed the wide river that curved around one entire side of the city providing a natural moat. He saw that below the city the river descended through a series of naturally tiered meadows until reaching a broad, lush valley. From there it formed a wide estuary that flowed down to the sea just a mile or so to the west.

A narrow road climbed up through the valley, eventually leading to a tall wooden bridge that spanned the river. The bridge rested upon huge wooden trestles. Beyond the bridge stood the city's fortified gates. They were double-towered, with a barbican extending out toward the high bridge, the last section also functioning as a drawbridge.

Now the youth noticed the dark specks that moved in and out through those massive gates and down onto the road below toward the valley, specks that were surely people on horses, on foot, in wagons and carts. Because it was the second week of May, the city and the surrounding area would be bustling with springtime activities.

The old horse, grateful for the pause in their journey, seemed perfectly content as he cropped the fresh spring grasses. Lute, though to all outer appearances likewise content, was in fact filled with anxieties. For this place he now studied so carefully offered him nothing but uncertainties. He'd been told to go there, and yet he knew not a single soul living there. He'd been told it was there he would discover his true destiny—for better or for worse—and that the time had come for him to seek out that destiny.

So, dutifully bidding farewell to his mother, he and the old roan had set out. Now, four and a half days later, he was nearly there, his only possessions being the few belongings in his knapsack and his loyal, venerable mount.

Inside his head Lute carried two additional things—two names. One was the name of the man who'd told him he must do this. The other was the name of the man he'd been told to seek out once he'd arrived in the great city. That second name was the name of his uncle, his mother's brother, though until just a few days ago he had never even heard of the man, let alone met him.

Having paused long enough, Lute gathered up his knapsack and re-mounted his stalwart horse. For another moment he gazed across the valley at the great city. Then it was time for Lute to confront his future.

In the broad meadow not far below the tall bridge, a huge gathering had assembled on this perfect May morning. As Lute approached, he could hear their cheering and jeering. They were watching some kind of athletic competition, urging on their friends and shouting good-natured abuse at their friends' competitors. Folks took scant notice of the youth, now on foot, as he led his horse up behind the crowd and stationed himself there. Being taller than just about everyone in front of him, he had a fairly clear view of what was occurring out in the meadow.

Lute saw right away that this was no noble competition, no jousting exhibition between knights or aspiring young noblemen. Not by a long shot it wasn't, for judging from their clothing, all the young men competing in the events appeared to be apprentices and working lads. And the variety of activities they were engaged in—wrestling, heaving the stone, foot races, and the like—were those only suited to commoners.

Apparently Lute had arrived just moments before the

completion of the games, for it wasn't long before the crowd began to disperse, with most of the folks moving back up the road toward the bridge and the city's gates.

One group amongst them, a group of lads whose headwear and bespattered aprons suggested they must be cook's helpers and kitchen knaves, was especially gleeful. "Beaumains!" they chanted, "Beaumains!" Towering in their midst was a grinning lad who stood even taller than Lute. This tall, broad-shouldered young man named Beaumains had obviously won many of the competitions just completed.

As the onlookers moved up toward the city, Lute noticed that amongst them were a few who stood in stark contrast to the others. Mounted upon impressive steeds, these men belonged to an entirely different social class. Clearly, these young fellows were knights, and their regal appearance suggested they might even be members of the king's royal court. Lute wondered why men of such high standing deigned to be here among the others.

"Look at 'em," he overheard a man say. "Never miss the games, they don't, not when Beaumains is competing. Well, ya gotta admit it, the lad's quite a sight to see."

As the knights spurred their horses on up the narrow roadway, the common folk parted to let them through. Lute watched them go with unconcealed admiration. As he did, he began to have thoughts about his own station and status within this world that was so totally new to him. Where, he wondered, would he fit in? Certainly not with the kitchen lads. He was, after all, of noble birth himself, even if the remote little hamlet from which he had just come was hardly a place of wealth, fame, or grandeur. He realized, though, that at the moment he looked more like a commoner than a nobleman. Would his uncle, once he found the man, be able to remedy that?

Lute fell in just behind the company of cooks' apprentices as they moved on back toward the city, rowdy but good-natured lads who continued celebrating the glories of their friend Beaumains. "Up the cooks!" they shouted gleefully, "Down the tailors! Down the saddlers! Three cheers for Beaumains!" He couldn't help smiling and sharing in their delight.

At one point the lad named Beaumains swung about, and for a moment his eyes lighted upon the tall, lithe, brown-haired youth who was leading the horse behind them. Beaumains gave him a nod and a grin, which Lute cheerfully returned. He felt comfortable in the presence of these raucous young men.

After crossing the high, wide bridge and entering the city through its huge and impressively fortified gates, Lute quickly realized that the city's inhabitants were enjoying some sort of holiday, for a festive mood prevailed throughout. Although he wasn't yet aware of it, he'd arrived on the first day of the fifteen-day celebration surrounding the Feast of Pentecost. And while Pentecost was a supremely important religious festival, it was also a time filled with joyful events and holiday exuberance, especially during the five days preceding the Eve of Pentecost.

The youth's deep blue eyes and keen ears drank in the sights and sounds of the city, his senses thrilling to it all. He and his old horse found themselves in a wide, cobble-stoned square filled with carts and barrows, colorful flags and banners, musicians and fruit-sellers. The square was lined on all sides with houses and shops whose upper floors extended outward beyond the lower ones. In the center of the great square stood a beautiful fountain; it was surrounded by a thigh-high wall.

Lute saw that a pair of narrow roads exited the square, one to the left and one to the right, roads that twisted and curved upward toward the great citadel; and he saw that straight before him rose a broad, steep set of stone steps on which many folks were ascending and descending.

The young man realized that the city, like the meadow below it, was built in tiers. The great citadel was its crowning glory, and he found that his eyes were constantly being drawn upward toward that great citadel and the towers that loomed above it.

For several minutes he stood off to one side of this large open square, partly to observe all that was going on and partly in order to collect himself. For as excited as he was by all he saw, he also found it a bit overwhelming.

"Do you need help?" asked a soft voice just off to his left. "You look rather like a lost sheep."

Lute turned and looked down into the face of a young woman whose wicker basket brimmed with fruits and vegetables.

"Thank you, but I'm in no position to be buying anything just now," the youth said to her. His remark caused her to laugh.

"You mistake me," she replied. "I'm not selling anything, only returning home from the market with my purchases."

Lute blushed at his foolish mistake. He'd assumed she was a young fruit seller, of which there were many wandering about the square. "Oh, goodness," he stammered, "how rude of me. Can I help you carry your heavy basket?"

Again the young woman laughed. "I stopped to see if *you* needed help. Not to *ask* for your help."

"Oh, well, yes," he stammered again. "Umm, actually, perhaps you *could* help me. You see, I'm entirely new to the city."

"Yes, I'd been getting that impression," she said, staring directly into his eyes.

"Umm, you see, I'm looking for the house of my uncle."

"Oh yes? And who might that be?"

"His name is Thomas," the youth replied, "Thomas the Earl. He is, or once was, the Earl of Sanham." At that the young woman's eyes widened.

"Thomas the Earl?"

"Yes. You see, Earl Thomas is my uncle, my mother's brother." Now she stared at him even more wonderingly.

"Here," she said, handing him the heavy basket. "You carry this, then, and I shall lead you straight to his door."

"I can't thank you enough," Lute said.

Striding off ahead of him, the young woman moved quickly across the square and began climbing the stairs leading up to the next tier of the city. The youth, still leading the old roan, hurried along behind her, the three of them drawing curious glances from many of the folks they hastened past.

After crossing the next, somewhat smaller city square, they began ascending yet another set of steep steps. Upon reaching the city's third level, the young woman swung to the left, the youth and his horse hustling along behind her. Finally she came to a halt before a high stone archway. A pair of thick oaken doors filled the archway, with a smaller door inset into the left-hand section. An ornate doorknocker, a huge golden bull's head from which was suspended a broad brass ring, adorned the smaller door. Above it was a small metal grille backed by a piece of wood.

"Here you are, then," the young woman said, the first time either of them had spoken since they'd set forth from the city's main square now far beneath them.

"Thank you so much," the youth stammered. "This has been most kind. I hope I haven't taken you too far out of your way."

"I don't often have a reason to visit the more rarified levels of the city," she replied, breathing hard from her physical exertions. "Anyway, it will be easier going *down* all those steps than it was climbing up. Well, young sir, I believe it's time to bid you adieu."

"Thank you kindly, miss. I do hope I'll be able to return the favor some time." He smiled at her, then turned his attention back to the smaller door within the gateway, carefully examining its metal grid and brightly shining doorknocker.

"Ahem," said a voice from behind him. When he looked around, the young woman was still standing there. "Young sir," she said, "might I trouble you for my basket?"

Blood shot into the youth's face. He hadn't realized he was still holding her basket. "Oh my word, please pardon my foolishness. Oh, and now that I know where it is I'm going, perhaps you'll allow me to carry your basket to wherever it is you are going."

But she reached out and took the basket from him. She gave him a fleeting smile, and then without another word she spun about on her heel and set off across the square.

Lute watched her neat, trim form as she strode quickly toward the central steps that descended to the lower levels of the city. As he did, it dawned on him that he had failed to ask her name.

CHAPTER 2

A long silence followed the youth's rather timid initial rappings with the doorknocker. Lute rapped again, this time more vigorously. He was about to give up when the wooden panel behind the small metal grille finally slid open to reveal a pair of eyes, part of a forehead, and a bony beak of nose.

"Yes?" came a creaky old voice.

"Oh, yes, thank you," replied the young man, "I've come to visit my Uncle Thomas. I believe he's expecting me."

The eyes stared suspiciously through the little grille. "No," came the creaky voice at last, "I don't believe he is. You are surely mistaken. *Now, go away!*"

The lad was taken aback. "But sir," he managed to stammer, "my mother wrote to him weeks ago. She told me she'd had a positive reply from him. You see, I'm the earl's nephew. My mother is his sister."

The eyes continued to stare at him through the metal grille. Finally the voice said, "Is that old bag of bones *yours?* If he is, then you'll need to lead him 'round to the garden gate at the back. I will let you in down there. Go down to the end of the wall, then follow the alleyway. It's easy enough. Even a simpleton can do it."

"Thank you. If a simpleton can do it, then perhaps I can as well."

The face disappeared and the wooden panel slid back across the door behind the grille.

Leading the old roan, Lute followed the directions he'd been given and soon found himself outside another wooden door which also had a metal grille in it, though this time with no sliding wooden panel behind it. When the lad stooped down to look in, all he could see was a terrible tangle of overgrown shrubbery. Someone appeared in need of a gardener.

Lute heard sounds approaching through the garden and finally saw the small man as he worked his way through the tangle of branches. There followed the sounds of a lock being opened and removed and of metal hasps being worked. At last the door creaked about halfway open, which was apparently as far as it would go, given the overgrown state of the garden.

The little man motioned with his head for the youth to come in. "The stable is ahead to your right. You can put your animal there. There are no others there at the moment. Maybe you'll find some old oats for 'im. Can't say for certain. If not, he can nibble where he will. When you're finished tending to your bag of bones, you may enter the kitchen up there." He extended his arm and pointed through the garden to where Lute could just make out the back of a sizeable gray-stone dwelling. "I will await you there."

"Thank you. You kindness is appreciated."

The little old man just scowled. Extending politeness to an unexpected visitor seemed to be beyond him.

In the large but neglected stables the lad did find both oats and barley, neither at all fresh, but they would have to suffice for now. He unsaddled the old roan, put him in a stall, and rubbed him down for a few minutes with a tattered blanket he found there. The gentle beast seemed content, so Lute navigated his way through the tangled garden and found the back entrance to which he'd been directed. He entered a cold, dank kitchen which appeared not to have been used in quite some time. Its flagstone floor was thick with grime and dust, its soot-blackened ovens and fireplaces matted with cobwebs.

"Come," said the creaky voice of the unwelcoming little man. Lute followed him through several narrow passageways until they finally emerged in a small and dimly lit room where a fire crackled in a goodly sized fireplace. Two people were sitting in the room on large and comfortable-looking chairs—a middle-aged woman and a man who appeared somewhat older. The lad assumed that the man, who seemed to be asleep, must be his uncle.

The woman looked up at the youth and smiled. She gestured toward a bench that ran along one entire wall of the small room. Lute set his backpack down on the bench and then lowered himself as well.

"He'll be waking up soon," she whispered. "He's been eager for your arrival."

Lute smiled, wondering who she might be. His uncle's wife? He knew little about his uncle, whose very existence he hadn't been aware of until quite recently. He didn't know why his mother had kept her older sibling a secret.

While his uncle continued to doze, the youth's eyes began taking in the room and the two people in it. The woman, who appeared to be maybe five or ten years older than Lute's mother, was rather plainly dressed, he thought, for an earl's wife—if that was indeed what she was. Just a few strands of gray showed in her dark and quite voluminous hair. The pallor of her unlined face suggested that she rarely went out of doors.

The elegant apparel of the sleeping earl contrasted somewhat with hers, though it seemed to Lute to be completely appropriate for a high-ranking nobleman. His wine-red tunic and dark silken hose, though perhaps a bit old-fashioned, bespoke a man of wealth and high social rank. He wore his thin, silvery hair at shoulder length, his beard short and neatly trimmed. As the young lad examined his face, he looked in vain for any resemblance to his mother's face. Because the man looked so much older than his mother, Lute wondered if he might have been aged prematurely by some ailment or illness.

As he waited for his uncle to awaken, Lute noticed that from time to time the grumpy little man who'd let him in kept sneaking peeks into the room. That fellow, the lad concluded, was probably his uncle's manservant, a fellow who'd long since grown protective of his lord. As far as the youth could tell, the grumpy little man and the woman sitting in the room were the only other people about. The large dwelling of the Earl of Sanham seemed eerily empty, eerily silent.

Turning his attention back to his uncle, Lute now realized that the man was awake and studying him. The lad didn't speak, but he smiled at the man, and as he did, he clasped and unclasped his hands unconsciously.

"I'm glad you've come," Earl Thomas said in a soft, kindly voice. "I'm sorry it's taken so long for us to meet. I've thought of you often." He smiled warmly at the youth, a twinkle in his eyes.

"Sir," Lute replied, "my mother never told me of you. I don't know why she didn't."

"She had her reasons," the man said sadly. "Oh yes, she certainly did. And although I wish things had been otherwise, I've always respected her reasons. I suspect she wanted nothing more to do with this place, and nothing more to do with the people she associates with this place—which includes me."

The young man sat silently for awhile, waiting to see if his uncle would offer any fuller explanation of those comments, but he didn't.

"Was it because of my father?" he proffered tentatively. "Was he the cause?"

"You know of your father?"

"No sir, in truth, I really don't. I know nothing at all about my father."

"She has never told you? Well, I guess I'm not so terribly surprised by that. She was hardly more than a girl back then, probably about the age you are now. And your father, he was little more than a boy, too."

"You know my father?"

It was the man's turn to pause. Finally he said, "Well, yes, I do know him, at least to some extent. He's quite a fine man, your father. Indeed, among the finest men I've known. Far finer than his father, whom I also knew. Because I admired your father, I chose to give him my service, service for which, in the end, I paid a considerable price." He glanced down for a moment at the thick woolen blanket draped across his thighs.

Lute sat still and pondered his uncle's words. He'd always assumed that his father had been some horrid villain, some vile high-ranking man of privilege at court who'd taken advantage of his mother before casting her aside. Apparently that wasn't necessarily so. Lute also wondered what service his uncle had given him and what price he'd ended up paying.

"Do you think, sir, that I might meet this man?" Lute said at last. "Do you think that might be possible?"

"Oh yes, it is quite likely that you will," his uncle replied. "But all in good time. But now, young sir, what about you? To begin with, what is it they call you?"

The young man blushed. "Sir, what most of my friends call me," he said with just a moment's hesitation, "is Lute."

"Lute?"

"Yes. It comes from some French phrase, I believe, some phrase that's been shortened down. I think it was once 'Le haut' something or other. Now it's just Lute."

"Lute," the man said. "I quite like it. May I call you that also?"

"Of course you may, sir. It used to embarrass me a little, but it doesn't any longer. I've grown used to it."

"Good. Nothing a bit wrong with Lute. Besides, it's the man who bears the name that matters, not the name he bears. Looking at you now, I think you have a chance to be a man worthy of bearing any name anyone might give you."

The youth blushed. "That's very kind of you, sir. And how may I address you, sir?"

"Thomas will suit me just fine."

"Would it be all right if I called you *Uncle* Thomas? Or just plain *Uncle*?"

The man smiled at the young lad. "If that is what you prefer, Lute, it will suit me perfectly well."

The woman, who had sat silently throughout this whole conversation, now spoke for the first time. "Lute, I believe it will be good for all of us to have you here. Life has been too quiet for us for much too long. It seems to me that you are already breathing new life into this tired old household. Anyway, perhaps now Gwilym"—and she glanced toward the door where the face of the grumpy little man could just be seen—"will show you to your own private chamber."

❖

During the next few days, as Lute became more comfortable living within his uncle's demesne, he began helping Gwilym with the household chores. Indeed, before long, with his uncle's permission, he began tackling many of the long-neglected things that needed attention both inside and out of the large stone dwelling. To begin with he set about making the large kitchen serviceable again, cleaning the ovens and flues, mopping the flagstone floor, emptying debris from the storage bins.

On the afternoon of his second day in the city, he turned his attention to the overgrown back garden—weeding, pruning, and clearing the pathways. As he worked and sweated, his old horse provided him with companionship. The beast found no lack of fodder in the overgrown garden.

On the morning of his third day, Lute declared his great desire to cook dinner that evening for his hosts.

"You are dissatisfied with Gwilym's modest culinary talents, Lute?" his uncle said with a grin.

"Oh no, sir, that's not it at all. I just thought it only fair I should take my turn."

"We once had a full kitchen staff, you know. Those days, alas, are behind us now. But yes, I would be pleased to have you cook for us this evening, if that's your wish."

His uncle's companion, whose name the youth now knew was Julianna, joined in. "That is most kind of you, Lute. And I suspect Thomas might enjoy someone else's cooking for a change also," a comment Thomas didn't contradict.

And so, provided with a large basket and a mental list of the items Julianna had asked him to bring back as well, Lute walked out through the front archway. For the first time since he'd entered his uncle's house, he found himself back out in the city. He knew just what he wanted for the meal he planned to cook—which vegetables, meats, herbs, and spices he would need. And he also knew what he himself had had a great longing for—fresh fruit. This early in the season not many kinds would be available, but surely there would be apricots, spring figs, and perhaps some early strawberries.

As he walked across the open square toward the first set of descending stair steps, in his mind he ran through Julianna's list, wanting to be certain not to forget anything. And as he did, he found his eyes once more being drawn upward toward the great citadel and the dragon banner above it. His uncle had told him it wouldn't be much longer before the two of them would go up to the citadel, a statement Lute found surprising, given the fact that his uncle, even with the help of a pair of stout canes, could barely walk across his own little chamber.

Lute quickly descended to the second tier of the city, where this time he noticed that one whole side of the square was taken up by the city's greatest church, called the minster. After studying this level for a bit, he passed on down to the lowest level, where Julianna said he'd find the largest number of shops and market stalls and where the food would be the cheapest.

Unlike the clothing he'd worn when he first arrived, he now wore a tunic more suited to his social class, even if it was only a faded russet-colored garment he'd unearthed from the chest of clothing his uncle had given him. Modest as it was, the tunic marked him for a nobleman. He'd expected his uncle's clothing to be too small, but that wasn't the case. Before the onset of his ailments, Lute decided, his uncle must have cut a more imposing figure than he did now.

For several minutes Lute moved slowly from stall to stall. He listened to the shoppers as they haggled and bargained, and as he did, he realized he was completely out of his depth. He could never bring himself to do what the others were doing. And since he didn't have a great many coins in his money pouch, he'd begun to fear he wouldn't be able to purchase all the items he'd hoped to.

"Are you, perchance, in need of help?" sounded a voice he'd heard before. "You still have rather the look of a little lost lamb."

"Oh, hello miss, hello. Yes, sadly, I have to confess that I could use your help yet again. But please, miss, before I say anything further, let me apologize for not having asked your name. It's been bothering me ever since. So please, miss, to whom do I have the pleasure of speaking?" The young woman couldn't help laughing at him.

"You would like to know my name, would you?" she said, with just a hint of flirtatiousness in her voice. "Why don't you tell me yours, and then I shall decide whether or not I wish to tell you mine."

"Actually, miss, I'm called Lute."

"Lute? Like the musical instrument?"

"Actually, yes, miss. Though it's really from some French phrase, I think."

The young woman stood there looking at Lute, a broad smile splashed across her oval face. What she saw was an open-faced young man with deep blue eyes beneath a broad brow, brownish hair that curled over his ears, and a hint of a cleft in his firm, square chin. He was tall and slender but broad-shouldered, and his russet tunic was just a little tight across his chest.

What Lute saw as he looked into the young woman's face was a light sprinkling of freckles across her nose and high on her cheeks. He noticed her hazel eyes and that the strands of hair that escaped from beneath her headscarf were the color of honey. The morning sunlight gave them a bright and lustrous sheen. Lute liked what he was seeing.

"My name," she said, pausing just for a moment, "is Gwendolyn."

"Gwendolyn," said Lute, "Gwendolyn. Well, Gwendolyn, I should be most grateful for your help. You see, I've come to buy . . . ." Lute ran through the long list of items he wanted to buy, the young woman nodding her understanding at each item.

"Let us see what we can do, shall we?" she said. "So, why don't we start with the baked goods, all right?"

Lute was hugely relieved to have an expert to guide him through the morning's purchases. And an expert she proved to be, bringing down the cost of every item nearly by half before she'd finished negotiating with each seller.

An hour later, Lute possessed everything he'd come for. And although his money pouch was now much thinner than before, there were still a few coins in it to clink together.

"Miss Gwendolyn," Lute said, "that's twice you've shown me great kindness. Now you really must give me a chance to pay you back. Do you have any ideas how I may do that?"

The young woman with the honey-colored hair and the sprinkling of freckles just smiled at Lute, a twinkle in her hazel eyes. "Young sir," she said, "I am sure I will be able to think of something. Allow me to reflect on it. For now I must be off—or I will be risking the wrath of my mistress, whose errands I must now be completing myself."

"Oh my word, I've kept you from your errands!"

"No need for alarm, master Lute. I shall dispatch them in a trice. Once again, young sir, I bid you adieu."

Lute's eyes remained upon the retreating figure of Gwendolyn until she'd finally disappeared amidst a thick mob of women thronging about the fish wagons.

CHAPTER 3

It was late afternoon on the Eve of Pentecost. Lute stood before the archway in the wall at the front of his uncle's dwelling, his eyes fixed upon the young men who were now crossing the square, young men who had trekked down from the citadel. There were seven of them, all on their way to the great church called the minster on the city's second level. Lute knew who they were—young noblemen who'd recently completed their training for knighthood. Tomorrow morning, as was customary on Pentecost, each of them would be given the accolade and would receive his sword and spurs.

All night long, Lute knew, those seven young men would keep vigil in the minster. For them it was a night of purification, their final act before taking their vows of chivalry at a great mid-morning ceremony. That ceremony was open to members of the nobility, and Lute had every intention of being there. One day, he hoped, he would be a man such as those he now watched, a man who'd been admitted into the holy fraternity of knighthood.

But for the time being, Lute would have to content himself with merely attending the evening service of Vespers. He and Julianna would go to the minster together, while Gwilym would remain behind to attend on Lute's uncle. The old earl had actually been feeling far spryer recently, but he still wasn't up to making the descent to the city's second level. "I am on the mend," he kept repeating, "I am truly on the mend. Lute's being here has breathed new life into these old bones of mine."

Even Gwilym, though he continued to show displeasure at Lute's presence in their household, considering him an unwanted intrusion, had to admit there was truth to the old earl's assertion.

As Lute and Julianna were about to reach the first set of stair-steps, he felt her grip tighten on his forearm. "Wait!" she said in a loud whisper.

It was at that moment that Lute, too, realized that several figures were walking toward them, a group of people who had just come down the steps from the highest level of the city. Lute halted where he was and turned his eyes toward them.

The lad caught his breath. It was the *king himself*—the king and his royal party! They were on their way to the minster. Once more Lute felt Julianna tugging on his arm. She'd already assumed a posture of genuflection, and Lute quickly did as well.

As the royal party was passing by, the king suddenly stopped. He turned toward Julianna and Lute and nodded to them, as was his custom. In the next moment his eyes found Lute's, and as they did, a slightly puzzled look came over the king's face. He tilted his head to one side and brought his hand to his chin, his brow knitted as if in thought. Then he patted his puffed-out lips a few times with the fingers of his right hand. Something seemed to be nagging at the king's mind.

"My liege?" said one the men beside him. "Should we not be moving on?"

"What?" said the king, still staring at Lute.

"Should we not be moving on, Sire?"

The king turned toward the man who'd spoken. "Yes, Ulfin, I suppose we should."

But before he and the others began their descent once more

to the city's second level, the king returned his attention to Julianna and Lute. He smiled at them and gave them a farewell nod. And as he did, his eyes lingered for another brief moment on Lute's awe-stricken face.

Julianna and Lute remained rooted where they stood until the king and his entourage had descended a considerable distance down the stairsteps.

"Oh, my word," Lute finally managed to say, "the king himself! Oh, my word."

"He did seem to take a special interest in you, Lute," Julianna said. "Did you notice?"

"Oh, madam, I was far too astonished just being in the royal presence to notice much of anything. Except how wonderful it felt! Oh, Dame Julianna, how I have longed to see the king! I've hoped for such a moment the whole of my life, and now I have truly seen him, standing no more than five feet away. Who would ever have thought it possible?"

"I believe the earl plans to introduce you to him quite soon, Lute. So I suspect you will be doing more than just admiring him from a short distance."

"Oh my!" said Lute, "*me* meet the king? Julianna, I would have no idea what to say to him."

"Lute, you'll do just fine. Your uncle will make sure of it."

"Me meet the king!" Lute muttered to himself. "I wonder what my mother would think about that?"

At Lute's remark, more intended for himself than for her, Julianna couldn't help taking a sideways glance at the young man, who had unknowingly posed a very good question.

A succession of glorious activities took place throughout the entirety of the next day. First, the high service of Pentecost in the great minster; and after that, the sacred ceremony in which the young men who'd kept vigil the night before officially entered the service of knighthood. Then later in the afternoon, for all the members of the nobility, came the royal banquet held within the great hall of the citadel. And not only was Lute in attendance at the great banquet, so was his uncle, who had been carried there atop Lute's own horse in a special sidesaddle ingeniously contrived by the grumpy Gwilym.

"Hope the old bag of bones won't drop you, my lord," Gwilym had muttered.

"Fortunately, the old bag of bones, like you, has a few more good years in him, Gwilym."

The earl's unexpected appearance at the royal banquet caused a minor stir, for it had been several years since he'd been able to attend any events in the citadel's great hall. When the earl, supported by Lute, hobbled into the large and magnificent room, several knights rushed forth to greet him and lead him and his nephew to sidetable seats quite close to the high table itself. The king's own steward, a knight named Sir Kay, made certain that Thomas and Lute were comfortably and appropriately seated.

"My dear sir," said Sir Kay, "it's been some time since we've set eyes on you! What a delightful surprise to see you once more. So this young lad is your nephew? It's a pleasure to welcome him to our joyous festivities."

Kay was a slender man of middle height, and his face and coloring struck Lute as being distinctly foxlike. Indeed, his amber-colored eyes bore a sly, cunning glint.

"Thank you, Kay," the earl replied. "I don't seem to recall your being so remarkably gracious to an old man such as I."

"My lord, I've made amazing strides since you've last seen

me. I've become ridiculously housebroken of late! Sadly, sir, I've traveled a great distance in the direction of becoming a semi-civil fellow."

The earl chuckled at Kay's remark. "I'm pleased to hear it, Kay, pleased to hear it."

After Kay had moved on, Lute looked at his uncle questioningly.

"Sir Kay has long been one of the court's great pranksters, Lute, not to say one of its troublemakers. Ofttimes, at least in the past, his pranks and gibes were borderline cruel, sometimes crueler than just borderline. If he's become semi-civil, it will be a relief to many, and not least to the king, for whom Kay has often caused embarrassment."

"Why would the king tolerate the man's cruel pranks?"

"Kay is his foster brother, Lute. The king once made a pledge to the man who'd raised him and Kay together that Kay would always be honored in his court and would always hold a position of responsibility. The king, Lute, is a man who never goes back on a pledge." Lute nodded his understanding.

Eventually the most honored members of the court began making their entrances, and as they did, Earl Thomas quietly informed the wide-eyed Lute who they were. Among those entering were some of the king's most revered knights, men such as Bedivere, Uwaine, Agravaine, Gaheris, Gryfflet, and Craddock.

Then walking alone came the king's own personal clergyman, Bishop Baldwin, bedecked in the robes of his ecclesiastical office. Following the bishop came the king's closest advisor, a venerable old sage whose name was Merlyn. A tall, shaggy-haired man attired all in black, he strode across the hall with surprising vigor, his long oaken staff held firmly in his left hand.

"Uncle," Lute said beneath his breath, "I know that man. That's the very man who told me I must come here!"

"If you know only one man in the king's court," came Earl Thomas's whispered reply, "he's the one to know."

Finally the king himself made his grand entrance. As he entered the court through the hall's great door, walking beside him was the most elegant, the most beautiful, woman Lute had ever seen.

Before the king and queen had advanced more than a few steps into the room, everyone rose to their feet. Then every person there dropped down to one knee, with head bowed. Everyone's head was bowed except for one. Lute was unable to take his eyes off of the king and his most beauteous wife.

Once the king and queen were seated at the center of the high dais, the feast began in earnest. Lute was so bedazzled he had trouble taking it all in. Servers glided past carrying a huge variety of dishes; minstrels sang and danced, juggled, performed skits and pantomimes. From time to time Lute's uncle asked him how he was doing, but all the lad could do was smile and shake his head in wonderment.

An hour or so later as the meal was finally winding down, the king left his seat at the dais to wander about the hall and visit with his guests. Having learned from Kay that the old earl was amongst them, the king hurried over to greet him. Standing before Lute and Thomas, he reached out and took the earl's hand in his and squeezed it gently with affection.

"My dear sir, how *wonderful* to see you," he said. "You are looking very well indeed. I doubt if we will be sending you into battle any time soon, but would you consider resuming your seat on the king's council? Thomas, we have missed you and your sage advice."

Earl Thomas smiled at the king's kind remarks. "My liege, I would be pleased to accept. This young man beside me, Sire, is my nephew, newly arrived in the city."

The king directed his eyes toward Lute and smiled. Then a look of recognition came over his face. "Didn't I see you last evening? On the way down to the minster?"

Lute nodded mute agreement.

The king studied him for a moment longer before saying, "I'm delighted you are here. I hope we shall soon become better acquainted."

Lute blushed with embarrassment. Finally he had the presence of mind to dip his head in acknowledgment of the king's words. As for words of his own, at that moment he had none at all.

After the king had moved on to greet others, Earl Thomas whispered, "Lute, those were not just polite words the king spoke to you just now. He's not a man who speaks empty words. If he says he wishes to make your acquaintance, he means it."

Lute remained speechless. Last evening he had seen the king for the very first time. Now the king had actually spoken to him. And the king actually wished to befriend him!

It was the king's custom that at the end of great feasts individuals with complaints or special requests could come before him and voice their petitions. Sometimes he was asked to adjudicate legal or financial squabbles, and sometimes to address personal grievances. Now and then someone appeared seeking the king's help with some great difficulty or challenge. The knights of the court eagerly anticipated such occurrences, for if the king granted the petitioner's request, he might select one or more of them to undertake the mission. The more dangerous and challenging, the more they relished it.

On this afternoon the king, after having addressed a few minor requests, suddenly found himself confronted by something far more significant. For it was then that a young maiden of noble mien entered the hall and stalked up in front of the royal dais. She was dressed as if for the chase, and she looked like someone who'd just arrived after a considerable journey. Her words confirmed that supposition.

"Sire," she proclaimed, dipping her head and offering a curtsey, "I greet you on behalf of my sister." Her voice was sharp and penetrating, and no one had difficulty hearing her.

"My sister, a lady of great worship, has sent me to request your assistance. At this moment, my lord, she is besieged by a hateful tyrant, a cruel and vicious knight who seeks to possess her lands and her person.

"Until now, Sire, through the bravery of her noble knights, my sister has held this tyrant at bay. But my lord, her men are exhausted, injured, or dead; my sister's resources are depleted, her straits dire. She stands in great need of your succor.

"We have heard, my lord, that in this court are some of the finest knights in the world. If that is so, we beg you to send someone with me who can challenge this tyrant and defeat him in single combat. My liege, that is our request." When she stopped, once more she genuflected to the king.

"Damsel," the king said, "what is your name? And what is the name of the woman for whom you are requesting our help? Tell us, too, where it is she dwells."

"With all respect, Sire, at this time I prefer not to tell you those things. But you have my assurances that she is a lady of great worship. To aid her would bring no slander upon your court."

"Then tell us, who is this terrible tyrant who is besieging your sister? Surely you can tell us that much."

"That much I *can* tell you. He is called Sir Ironsides. He is also known as the Red Knight of the Red Laundes."

The king considered her words for a moment before replying.

"My lady," he said at last, "I know nothing of this Sir Ironsides, this Red Knight of the Red Laundes. I have never heard of such a knight. How can I be sure he is what you say?"

"Sire," said a knight seated just at the king's right hand, "I do know of him. He is one of the most perilous knights of the world. Some say, my liege, that he possesses the arm strength of seven men. I once encountered this man and did battle with him. He inflicted severe wounds upon me, and I was hard pressed to escape with my life."

The king turned to look at the speaker. "If that is so, Gawain, then he must be a formidable foe. How did he conduct himself?"

"Most nobly, my lord. It was a fair fight, start to finish."

The king nodded, then turned his eyes back toward the maiden before him.

"My lady, will you not honor my request to tell me your name and the name of your sister? Will you not tell me from whence you have come?"

"At this time, Sire, I must decline to do so."

The king sighed. "If you decline to do so, my lady, then I must decline to fulfill your request, though I do so with heavy heart. If you are unwilling to provide such essential information, I cannot in good conscience place the lives of any of my knights in jeopardy."

"Then I must bid adieu to your *most* noble court and seek succor elsewhere," she replied, scornfully. "I was told that in *this* court I would find the most valiant men in the world. That is something I no longer believe to be true."

"Wait!" came a voice from the back of the great hall. Striding out into the center of the room was a tall young man. He was not nobly attired but wore the garb of a kitchen knave. Lute immediately recognized him—as did almost everyone there—for he was the same young man who had performed so brilliantly in the games the day Lute arrived at the city. Lute racked his brain to recall the young man's name. Then he had it. *Beaumains.*

"My liege," said this broad-shouldered young man who bowed on one knee before the king. "When I arrived at your court a year ago, you granted my request for three boons. As you surely remember, I chose to delay asking two of those boons until a later time. Now, Sire, I wish to make those requests."

The eyes and ears of everyone clung to the words and person of this splendid young fellow, whose brownish-red locks glistened in the torch light. His humble kitchen-knave's clothing couldn't conceal his innate nobility.

"I remember my promise. Make your requests."

"First, I request to be knighted. My lord, I assure you that despite my appearance I am of noble birth"—a claim no one in the court doubted. "I wish for Sir Launcelot to be the one to confer those honors upon me—if he is willing to do so."

"It would be my great honor to do so," said a knight seated only a few seats away from the king.

When Lute studied this man, he felt sure he was one of those he'd seen that first day, one of the knights who'd come down to the meadow to watch the games being played by the working lads.

"Sire," the knight continued, "if you allow me this privilege, I will happily bestow the mantle of knighthood upon a young man of such outstanding promise."

"Let it be so," stated the king. "And now, Beaumains, what is your final request?"

"Sire, I wish to undertake the rescue of this damsel's sister."

"Young sir," the king said, "I have already declared that no knight of mine shall be sent on an adventure of such uncertainty. Indeed, this undertaking is hardly one well suited for someone just entering the knightly ranks. It would please me if you would make a different request, one I can honor."

"Sire, I mean no disrespect, but you promised me three boons. Two of my requests you have honored. Will you not honor the third? Sire, is not a king's promise a sacred pledge?"

The king looked discomfited by the lad's indirect rebuke. "Beaumains," he said, "I have watched you for a year now, and like Launcelot, Gawain, and others, I believe you are a young man of immense potential. I hope to see that potential fulfilled. Do not throw it away at the very first opportunity."

"Grant me my boon, Sire, and I assure you it will not be thrown away."

The king expelled his breath. "So be it, then," he said. "And God speed you, Beaumains, in all your endeavors."

"*What?*" cried the damsel, who had remained in the court and had watched this little scene play out. "My liege, have you denied me the aid of your finest knights, only to agree to send back with me naught but this stinking kitchen knave? That, sirrah, is the vilest insult I have ever experienced. Fie on *him*, sir, and fie on *you!* I shall have nothing further to do with either of you."

She spun about to take her leave, and at that very moment through the great door stepped a tiny man who was leading a huge charger. The warhorse was trapped in harness and bridle of gleaming gold.

"Sire!" the little man cried out, "here I bring Beaumains his destrier. And here I bring the sword with which he shall receive the accolade of knighthood!"

"Well, good for you, little man!" cried the damsel. "Now, get out of my way!" She brushed the tiny fellow aside and exited the hall.

Chapter 4

It was evening on Trinity Sunday. The two-week celebration of Pentecost was over.

Lute, Earl Thomas, and Julianna sat in the earl's small chamber enjoying a light supper. Gwilym, as usual, hovered within earshot just outside the room.

"Lute," the earl said, brushing a few last crumbs from his beard, "I wish to make a request of you." The urgent tone of his uncle's voice brought the youth to attention. "I do, Lute, and I am afraid it is no minor matter."

"Sir, I hope you know that I will do anything you ask of me if it be within my power."

"You are surely aware of how modestly we have been living here, the result of our much diminished means. How, you might ask, does it happen that a nobleman who was once wealthy and important finds himself in such impoverished circumstances? Lute, that is a most pertinent question."

"Sir, I have no complaints about how we live here. You've been extremely generous, and I am quite comfortable."

"Perhaps *you* have no complaints, but I certainly do. How is it, I ask again, that our means have become so reduced? I myself do not know the answer. I *want* to know the answer. That, my nephew, is the task I wish to place before you.

"So Lute, I would be most grateful if you would go and find out what's been happening on our granges. I need you to discover why the income from our farms and lands, once so considerable, has dwindled so drastically. My reeve swears it is through no fault of his own. He swears it is because the crops have suffered from drought and infestations. Nature, he says, is responsible, not mismanagement. I cannot help wondering if—because of my infirmities—certain people have been taking great advantage of us, knowing there is little I can do about it."

"Uncle, if you wish me to go to the lands in your earldom and investigate matters, I am quite willing to do that."

"You have been here such a short time, Lute, I wish I didn't have to ask you to depart again so soon. You are just now beginning to learn about life in the city and life at court, only just now enjoying a small taste of what the future may hold for you here. But sadly, our situation has become quite dire. I've no one else to turn to."

"The king would grant us his largess, were we to request it," Julianna added. "Indeed, he would probably assign someone important to look into things for us. Your uncle's pride forbids him to make such a request."

"Of course it does," the youth replied. "We must cope with matters ourselves if we possibly can."

"You speak like a younger version of your uncle, Lute."

"I would be proud to be a younger version of my uncle, Dame Julianna," Lute said fiercely. "Uncle, tell me what I must do. Tell me where to go and who I must see."

"I shall. But first, go over to the great chest there by the fireplace. Open it and take out everything in it."

Lute lifted the heavy lid of the huge ornamented oaken chest. One by one he extracted the items it contained—a hauberk of chainmail, a short sword and a long sword, a shining helmet, a pair of greaves, a surcoat and a mantle, a pair of golden spurs, a pair of daggers, and several other small weapons.

"All of these items, Lute, I bequeath to you. For your immediate undertaking you will only need a few of them, but when you return you will want them all."

"Uncle, these are the accoutrements of a knight."

"Yes. From henceforth, Lute, you are my knight."

"Sir, I haven't yet begun my training in the art of knightly combat."

"Your training will be of a different kind, Lute. You will learn by doing. After you've returned, then we shall see to the finer points. Now listen to what I am about to tell you, for it is of the utmost importance.

"There is just one man I wish you to seek out, a man who will know the truth of the matter and who will be your ally. Trust him only. Trust no one else, no matter how honest they may seem to you."

Late into the evening Earl Thomas continued speaking to his nephew, telling the youth everything he would need to know in preparation for the task he was about to undertake.

Lute listened carefully, absorbing every detail about the place he would be going and the people he would encounter there. He and the earl both assumed that Lute's journey to his land holdings would be a solitary one. But that assumption would prove to be incorrect. For the youth would not be making his journey alone. He would have an unexpected traveling companion.

As Lute, mounted once more on his gentle gelding, moved across the lowest tier and through the city's main gateway, he was unaware of the fact that several pairs of eyes were on him. One pair of eyes belonged to the man who would soon be joining him. Another belonged to the young woman whose name was Gwendolyn. And there were other eyes upon him as well.

"What are you looking at?" The voice belonged to a young fellow who was standing close beside Gwendolyn.

"Oh, nothing, really," she replied.

"You were staring at the youth on the horse," he replied, a slight edge to his voice.

"Do you know him?" she said.

"No. Do *you?*" The speaker, who was about the young woman's age, was a sturdy lad whose apparel suggested he was probably a blacksmith's helper.

"Not really," she said, "though I've noticed him once or twice during the last few weeks doing errands in the market."

"It appears he's leaving. Probably a good thing. One less snot-nosed nobleman around here is always a good thing."

The young woman did not reply to the youth's bitter remark. But her thoughts did not match the sentiments just expressed. She very much hoped that Lute wasn't leaving the city, at least not for good. And if he was, she didn't agree that it was a good thing. From her point of view, it would not be a good thing at all.

When Lute reached the end of the high wooden bridge that crossed the river beyond the city's main gate, he noticed a solitary figure standing by the side of the road, a tall, lean man dressed all in black. In his left hand the man held a long, oaken staff. It was the man his uncle had called Merlyn, the same man who'd told Lute to come to the city in the first place.

The man held up his right hand, signaling Lute to stop.

"You're on your way to Sanham, are you?" Merlyn said.

Lute's uncle had told him to trust no one other than the man whose name he'd given him. And that name wasn't Merlyn. So Lute wasn't sure how he should respond to Merlyn's question.

"It's all right, Lute, I already know the answer to my question. Lad, I plan to go with you. Well, sort of, anyway. I'll be going on foot, so I won't be able to keep up with you—though I am not a slow walker. But here's my advice, should you wish to take it. On the road you'll be following, it will take you about three days to reach your destination. Tonight, thirty or so miles up the road, you should stop in the small village with an inn called the Black Dog. You will be safe there."

Safe? thought Lute, his eyes widening at Merlyn's words.

"The innkeeper is a friend," Merlyn continued. "I will catch up with you there. Tonight we must have a serious chat. Do not stop anywhere else. If you do, you might place yourself in grave danger. I will see you tonight."

At that the old man turned away and set off taking long, quick strides. He wasn't jesting when he said he was a fast walker.

Lute, still wondering about the old man's ominous words, put the venerable roan into motion once more. It took him a full five minutes before he'd overtaken the lanky figure garbed in black.

Although there were few folks about, the little meeting out on the road between Lute and Merlyn hadn't gone unnoticed. Three men standing high up on one of the towers that flanked the city's main gateway fixed their attention on the pair of figures out on the road.

Soon mounted, the three men spurred their steeds swiftly. As they rode across the high bridge, their horses' hooves clattered on the thick wooden planks.

CHAPTER 5

Merlyn watched the dark speck that was Lute and his gelding as it receded in the distance. Small clouds of dust hung briefly in the air marking their passage. It was a sparsely traveled road, and after the first two or three miles, Merlyn had yet to meet anyone or be overtaken by anyone.

But his instincts told him he was not alone. So when he crested a low hill and saw a thick area of overgrown hawthorn hedge, he stepped quickly off the roadway and burrowed himself down carefully beneath the lowest branches, branches now bedecked with a profusion of white blossoms.

Ten minutes later a trio of riders appeared. Their horses were moving slowly, and to a normal observer they probably wouldn't have seemed threatening. But Merlyn was no normal observer. He lay unmoving beneath the snowy hawthorn branches, watching the riders with narrowed eyes, studying them intently. He didn't recognize them. That fact alone gave him pause, for there were few people in the entire kingdom that Merlyn didn't know. Once Merlyn had seen someone, he remembered him.

They were large men wearing leather jerkins. They weren't heavily armed, though each of them wore a short sword on his left side, a dagger on his right. They rode well-muscled steeds of superb quality, another fact that caused Merlyn concern. Who were they and what were they up to? Merlyn knew he must find out. And he suspected they might have some of the same interests as he and Lute. He had no doubt that they were following Lute.

Merlyn crawled out from beneath the tangle of hawthorn branches and set off at the fastest pace he could make his long legs go. It was no mean pace, but even so, he couldn't keep up with either Lute or the trio of men who were probably pursuing him. Well, Merlyn thought to himself, perhaps we will soon see what kind of stuff this young lad is made of.

Merlyn's words continued to nag at Lute. He'd known from what his uncle had told him that he might face some real dangers when he neared his uncle's holdings. But he hadn't expected any special troubles to surface during his journey. Now he'd better stay alert, better be even more cautious than ever. So he decided it was important that he follow Merlyn's advice and find the Black Dog Inn. Then maybe tonight he and the old man could sit down and have their "serious chat."

Perhaps ten or so miles along the road Lute, always attuned to his horse's needs, sensed that the old roan would welcome a respite. So, veering off from the narrow roadway, they meandered across a meadow toward a lively stream that splashed along between low, grassy banks. The horse soon drank its fill, then began grazing contentedly on the fresh spring grasses. Lute, after refilling his water pouch, sprawled out on a sunny patch of grass. He shut his eyes for a moment. Without intending it, he dozed off.

Two hours later he suddenly sat up and rubbed his eyes. He'd napped so long that the sun was now well past the zenith. It had to be at least mid-afternoon. Knowing that he still had many miles to go to reach his destination for the night, he felt himself a fool.

Rising to his feet, he ran his eyes over the meadow in search of his horse. For a moment he didn't see him. Then there he was, grazing thirty or so yards away. And the old gelding *wasn't* alone.

Also cropping the grasses beside the old roan was an elegant stallion. Its coat was a glossy black, and it had three white stockings and a white blaze on its forehead. Its saddle and bridle, finer than any Lute had ever seen, were trimmed with silver. It was an astonishing sight.

Lute slowly walked up to the glossy stallion. So as not to startle the horse, he ran his hand along its withers as he moved forward toward the bridle. The horse seemed unconcerned, and Lute began to rub its neck affectionately.

"You are a beauty," he said softly. The horse raised his head and whinnied softly. "Oh yes, you certainly are. And you know it, too," he said with a grin. "But where is your master? Or did you just magically appear, newly come from the faerie otherworld? If you did, where is the beautiful princess? Don't you know you're supposed to bring me a faerie princess, a faerie princess most desirous of receiving my love?" The horse just nickered again softly and tossed its elegant head, causing its silver bridle to jingle. "Okay, then," Lute said, "I guess there's no faerie princess."

Lute spent several minutes searching about the meadow for the horse's master, regularly calling out "hello?" He got no response. He wondered if perhaps the horse's master had been thrown and was lying somewhere unconscious; but search as he did, he found no one.

Knowing he'd squandered far more time than he'd intended, and knowing he had a goodly distance still to travel, Lute decided to ride the stallion and lead the roan behind him. If he couldn't find the owner, perhaps he could leave the stallion with the inn keeper at the Black Dog Inn.

Back out on the road, Lute set off at a much faster clip. He felt confident that the old roan, now riderless, would do just fine cantering along behind the stallion.

The trio of riders who'd set off from the city after Lute and Merlyn were thoroughly confused. To begin with they'd been following two sets of tracks, one of a horse and one of a man on foot. Then the man's tracks had disappeared from the roadway. Perhaps he'd turned off to go to some other destination. And after another six or seven miles, so had those of the horse. Now no tracks of any travelers appeared in the dusty road. No one had passed this way for at least a day or two.

The three riders hadn't known the identity of the man who'd left his footprints on the road, though they knew it had to be the man they'd seen speaking to the youth just beyond the city's bridge. But their concern wasn't with him anyway. Their only interest was the youth. And in regard to him they had a very simple plan—keep close behind him till they had the cover of darkness, then bring the youth's journey to a quick and permanent termination.

They didn't know that Merlyn, moving with remarkable swiftness, remained just a short distance behind them.

For four hours Lute rode rapidly, and he did so without hesitation or reservation, for he could tell that the two horses, both well-rested, enjoyed being put through their paces.

The late May sun hung low above the western horizon as Lute came over a small hill. Now in the distance before him he could see the sun reflecting off of a weathercock high above a good-sized structure. About the large building was a scattering of smaller buildings. "It's the village with the Black Dog Inn," he said to himself. "It can't be anything else."

The road ahead of him, he saw, swept in a long, wide curve toward the small village, still at least three miles distant. But Lute saw that if he swung off to the right at the bottom of the steep incline and then cut across the fields, he'd halve the distance and save several minutes. Perhaps he might yet reach the inn before dark.

Looking out from the hilltop, Lute also saw that part way along that broad sweep of the roadway were three mounted men riding abreast. They were trotting toward the village.

Unbeknownst to Lute, half a mile behind those men, his long legs taking mighty strides, walked a tall man in black.

Lute rode quickly across the fields to the right of the trio of men. He paid no attention to the riders, and they were completely unaware of him.

But the tall walker in black was aware of both Lute and the riders. And when he saw their paths converging, the sight created in him a great sense of urgency, for all of them would reach the village well before he would.

It was the youth who got there first. Leading his old roan, he trotted the black stallion in through the central archway between the two long wings of the Black Dog Inn. They clattered across a cobblestone courtyard to the stables behind it. As he passed through the arch, Lute cast a quick glance over his shoulder and saw the sun disappearing behind the hill he'd ridden over ten minutes earlier. He'd done it. He'd arrived at the inn by sundown.

Only moments later the three riders entered the village. They rode directly toward the inviting-looking inn. Smelling the wood smoke from the chimneys and the tantalizing fragrance of meat sizzling over coals, they were sorely tempted to stop. But knowing they now had little hope of finding the rider they'd been pursuing, they didn't. No, they would push on toward Sanham. If they didn't encounter him out on the road somewhere, they were certain to find him there. For now, they would postpone the little bit of business they'd been hired to perform. In another day or two, they would complete it.

Seeing the riders move off down the road away from the village, the old man breathed a sigh of relief. Had he been forced to, he could probably have dealt with the threat posed by the trio of riders. He was happy it hadn't come to that.

Tired from the long, hard walk, the man's steps were heavy as he entered the doorway to the Black Dog Inn. Before even slinging down his cloak and staff, he called out for the serving girl to bring him a tall mug of a dark and frothy beverage.

CHAPTER 6

As Lute climbed off of the black stallion near the entrance to the stable, the hostler's lad greeted him cheerily. But then the boy looked more closely at the horse Lute was riding. When he did, his eyes grew big.

"Hello," Lute said. "Got two more hungry customers for you. Busy night thus far?"

"Oh, no, hardly any f-folks here a-tall," the lad said distractedly, barely able to take his eyes off the stallion.

"He's a beauty, isn't he?" Lute said. The stable lad just nodded, all the while rubbing the horse's neck in awe.

"You wouldn't happen to know who he belongs to, would you?" Lute asked. His question seemed to startle the lad.

"B-belongs to?" stammered the lad. "Oh no, sir. I just takes c-care of 'em. That's about all I knows about." But it seemed to Lute that the lad looked nervous.

"He's not mine, actually. I found him riderless back on the road a ways. No sign of any rider, so I thought I'd better bring him along. Are you sure you don't know who owns him?"

"Oh no, not me, sir. I just t-takes care of 'em." The lad shuffled his feet uncomfortably.

"Would you mind putting them together in the same stall? Would that be all right? They seem to like being in each other's company. Good thing the old roan is a gelding, I guess, or they'd probably be at each other's throats."

"You g-g-go on inside, sir. G-g-get yourself some food. I'll be takin' real good care of 'em. You can surely c-count on that."

"Thank you. I know you will." Lute patted each of the horses, nodded to the lad, and then stepped off toward the back entrance to the inn.

Only a few people were seated at the several tables scattered about the dark dining room. Off by himself in a far corner sat Merlyn. It took Lute a few moments for his eyes to adjust to the dimness, but then he spotted the old man, who was leaning back against the wall, his long legs splayed out before him. Lute walked over to join him.

"Before you go and get too comfortable, Lute, would you mind helping out an old fellow by getting this tankard filled once again? Whilst you're getting something for yourself?"

"Oh, I expect I could," Lute said with a grin. The serving girl knew what Merlyn had been drinking, and Lute asked for the same.

"So, lad," Merlyn said, when Lute returned, "you seem to've added a horse since I saw you last. When I watched you arrive, you were riding one and leading another. How did that come about? "

"It was the oddest thing, sir. After traveling ten miles or so we stopped to take a little break, and I blush to admit that I fell asleep for a bit. When I woke up, this beautiful stallion was grazing right alongside my old roan—saddled and bridled and everything. Don't know where in the world he came from. I wondered if he could've thrown his rider. But I searched all around and didn't find anyone. Couldn't just leave him, so I brought him along. I asked the hostler's lad if he knew who the horse belonged to, but he said he didn't. I wondered, though, if he was telling me the truth."

"Perhaps it was just your lucky day. Even from a distance, he appeared to be quite a fine animal."

"My lucky day? Oh, no, sir, I've never been a finder's-keepers kind of person. I'd much prefer to return the horse to its true owner. I certainly don't plan to keep him."

Merlyn smiled at the earnest lad. "You seem to share many of your uncle's ideas about things, don't you now?"

"I really couldn't say, sir. I've only just begun to know my uncle."

"What you said just now was much the kind of thing he might have said."

"Would you tell me about him, sir? And could you tell me why, if it's something you know, that my mother never once mentioned him to me all the while I was growing up? And could you tell me what happened to cause her to leave the city for good and never speak of it?"

"Oh, dear, Lute, you want me to tell you all that? Well, perhaps it wouldn't hurt to tell you a few of those things. But some of them I'll leave for your mother to tell you—if she chooses to."

"At least tell me about Earl Thomas. What happened to make him so crippled? Was it in a battle?"

"Maybe I'll start a bit earlier than that, Lute. Perhaps I should start with Uther Pendragon."

"You mean the king's father?"

"Yes, that's who I mean. Your uncle was a young nobleman in Uther's court, an extremely promising young knight. But Lute, he was also a man who always spoke his mind. That often is a good quality, but sometimes it can be just the opposite. Thomas sometimes found himself in disagreement with the king's decisions and actions, and when he did, he couldn't help saying so—which didn't endear him to King Uther. On one particular occasion his outspokenness almost got him banished.

"But then the king suddenly died. And after that there was great turmoil in the land over who would replace him. There was great uncertainty about whether or not he had ever had a true heir. As you surely know, after a time our present king proved himself to be the rightful heir, though many of the lesser kings and barons refused to accept him. Your uncle, to his great credit, was one of the brave few who stood by the young king. That was especially noble, Lute, given how much your uncle had been misprized by the new king's father.

"Eventually things boiled to a head, and a great and terrible battle was fought with the king and his loyal supporters on one side and a huge confederacy of rebels on the other. Perhaps you have heard of the Battle of Bedegrain Forest?"

"Oh yes," Lute said, with rapt attention, "I have indeed."

"Your uncle was one of its true heroes. And he was also one of its greatest victims. In the battle he personally downed ten of the king's chief foes. But just before the battle concluded, he received a lance thrust that passed through his right thigh, a thrust so vicious it killed his horse and went through most of his left thigh also. Thomas was fortunate not to be killed.

"When the battle was over, he was found unconscious amongst the dead and the dying. He was close to death, but the leeches miraculously saved him. He remained bed-ridden for weeks, but in time his wounds healed, at least after a fashion.

"Those days immediately after the battle were filled with great joyousness and great sorrow. Many fine men had died and many more, like your uncle, had suffered crippling wounds. But the king's forces had won, the rebels had been put down, and the kingdom was well on its way to being pacified.

"It was also, I confess, a time of riotous celebration. I confess it because I, too, participated in it. As did many of the young men of the king's court; and as did the king himself, and even your grandfather, the Earl of Sanham. He'd come to the great celebration accompanied by his lovely young daughter, who was hardly more than a girl. She was a delight to the eye, and she attracted attention from all the men present, including me. Oh yes, Lute, your mother was quite a lovely young woman." A faraway look came into the old man's eyes, and for a long moment he remained silent, lost in his recollections.

Lute, wanting to know more, finally said, "And what happened after that, sir?"

"Oh, yes, well, there was one young man amongst us who was especially enchanted by your mother. He became enthralled by her innocence and her loveliness. And it wasn't long before both of them, despite themselves, gave in to their awakening desires. They shared a brief but ardent relationship. That, Lute, was when you were conceived."

Merlyn's words had been pouring out in a spate, but suddenly he grew silent. He realized he'd gotten carried away with his recollections and that he'd probably gone and said more than he should have. He glanced sheepishly across the table at the young man he'd been addressing. Lute sat there as if turned to stone.

Finally Lute said, "And then what?"

"Why don't I get back to telling you about your uncle, Lute, that's who I'd meant to be telling you about. Those things I was just nattering about, they're all true. But if you wish to learn more about them, it's really your mother you must ask. She's the proper one to be telling you more—if she wishes to do that.

"But I hope you can understand. We were excited, we were jubilant, we'd just crushed our foes and won the kingdom back once and for all for the young king. We couldn't help ourselves.

For many of us, me included, our joyousness gave way to folly, and in some cases, to total debauchery. Your mother was not the only one who awakened our desires or who fell victim to our lustings. Not by a long shot. Nine months later when your mother gave birth to you, you were just one of many young babes born on or about the very same day."

"Do you plan to tell me about my father?" the young man asked quietly.

Merlyn sat stilly, pondering the matter. Finally he said, "Do you not know?"

At last the lad answered, looking the older man straight in the eye. "No, sir, I don't. I honestly don't."

The older man stared for a moment at Lute. Then nodded his head slowly, lips compressed. Finally he gave a little shrug. "Well, in time you surely will. But it isn't for me to say."

"Is it so bad, sir?"

Merlyn hesitated before answering. "Well, no, not really. No, Lute, it isn't really so bad."

Lute's eyes remained on the old man's impassive face.

For the next hour the two of them sat there together in the gloom of the Black Dog Inn eating their suppers and downing additional tankards of the dark and foamy ale. Neither of them said a whole lot more during their meal, though both of them did quite a lot of reflecting upon the previous, rather one-sided, conversation, especially the young man.

"All right then," Merlyn said after they'd finally finished eating, "why don't we go and have a look at this horse—this horse you say you found—before we head off for our beds."

"Say? Sir, I *did* find him. I certainly didn't steal him!"

"I'm just joshing, Lute. I know you're not the thieving kind. Leastways, I don't *think* you are." The old man was still smiling at the youth.

"Well, that's quite a relief to hear it, sir."

They were soon walking down the center passage in the darkened stables between the two rows of stalls, many of which were empty on this quiet night at the inn. Toward the far end of the passage they came to the stall containing a pair of occupants. "This'll be them," Lute said.

Merlyn leaned into the stall to take a good look, and when he did, the old roan started to come over to him, then suddenly shied away. But it wasn't the old roan that captivated Merlyn's attention.

As his eyes took in the wondrous sight of the glossy black stallion with the three white stockings and the white blaze on his forehead, the old man groaned audibly.

"Oh my goodness," he finally said. "Lute, what have you done?"

THE RIDERS

CHAPTER 7

The lad's no good. Pains me ta say it, but I tell ya, the lad's just plain no good. Never has been, never will be. And that's the truth of it."

"And I say you're wrong. He's got a lot o' good in 'im, that lad. Oh yes, he's a wild one, no doubt about that. But I've seen 'im perform a few good turns. P'rhaps the good be buried far deep inside o' him, but he ain't so wicked as you make 'im out ta be. There's a good bit o' good in that lad, there surely is."

"That's what *you* say."

The two speakers, clad in the homespun garb of husband-men, were watching a young lad as he put his horse through its paces out on the green grassy expanse behind the manor house. He was a bold and reckless rider who gave little thought to his own safety or to that of his horse. Whenever the lad was out there careering and careening about, it was a brave man, or a total fool, who dared set foot anywhere near the same patch of ground.

"He'll break his bleedin' neck one o' these days, sure as I stand here. He's done in two o' the lord's finest horses a'ready. Like as not, that there one'll be next."

"But you've never seen a finer rider for his age, have ya now," said the second man. "I'll bet you never will, neither."

"No, I'll give you that. The lad can surely ride."

"Oh yes, that young feller can ride like the very devil his-self."

Both men chuckled.

The two husbandmen continued watching the young rider as he took his mount over three high jumps in succession, the elegant, exquisite horse sailing over each of them almost effortlessly.

Letting out a loud cackle, the youth whacked the horse on the rump with a small whip in his left hand, then pushed the steed as fast as it could go back toward the stables. Even before the horse had skidded to a halt, the rider had hurtled his slim, lithe body off its back and dashed on foot toward the manor house. A stable boy, used to the reckless ways of the young lord of the manor, was there to grab the reins of the sweaty horse the lad so casually abandoned. He led him off to the stables to be properly attended to.

"He be just fifteen," the youth's defender said to his fellow observer.

"Maybe he be just fifteen, but he's been the way he is ever since he was a little bitty 'un. He's never changed and he never will."

"Nah, he ain't nearly bad as you make 'im out ta be."

"P'rhaps not, p'rhaps not. Though maybe . . . he be even worse than I say."

The lad being observed and commented on by the two men was the son of the Earl of Oakdon, a lesser nobleman whose small earldom occupied a corner of land projecting into the great North Sea not many miles north of The Wash. It was a remote yet beautiful area of woods and dales, scattered amongst which were the holdings of many small tenant-farmers, farmers who kept half their crops, the other half going to the earl.

In actual fact, the young man was the foster son of the earl, for the earl and his wife had had no children of their own. But he'd been treated like royalty ever since he'd come to the earl as a wee babe.

One morning an ornate wooden cradle containing the child had been found by a fisherman washed up on the seashore. Where the cradle had come from, no one knew. Perhaps it had been washed overboard from a ship. The man who found it could tell by the fine quality of the cradle and the silken garments in which the babe was wrapped that the child was of noble birth. Hoping to ingratiate himself with the old earl, he delivered the child to him. Indeed, his act not only earned him the earl's good will but a leather purse stuffed with coins.

From his first arrival, the boy had been petted and pampered. Having no siblings with whom to share the earl and his wife's affections, he'd quickly become their darling, the apple of the old earl's watery eye.

The lad soon proved both extremely bright and extremely athletic. By the time he was three, he was tearing around the fields on the back of his pony. By the time he was five, he could recite the Creed and the Pater Noster in Latin. By the time he was twelve, he was fluent in French—and he'd also beaten up his tutor for daring to correct his pronunciation. By the time he was fourteen, he'd become a real danger to every young female within thirty miles.

Now at age fifteen, he was a slender youth of slightly more than middle height. But slender though he was, his physique belied an unexpected strength, as many a local lad who crossed him soon discovered. The youth was quick and strong and blessed with remarkable agility. He became a left-handed fencer, and before he'd reached fifteen his prowess at that sport surpassed that of most mature noblemen.

He was a handsome young man, his face and skin as pale

as those of a romance heroine. His hair was such a dark shade of red that in most lights it appeared to be black. His nose was long and narrow, his lips wide and thin, his close-set eyes a startling shade of light gray-blue. When he directed his gaze at someone, he did so with an unblinking stare, often causing the recipient to experience a cold shiver.

His name was Mordred.

The Earl of Oakdon was as proud of his young son as any father could be. While he wasn't entirely oblivious to the young man's passionate nature and his frequently misdirected energies, he was a tolerant and loving man, willing to overlook the lad's faults and to cherish his many talents. Now that Mordred was fifteen, the earl knew the time had come for his son to begin training for knighthood. And he knew that to do that properly, the youth must leave the earl's domain and go to the king's greatest city in the land of Logres, there to begin his tutelage under the guidance of one or more of the king's most celebrated knights. The Earl of Oakdon had high aspirations for the lad he considered to be his son.

And the lad, though never one to reveal his innermost desires, secretly possessed even higher aspirations for himself than did his father. He considered knighthood a given. He considered his joining the ranks of the Knights of the Round Table a near certainty. He even dreamed of some day being invited to join the king's inner circle of advisors. And he had another dream, a secret dream, one he would never share with anyone. But in his heart, he believed it was something he was *destined* to achieve—and achieve it he would, he told himself, by whatever means were required.

The earl was fortunate to have several trusted retainers

working for him, men who were responsible for overseeing the well-being of his small domain, and men with much worldly experience as well as considerable martial prowess. When it came time to send the lad away to be trained, the earl would select two of them to accompany the youth as he journeyed to the king's great city.

After considering the matter, the yeomen the earl selected were men called Tib and Grim, a pair who complemented each other well. The earl prized Grim for his strength and outdoor skills, Tib for his quick intelligence and his ability to cope with unexpected challenges. With them, he believed, Mordred would be in good hands. He would, that is, so long as he didn't do anything to take himself out of those good hands. But with a lad such as he was, there was always that danger.

So only a few days after the Feast of Pentecost, Mordred and his yeomen attendants set off on their journey to the south. Their destination was the great sparkling city that lay near the country's southwestern coast, the great city that had been completed thirty years earlier at the bidding of the king of Logres, King Uther Pendragon.

For the earl and his wife, it was a tearful departure. Their son shed a few tears also, though by the time he and his companions had ridden no more than a furlong they'd long since dried. His parents' eyes remained upon the riders as they receded into the distance, but the young man they so adored cast no glance behind him. His eyes were on the future, a future he saw filled with a succession of brilliant achievements. And the last of those achievements, he privately vowed, would be the most brilliant achievement imaginable. He would allow nothing and no one to stand in his way of achieving it.

That first morning, with Mordred setting the pace, the three men covered a great deal of ground. Tib rode close behind Mordred, holding the lad's massive warhorse on a lead behind him; while Grim, riding last and in charge of their laden packhorse, had to labor hard just to keep up. The youth himself was mounted upon a sleek, berry-brown palfrey, the finest horse in his father's stables.

Their journey would take them slant-wise across the middle of Logres in a southwesterly direction. The first main city they would come to was Nottingham, and then it would be on to Coventry and then Gloucester. Before reaching their destination they would need to travel roughly 200 miles; their journey would probably require four or five days—though far less if they continued at their initial pace.

Toward late afternoon on their first day, after eight hours of steady riding, they found themselves approaching the outskirts of Nottingham.

"Young sir," Tib inquired, "are you perhaps ready to take a break?"

Mordred just smirked. He knew that taking a rest break was what his companions wanted and needed. As for himself, Mordred was neither hungry nor tired.

"Yes," he agreed. "Why don't we do that? We don't want to run the horses into the ground, do we?"

His remark brought no reply, though both Grim and Tib knew that their young charge had never been one to worry over-much about the condition of his horses.

So they stopped at the first roadside inn they came to, where they turned their mounts over to the care of the hostler's lads. Moments later they'd settled themselves at an old plank table made of three rough, broad boards laid upon sturdy saw horses. It was a dark and grungy little place, but the smells emanating from the kitchen set their juices to flowing just the same. As for Mordred, so did the sight of the young lass serving them, whose blouse and skirt didn't conceal the rounded contours of her ripe, young body.

When they'd nearly finished their meal, Mordred excused himself to visit the inn's primitive loo, located far out in the field behind the building. After ten minutes or so, when the lad hadn't yet returned, Tib asked Grim to go and see what was keeping him.

"He ain't there," was Grim's reply when he returned. "Don't know where he is. Looked all about. The horses still be there, so he can't've gone so far."

"Have you seen anything of the serving girl recently?" Tib asked, his eyebrows raised.

"Can't say as I have." Then, realizing what the other man was suggesting, he grinned and shrugged his shoulders. "What'd'ya s'ppose we should do, Tib?"

"Nothing we can do, I think," Tib replied. "Just wait until he decides to come back."

"He's usually a quick one at that kind of business," Grim said. Tib said nothing; with lips pursed, he simply nodded his agreement.

Indeed, just over half an hour later the lad returned. "Ready to be off, then?" he said, cheerily.

"All ready sir," they both replied with straight faces.

Now it was Tib who took the lead, for he said he knew of a way to go that would keep them from having to pass through the midst of the small city of Nottingham. They rode for an hour along a trail that cut through deep woods and occasionally passed through small open meadows filled with tall grasses and wild flowers. They saw few folks along the way, and the few they did see eyed them with caution and gave them a wide berth. It wasn't until they'd emerged back into the open fields beyond the city that they realized that all this time they'd been followed.

Now, no more than a hundred yards behind them, rode a small group of armed men. There were five of them, and they were making no effort to conceal their hostile intentions, for all of them had begun shouting vicious slurs and insults, all directed at Mordred.

Tib, Mordred, and Grim stopped and swung their mounts around. They sat still, watching the small group of men who were approaching, men who continued hurling vile epithets at Mordred, the least vile of which was "lecherous jackanapes." As the riders drew nearer, Tib and Grim dropped the leads to the extra horses and loosened the swords in their scabbards.

Now the five men slowed their approach and spread out into a single well-spaced line, all the while still hurling insults at Mordred.

When they'd reached a point where they were no more than twenty yards away, Mordred suddenly spurred his mount straight at them. With his sword arm raised, he took aim at the man who was riding in the center of the line.

That man whipped out his weapon and prepared to fend off Mordred's threatened blow. But his reactions were too slow. As the young lad neared him, it appeared that his blow would be directed right at the man's head; but as soon as the fellow lifted his sword to ward off the youth's blow, Mordred suddenly redirected his sword and swiped the razor-sharp brand straight across the man's unprotected mid-section. The sword fell from the astonished man's hand; he cried out in pain and slumped forward on his horse's neck.

The rider next to him charged at Mordred, who simply parried his overhand blow and then buried his slender blade deep in the man's chest.

The other three men, quickly weighing their options, decided upon flight. For two of them that turned out to be a wise decision. For one, perhaps not. Because it happened that that fellow was the one Mordred chose to pursue, his vastly superior horse running the man down within a hundred yards.

The little skirmish was over in less than a minute. Tib and Grim had remained right where they were during the entire thing. When the youth finally returned to them—his eyes gleaming, his cheeks flushed with excitement, his exquisite horse barely breathing hard—they offered him no words of congratulation.

They had just observed their young charge dispassionately chop down three men who would surely die, men whose anger toward young Master Mordred was no doubt justified.

But theirs was not to reason why. Their purpose was to see the lad safely to Logres' great city.

Tib and Grim had never felt any great fondness for their young charge, and what they'd observed had done nothing to improve their opinion of him. It had, however, reinforced their belief that Mordred was far from being an ordinary young man.

CHAPTER 8

Down the dusty road rode three grim-faced men in leather jerkins. They were the same trio of men—hired mercenaries—who'd set off from Uther Pendragon's great city two days earlier in pursuit of Lute. Thus far they'd been thwarted in their intentions. It would probably take them another day or two to complete their mission, now that Lute had slipped through their fingers. But surely no longer than that.

Toward the three rode another trio of swiftly moving riders, two of whom were leading additional horses. The young man out in front was mounted upon an impressive stallion, and the three mercenaries eyed it with envy. Under other circumstances, they might have acted upon their envy. But this was no time to swerve from their original mission, one that promised them a lucrative payday.

Mordred slowed his mount as he approached the three unknown riders. He sized them up at a glance, sensing they might pose a real danger, one far greater than that posed by the foolish men who'd pursued them the day before. Tib and Grim made similar assessments. Readying themselves for what might occur, they pushed back their cloaks and loosened the swords in their scabbards.

But the two sets of riders passed by each other without incident, each making token acknowledgments of the others. Once they'd ridden a bit farther, however, all of them cast quick glances back over their shoulders, just in case the other riders' intentions weren't as benign as they'd appeared.

Feeling secure once more, these two small groups hurried along their way, neither having any further concerns about the other. Nevertheless, Mordred filed away a picture of these men in his mind, as was his wont. He wanted to be sure that if he ever encountered them again, he would remember having met them.

Several hours later another curious incident occurred, and for some reason this one alarmed Mordred far more than the previous one. For as Mordred, Tib, and Grim were passing through a narrow combe between two gently sloping hills, atop the hill to their right a rider suddenly appeared. He sat silhouetted against the late afternoon sun upon a magnificent black stallion. As the steed stood stock still on the crest of the hill, some seventy-five yards distant, its lanky rider stared down at them with obvious interest. Tib, who'd noticed the fellow also, lifted a hand in greeting. The distant rider, however, offered no gesture in reply.

"Friendly bastard," Mordred muttered, as the three of them continued along the road.

In only another minute, the black horse and its rider were lost from view. But for Mordred, the sudden appearance of this horse and rider had sent a chill up his back—not a common occurrence for the intrepid youth.

"Tib," Mordred asked, "that fellow back there on the hill. Did you recognize him?"

Tib hesitated before replying. "Perhaps, young master, though I can't be sure. I thought he looked a bit like someone I've seen in the city, an old fellow rumored to be a close confidant to the king. I can't say for sure if it was him."

"The king's confidant?"

"So they say. Quite a strange old bird. Most folks find him a bit frightening."

"That was a truly magnificent steed."

"That there steed," Grim said, joining in, "magnificent though he were, he surely did give me the jitters."

"Me, too," Tib admitted.

"Didn't know my father sent me on this journey with a couple of old women," Mordred said with a chuckle.

Tib and Grim guffawed at Mordred's remark. But the truth was, that great black steed they'd glimpsed on the hilltop had given all three of them the jitters.

Two days later, on a wet, gray afternoon, Tib, Grim, and Mordred reached the end of their journey. A light drizzle fell upon them as they rode slowly up the winding road toward Uther Pendragon's great city. The city did not glow as it had on that May morning three weeks earlier when Lute had arrived; nor were any great festivities going on.

The sound of their horses' hooves on the high wooden bridge was muffled by the dampness of the planks, and when they passed through the city's main gates they were met by no great flurry of activity. Most of the booths and carts in the cobblestoned square were covered with canvas or oilcloth tarpaulins; still, a certain amount of subdued activity was occurring, and the riders paused to view the entire scene. All three of them ran their eyes over the buildings around the square and the few people who were milling about. Then, inevitably, they raised them toward the great citadel that towered above them, a great gray fortress now enshrouded in mist.

For a moment Mordred sat quietly on his mount, his eyes

remaining upon the dark, looming castle. Then he began whispering softly to himself:

> *"Stark gray towers, rising in mist,*
> *Stone upon stone,*
> *The masons' soaring work . . . "*

Tib and Grim exchanged glances. They'd seen the lad behave similarly before. And as before, his little waking reverie lasted only a brief moment; when he came out of it, he turned his eyes toward his companions. "Lead on?" he asked Tib.

Each of them knew that the place where they'd arranged to lodge was located on the city's second level, one level up from where they now were, but at that moment they were in no hurry to get there. Indeed, that was because the several alehouses on the city's lowest level had snared their attention.

Tib pointed across the square toward a vine-covered establishment not far from the central stairway. The sign hanging before it said "The Fox & Grapes." It certainly didn't look like a high-class establishment, but Mordred had no qualms about rubbing elbows with his social inferiors. There'd never been anything touch-me-not about the lad. Besides, in his mind just about everyone was his inferior, regardless of a person's position or social status. So he was quite accepting of the lower social classes, because *of course* they were lesser beings.

So while Grim, holding up a shiny coin, set about luring a young boy into watching their horses, Tib and Mordred went on into The Fox & Grapes.

"You've been here before?" Mordred asked Tib as they looked over the occupants of the crowded room.

"Oh yes. Best ale in all Logres." He grinned at the young man, relieved that their journey was now over. His responsibilities weren't yet fully discharged, for he and Grim would need to keep a close eye on the youth in the coming days; but soon now two of the king's own knights would begin mentoring the lad in matters that were beyond Tib and Grim's purview.

Grim soon came to find them, shouldering his way through the rough crowd, a crowd mostly made up of young apprentices from the nearby shops, as well as a wide variety of rather dubious-looking women. Moments later a stocky young man, still wearing his ironmonger's apron, came over and plopped himself down at an empty place beside Grim at their rough plank table.

"Ya mind?" he asked.

Mordred gave him a welcoming nod, and the young man nodded back. Then he buried his nose in his tankard of ale and drank deeply. When he looked up again, he discovered that Mordred's cold, gray-blue eyes were still on him. The young man tried locking eyes with Mordred, but Mordred's steely gaze so unsettled him that he looked down at his tankard. When he did look up again, Mordred's eyes were still on him.

"You wantin' sumpthin'?" the young man blurted out at last. "Why you keep lookin' at me?"

Tib and Grim shifted in their seats, not happy about the direction things seemed headed.

But Mordred quickly retrieved the situation. "Excuse my rudeness," he replied graciously. "I'd no intention of giving offense. I was staring at you, friend, because I was trying to figure out what it is you do. I've decided that you must be a blacksmith. Am I right? Your clothing, as well as your forearms, with all their burns and scars, seem to suggest that."

The young man, who was not a young man of particularly

great intelligence, stared back at Mordred, not quite sure what to make of him. Finally he said, "Aye, I am a blacksmith, leastways almost."

"Are you a maker of swords, by any chance?"

"Nah, not no sword maker. Just general ironmongery. My master, though, he sometimes gets called upon to make weapons—pikes and halberds and such like. But nah, the sword makers, they be mostly up at the castle. They don't like ta dirty their hands with what us workers down here hafta deal with." The lad lifted his tankard again and swilled the rest of his drink.

"I'd like to come and watch you work," Mordred said. "I've always believed that the kind of work you do has great value. Every bit as important as what those fancy sword makers do up at the castle."

The young man shrugged, not really understanding what Mordred was getting at. Tib and Grim weren't following Mordred's drift either, though they'd long since realized that their young charge often did and said things that defied easy comprehension.

All the while they'd been sitting there, the greater part of the conversations going on around them appeared to concern someone named Beaumains. The whole room seemed rife with rumors of his glorious deeds. This Beaumains, whoever he was, had gotten many of these young men extremely excited.

"Who's this Beaumains fellow they all seem to be talking about, friend?" Mordred asked their new acquaintance.

"Hah. These fools're all so keen on Beaumains. They all seem ta think of him as one of them. Let me tell ya, he ain't. He's no more one of them than you are." His words sounded a bit like an accusation.

"Sure he is," said a fellow at the next table who'd overheard those words. "He be one of us sure as I sit here. Didn't he live up there in the castle with all the kitchen lads for a whole long year? Didn't he eat and sleep and work right alongside 'em? And never a single complaint, neither. Worked his fingers to the bone, so they says. Never lorded it over 'em a bit. Why, if he don't be one of us, then I'm a horse's arse."

"Not much question about that," another man said.

"Beaumains did every blessed thing the lads did, every blessed thing," another man said.

"Every blessed thing except one," came a new voice, prompting good-natured laughter.

"Oh yeh, right enough he didn't do that," another man said. "Not that there wouldn't've been many a maid a-willin'."

"Where is he now?" Mordred asked.

"They say he's about to take on the Red Knight of the Red Laundes," one man said. "They say that after Launcelot knighted him, the two of 'em tested their strength against each other and fought to a draw!"

"They say," came another voice, "that he's defeated Sir Perimones, Sir Pertelope, and Sir Persaunte of Inde."

"All the while being reviled by that Savage Damsel, a-callin' him nothin' but a smutty, stinkin' kitchen knave!"

"He'll sure prove her wrong!—the vile-mouthed trollop, the filthy scut!"

"Done it already, he has. Look out, Red Knight of the Red Laundes, Beaumains is a-comin' for ya!" All the lads within earshot gave a hearty cheer.

"*Pah!*" scoffed the young blacksmith's apprentice sitting across from Mordred.

"He sounds like quite a fellow," Mordred said, cocking his head to one side.

"And all I says to that is *pah!*" exclaimed the youthful ironmonger. Then he got to his feet and stomped out of the alehouse.

Outside, the blacksmith's apprentice pulled his hood over his head, hunched his shoulders, and stepped quickly back out into the drizzle. He didn't notice the young woman who was just then coming across the square with her basket, the young woman named Gwendolyn. If he had, he would have surely stopped to speak with her, for he was more than sweet on her. Lately, though, he'd been worried about her affections, ever since the arrival in the city of that young nobleman a few weeks ago. Although she denied it, he wasn't so thick as not to know he had a serious rival.

Gwendolyn paused for a moment outside The Fox & Grapes and watched as the young fellow strode quickly toward the smithy. She quite liked all the attention Rafe had been lavishing on her. It was nice knowing that someone was totally captivated by her. Still, she knew she should really be setting her sights a bit higher. That young man named Lute, now, he was someone she believed she could be very interested in, if she dared go down that path. There were serious obstacles on that path, no doubt, but she was sorely tempted to see if she couldn't surmount them. She recalled her old mum's oft-repeated dictum—"nothing risked, nothing gained."

As she stood beneath the overhanging roof of The Fox & Grapes just out of the drizzle, another young man stepped out from the doorway. He too, she thought, had the bearing and appearance of a nobleman. He wasn't quite as tall as Lute and was slimmer in build, but, even at a glance, she could see that he was confident and self-possessed. And his face, she realized, was strikingly handsome.

"Excuse me," he said to her, noticing her standing there alone beneath the cornice, "are you by any chance familiar with a lodging house called The Willows? It's supposed to be on one of the lower levels of the city." Mordred already knew the answer to his question.

She placed her hand on the side of her face and tilted her head as if giving the matter serious thought, though in fact she knew well the lodging house he meant.

"Let me see. If I'm remembering correctly, it's on the next level up. In front of it are the two wide-spreading trees that give it its name. If you go up the central stairs, it will be off to your left, over on the side of the square opposite the great minster."

"Thank you, miss," Mordred said with a smile and nod of acknowledgment, "it shouldn't be so hard to find, then. And would you happen to know if there's a public stables close by? My men and I have five horses that will need caring for."

"No, I don't know about that. But I would be very surprised if The Willows doesn't have its own private stables. It's reputed to be one of the finest lodging houses in the city."

"Even better," said the young man. Then he suddenly stuck out his hand to her. "I'm Mordred. Soon to be the Earl of Oakdon. Though you've probably never heard of tiny little Oakdon."

"It's off to the northeast, I believe," she said, "perhaps not so far from Lincoln and Nottingham?"

"You are educated as well as beautiful," Mordred said, grinning. "But you still haven't taken my hand."

She reached out shyly and grasped only the tip end of his fingers. "I'm Gwendolyn," she said, softly.

Tib and Grim came through the doorway just as the young woman was withdrawing her hand from Mordred's.

"Good God," muttered Grim, "the lad don't waste no time, does he?" Then he stepped off into the drizzle to track down the boy he'd hired to watch their horses.

"These are my men," he said to Gwendolyn, clapping Tib on the shoulder and pointing after the receding figure of Grim. "Tib, she's given us directions to the lodging house."

"Thank you, miss," Tib said, "most kind." Directions to the lodging house were something he wasn't in need of either.

By the time Grim was back with their horses, the young woman named Gwendolyn had stepped quickly away through the light rain.

As she did, she found her mind going back over the little scene she'd just been a part of. And she found herself wondering about this young man she'd just met, this confident and handsome young man. He was handsome all right and extremely self-assured; not at all shy like Lute. She realized that she found herself feeling rather disturbed by her brief meeting with this handsome young nobleman. She wasn't quite sure why.

CHAPTER 9

Lute slept fitfully at the Black Dog Inn. What had Merlyn meant when he'd suddenly bellowed, "Lute, what have you done?"

As far as the lad knew, he'd done nothing he shouldn't have. Yet Merlyn had spat out that remark like some terrible accusation.

Merlyn was already breakfasting when Lute entered the room. When Lute offered the old man a soft-spoken greeting, all he received in return was a tight-lipped nod.

Finally Merlyn said, "That *creature* you brought here, Lute . . . ." But then his words trailed off.

"Yes?" Lute finally replied, feeling somewhat abashed. "Sir, what's so bad about that creature I brought here?"

"Apparently you don't know the truth about him."

"The truth about him? Sir, all I know about him is what I've already told you."

Merlyn sat silently, scratching nervously at his beard.

"Well," he finally said, "to be honest with you, I don't know the truth about him either. But I feel very, very strongly that he is a creature you must have no further dealings with. Lute, I pray to God the time you've already spent with him won't have harmed you irreparably."

"Goodness, sir, I really do not know what you mean. With respect, sir, he is just a horse."

"No, he *isn't* just a horse." For a long moment the two of them stared at each other rather sullenly.

"Then I guess you know something that I don't," Lute said at last.

Merlyn breathed a deep breath. "As is often the case," he mumbled into his beard.

After finishing their none-too-cheerful breakfast, the two of them headed once more toward the stable, but they were intercepted in the courtyard by the hostler's lad, the same lad who'd helped Lute the night before.

"The m-master," the boy stammered, "he says ya c-can't leave the horse here. I knows you were a-hopin' ta do that, but he says ya c-can't. He wants 'im out of here, s-s-sooner the b-better." Lute and Merlyn nodded their understanding.

"That new horse of yours, Lute, he certainly isn't too popular. *You* don't want him, *they* don't want him, and it seems that even his own *owner* didn't want him. Now, I wonder why that might be?"

"There's only one reason I don't want him," Lute replied. "He isn't mine. If he were mine, I wouldn't give him up for all the rubies of India." Despite himself, Merlyn chuckled at Lute's hyperbolic remark.

Feeling a bit more companionable once more, the two walked side by side down to the far end of the stables where the horses were stalled together. Seeing Lute and Merlyn, both of the large beasts came over to the opening to greet them.

But as Merlyn reached out to pat the old roan, the horse shivered and then shied back away from his outstretched hand. The black, however, did not. He extended his neck and noble head out through the stall opening and rubbed it against the side of Merlyn's gray-bearded face. Lute was startled by the animals' very different reactions.

"Well, Lute, it appears that I may have to learn to ride a horse."

"*Learn* to ride a horse? Sir, are you saying you don't know how to ride a horse?"

"Yes, that's what I'm saying. I've never learned to ride, lad, because no horse I've ever encountered would let me ride him. Not until now, perhaps. No, every horse I've ever been near has had an instinctual fear of me—just like your gelding. Can't say I blame them, really. Sensitive creatures, horses; feel things most of us can't. And in my case, there's something about me that frightens them. But the black here seems to be an exception.

"Whether that's good or bad, I can't say. Anyway, since we can't leave him here, and since I can't have you riding him ever again, it seems that I will have to try it myself."

Lute watched as Merlyn patted the black affectionately. The roan eyed the old man warily from a safe distance.

"Well," Lute said looking around, "it seems we're on our own this morning in regard to doing things. I'll go ahead and get the both of them saddled and ready to go."

"And I'll try to work up my courage in regard to riding a horse. Given a choice, I would much prefer to walk."

"When you get used to it, you'll be surprised. Honestly, sir, there's nothing in the world as wonderful as tearing along on a truly fine horse. And that, sir, is a truly fine horse."

"Well, Lute, I suppose I'm about to find out if it's as wonderful as you say."

Half an hour later the two of them were ready to set off. They could see that the innkeeper and the hostler's lad, while keeping their distance, were also keeping a keen eye on them, both of them eager to see the last of the great stallion on which Merlyn was now rather precariously perched.

"I'll ride slowly alongside of you for a while," Lute said, "until you get the knack of it."

"No, Lute, I didn't tell you this before, but we won't be traveling together for the next day or two. My plans will be taking me on a different route. So for the time being, lad, you'll be on your own. But do try to get there as quickly as you can. And when you do, go and find the man your uncle told you to find. Try not to do anything to call special attention to yourself. Once you're there, take your time as you begin to get the lay of the land. Don't rush into things.

"I won't be too far away, so if any unexpected crisis develops, I might be able to lend a hand. But remember, Lute, this is your adventure. You are, no doubt, going to face some challenges, challenges neither of us can anticipate. But your uncle and I have confidence in you. I feel sure you'll come through just fine."

Lute didn't feel so happy about having to proceed alone. But, when he'd first agreed to undertake this mission, as far as he knew he'd be doing it completely on his own. He never expected to have any help from anyone, let alone Merlyn. So even if Merlyn was leaving him for a time, he was still better off than when he'd started out. And anyway, as Merlyn had said, this was *his* adventure.

So all that long day, Lute and his old horse ate up the miles. Lute didn't dare stop to take any naps, as he'd done the day before, and he didn't give the ancient gelding many chances to rest. Throughout the day they met few others on the road, and, by day's end, Lute felt sure his destination wasn't far away.

Since Merlyn had warned him about drawing attention to himself, Lute decided not to stop at an inn. Spotting a thick grove of alders a quarter mile or so off the road, he decided that was where he and the roan would quarter that night.

While Lute moved steadily along the road toward Sanham, Merlyn jounced along atop the elegant stallion; and he hated every minute of it. But as the day wore on, Merlyn gradually grew more accustomed to it, and his initial belief—that riding a horse was both physical and mental torture—began to subside. By mid-afternoon, he'd begun to gain at least a tiny bit of confidence in his abilities. If only riding a blasted horse didn't make his inner thighs and his bottom quite so sore!

And just as Merlyn was beginning to feel quite a bit more confident about his riding skills, the black suddenly bolted.

"Stop! You dratted creature, stop!"

But the dratted creature had no intention of stopping. Merlyn drapped both arms about the creature's neck and held on for dear life. Finally, after maybe half a mile of frantic dashing, the beast slowed to a steady trot, allowing its terrified rider to breath a sigh of relief.

"What are you to up, you accursed creature? Where are you taking me? Oh, lord, why did I ever climb up on a damnable brute like you?" As if in reply, the horse snorted.

The great black steed suddenly halted atop a knoll, a place from which they could look down upon the narrow road that passed between high hills.

And only a moment later, along the road beneath them came a trio of riders. Was this what the horse had wanted him to see? Was there some strange method in this accursed creature's madness?

Once more the old man failed to recognize the riders, just as had happened the day before. From their travel-stained appearance, Merlyn guessed that this threesome had already traveled for quite some distance. In all probability, they were headed toward King Uther's great city, a day and a half's journey ahead of them.

When one of the riders glanced up and saw the figure on the black horse, he raised a hand in greeting. But Merlyn was too deep in his thoughts to respond—for a feeling had begun to grow inside him, a feeling that these three riders were no ordinary folks. As sometimes happened, the old man was experiencing some kind of premonition. But a premonition of *what?* Merlyn was rarely frightened. But suddenly, he was.

Only moments later the trio of riders passed beyond Merlyn's view. But the old man and the horse remained rooted where they were.

"So why did you bring me here, hmm?" Merlyn finally whispered into the ear of the black. "You did that on purpose, didn't you? What *are* you?" he mused more to himself than to the horse. "Do you mean *well?* Or do you mean . . . *something else?*" The black horse only snorted.

For the remainder of the day, Merlyn wondered about this strange and rather frightening creature he was now stuck with. Where had he come from? Why had he suddenly appeared to Lute? Was that by accident or design? And if by design, *whose* design? Was the horse meant to present some special temptation for Lute? If so, had the lad avoided the temptation and passed some sort of test? Or had Lute's association with the horse, brief as it had been, caused the youth real harm?

Most perplexing to Merlyn was why the horse didn't fear him the way virtually every normal horse had always done. Clearly, this was not a normal horse. Was it perhaps, Merlyn wondered, in some sense a demonic horse? Did it not fear him because the two of them shared some deep-seated kinship?

As he pondered these matters, Merlyn reached down and patted the horse's side.

"Beneath our differing flesh," he said, "it seems that you and I may have some things in common. Anyway, whatever the case, for now it appears that we are stuck with each other."

As if in answer, the horse let out a mighty snort.

❖

Standing behind a dry-stone wall, a man in a leather jerkin kept watch on the dusty road. Evening was drawing on, and he was about to leave his post and return to the inn in the nearby hamlet when a solitary rider came into view some half mile away. The man watched as the rider veered off the road to the right, directing his mount toward a coppice of tall trees.

For a moment he wondered if he should ride back to the hamlet and report what he'd seen to his companions. It would be easy for the three of them to dispatch the young man during the night. But then, he thought, why not just complete the deed himself? Why share the honor with his so-called friends, two men for whom he had no special affection? All he had to do was wait a bit until the youth had settled down for the night, then steal up and stab him as he slept. Easy as anything.

So he sat himself down out of sight and leaned back against the stone wall while he chewed upon a cold and greasy capon's leg. He would wait for a couple of hours and then creep over to the coppice on foot. Yes, the whole thing would be as easy as one, two, three.

Within the grove, Lute found a level spot thick with fallen leaves where he could bed down for the night. There was no need to hobble the old horse. He knew that the loyal old beast wouldn't stray far. He removed the saddle and spent a few minutes rubbing the gelding down. The youth and the horse shared a deep affection, and both of them enjoyed the physical contact. Lute readily admitted that he had lusted after the beautiful black; but he knew he could never forge so close a bond with the black as he had with the old roan.

Knowing it would be risky to do anything to reveal his presence, he made no fire but ate a cold meal of cheese and bread, washed down by the water in his drinking pouch. The early June night shouldn't be too chilly, and he had his thick cloak to wrap about him. After making a final check on the horse, Lute settled down in his leafy bower. It was a clear night, and the light of a gibbous moon shone down on him, filtered by the boughs that arched above him.

It was a couple of hours later that Lute was startled into wakefulness by the whinnying of his horse. Wolves, was Lute's first thought. But surely not this far south in Logres! He rolled over quickly and snatched his knife from its sheath. And, as he leapt to his feet, his attacker came at him.

The man came charging through the trees and hurled himself at Lute. His shoulder crashed into Lute's chest and knocked him flat on his back. As Lute fell, his head banged hard against a thick tree root. The man dropped down on top of him, pinning the youth's arms to the ground with his knees. He was a large and powerful man, and Lute could smell the odor of his body and his fetid breath. Lute still grasped his knife in his right hand. But with his arm so firmly pinned to the ground, it was useless.

"Easy as one, two, three," he heard the man muttering through clenched teeth. "Sorry 'bout this, lad, ain't nothin' personal—business, strictly business."

As the man lifted his right arm to strike the fatal blow, there was a sudden commotion in the trees just behind him—the sounds of someone approaching. The man cast a swift glance back over his shoulder and found himself staring straight into a huge and hideous face. It was the face of Lute's horse.

For the briefest of moments, the man's sudden fright and confusion caused him to ease the pressure on Lute's arms. And Lute, using every ounce of his strength, jerked his torso to the left. Lute's sudden twisting caught the man off guard, and he nearly toppled off of the lad.

Lute realized his right arm was free. With a vicious swing of his knife-wielding arm, he slashed at his attacker's face. Emitting a great cry, the man rolled away from Lute. Then he scrambled on all fours toward an opening in the trees.

In a trice, Lute was on his feet. He took two steps and leapt onto the man's back. Lute's body flattened him to the ground, knocking the wind out of him.

"Lie still," Lute hissed, "or I will finish you."

The man did lie still, but only for a very few seconds. As soon as Lute was no longer on top of him, the man leapt to his feet and tried to make a dash for it.

In the next instant, Lute's knife was spinning through the air in pursuit of the fleeing figure. It was a completely instinctual reflex for Lute. As soon as he'd done it, he wished he hadn't.

The knife caught the man square in the back. He took only two more steps before sprawling forward, landing face down, the haft of the buried knife pointing skyward. The man's body twitched for a few seconds. Then the twitching stopped.

An eerie silence enveloped the grove. Lute was stunned. He stood there silently, trying to collect his wits. Finally he looked over at the old, innocent-looking roan still standing just a few feet away.

Lute walked over to horse and draped his arm about the horse's neck.

"Thank you, old friend," he said, "thank you."

CHAPTER 10

As soon as Tib, Grim, and Mordred had settled into their rooms in the Willows—Tib and Grim sharing one small chamber, Mordred enjoying a larger one next door to them—the lad went straight to bed, not even bothering to eat any supper. He was a youth of inconsistent habits, sometimes going two full days without sleep, other times sleeping for as long as sixteen hours at a stretch. On this evening, he was asleep long before dark, and he slept a solid ten hours.

Eschewing breakfast the next morning, Mordred was dressed and away from the lodging house shortly after dawn. He headed straight for the central stairsteps and climbed to the city's third level. He studied the residences of the lesser nobles and wealthy merchants, then bounded on up the final set of steps to the city's highest level—occupied entirely by the great royal fortress and its surrounding complex of buildings and grounds.

Few folks were up and doing at that hour of the morning, and those few were men with a variety of mundane tasks ahead of them, and so it appeared that the lad could wander freely and explore the outer areas of the great complex without challenge or impediment. He was especially eager to see the athletic fields where he knew the young men who aspired to knighthood spent much of their time training.

He found the large grassy area after just a few minutes of searching, and he climbed to the top of the three-tiered rostrum that overlooked the green expanse. He estimated that the entire area was perhaps 150 yards in length and 100 yards in width. At this early hour of the morning it was completely unoccupied. As he looked down at it, he imagined himself out there riding against the finest competitors. And he felt sure it wouldn't be long before what he envisioned would become reality.

And then he turned his eyes again toward the looming citadel. He saw that its four great corner towers were connected by high curtain walls, walls upon which even now armed guards paced; behind those walls and rising up in the center of the fortress was its massive central keep. At the very top of the keep rose a smaller tower above which floated King Uther Pendragon's famous dragon banner.

Separate from the main fortress and located not far behind it was another, much smaller, castle—an edifice in many ways more a palace than a castle. It too had many towers and turrets. Mordred saw that this smaller, quite self-contained structure, was encircled by a deep, water-filled moat. He also saw that it was connected to the main fortress by a crenelated walkway that passed high above the moat. The lad surmised that it must be the private residence of the king and his queen—their fortress within a fortress—where they lived in privacy with their most trusted associates and personal servants. It would not be a place where public functions were ever held, Mordred guessed. No, they would surely take place only in the great hall that occupied the ground-level floor of the fortress's great central keep.

Although Mordred wasn't easily awed by things, he found himself viewing all of these sights with both delight and envy. Wouldn't it be wonderful, he thought, to be the lord of all he surveyed. Of course such a thing was far from his reach, at least for now. But it never hurt to dream. And then he lapsed into one of his reveries:

> *"The lord of all Logres, mighty and munificent,*
> *Looked down from his tower*
> *Upon his green land:*
> *All who abode there were at his beck and call.*
> *It was he who decided*
> *Who rode, who strode,*
> *Who labored, who leisured.*
> *It was he who decided who lived and who died."*

"Hello," came a voice from behind him, startling Mordred and bringing him back to the here and now. He turned around to see who was addressing him and found himself looking into the smiling face of a tall man who appeared to be in late young manhood or perhaps early middle age. The man wore a hooded woolen cloak that enveloped his head and shoulders; but when he loosened it for a moment, Mordred could see beneath his hood the gleam of a small circlet of gold.

"Oh, Sire," said the astonished Mordred, quickly dropping down upon one knee. "My liege, forgive me if I have wandered into forbidden territory."

"No, you haven't," the king said, still smiling. "These grounds are open to members of the nobility. Nonetheless, it would interest me to know who you are and what you are doing here at this time of day."

"Oh, most certainly, my lord. My name, Sire, is Mordred. I am the son of the Earl of Oakdon and his heir. I've just arrived in the city to begin my training for knighthood. I was so very eager to see the place where my training would take place that

I didn't want to wait until tomorrow morning when it will actually begin. I was so excited last night that I couldn't sleep. I just had to come here, Sire, as soon as I possibly could."

The king couldn't help laughing. "I know what that's like," he said. "I had many of the same feelings not so many years ago. I'm sure that I have met your father, Mordred, though I can't say we're well acquainted. As for your training, do you happen to know which knights will be in charge of it?"

"Oh yes, Sire. Their names are Sir Ascamour and Sir Mador de la Port."

"Excellent fellows, Mordred, quite good choices. Ascamour for swordsmanship and Mador for horsemanship, I suspect?"

"Indeed, my liege. They were highly recommended to my father by a friend of his, an older knight named Sir Jordan."

"Who is also a close friend of mine. How is your horse? Will you be well mounted? If not, perhaps I can help."

"Oh, Sire, that is most generous. But I've brought two very fine horses with me, the best in my father's stables, an elegant palfrey and a sturdy destrier."

"Excellent. Well, Mordred, I believe I'll continue my morning stroll now. You may freely continue your explorations. I only ask that you not go any closer to the royal residence. The queen and I are very particular about preserving our privacy."

Mordred dropped to one knee again and dipped his head. "Of course, my liege," he said, with all the respect he could muster up.

"Perhaps we will meet again soon," the king said. He nodded his farewell, then stepped out quickly in the direction of the main fortress.

Mordred watched his liege lord walking away. And as he did, a sly smile slid slowly across his face. He felt quite certain he'd made a favorable impression on the king. Imagine his luck running into the King of Logres within the first hour of his first morning in the city. "I do believe this is going to be a very good day," he mused, "a very good day indeed. This has been a most propitious beginning."

The king, as he strolled on toward the citadel, found himself reflecting on the young man he'd just encountered. All in all, he'd found him quite appealing. He liked his eagerness and he liked his looks. He was certainly a handsome lad, this young Mordred, this son and heir to the Earl of Oakdon.

At the same time, though, there was just a little something about the young fellow that disturbed him, something he couldn't quite put his finger on. It wasn't so much that the lad had seemed a little too good to be true, that he had been putting on an act . . . or . . . or *was it?* Anyway, the king thought, this young man would certainly bear watching.

Mordred remained at the combat grounds for another hour. Wanting to discover as much about it as he possibly could, he walked slowly from one end of the field to the other, studying the ground carefully, memorizing the places where the turf was firmest and where loosest, where the ground was just a little bit uneven, where the grass was thickest and where thinnest. He knew that individual combats sometimes turned on the smallest of things. Any edge he might be able to gain over an opponent who didn't know what he knew was an edge he wanted to have.

Mordred had supreme confidence in his skills as a swordsman; and he thought it highly unlikely he'd come up against anyone within a few years of his age who could best him in a one-on-one fight. And while he similarly doubted there could be any young man in all of Logres who possessed his skills in riding, he had to admit that he had yet to be tested in mounted combat against lads with real experience and ability. Here he would certainly be tested. And it was in that one area that he felt unprepared. He hoped that this man named Sir Mador de la Port would prove to be a truly fine instructor. Mordred was relieved to hear the king assure him that he would.

During the following hour Mordred wandered the paths that meandered through the grounds surrounding the great citadel, stopping at intervals to admire the fortress from different perspectives. Tomorrow he and a small number of other youths new to the city would be taken inside and shown around, but for now he was content to study its external fabric. He'd had little experience of actual castles, but he knew that a good knowledge of castle defense was something well worth having.

Eventually he moved as close as he dared to the private castle of the king and queen, being mindful of the king's warning. At one point, when he noticed movement in a high window, he slipped behind a tree so that he could see and not be seen. For the next ten minutes he remained there, sneaking surreptitious glances around the tree when he felt it was safe to do it.

Every now and then through that open window he caught glimpses of a pair of women who sometimes stood there for a moment before moving on past. Even from that considerable distance it seemed to him that they were both quite lovely, though one much more so than the other. Was one of them the queen? If so, she was surely the more lovely of the two.

When Mordred fell asleep that night back at the lodging house, he experienced delightful visions involving each of the women he'd seen at the high window—visions that especially involved the more lovely of the two.

CHAPTER 11

Merlyn—his long, lean body sore and aching from a hard day in the saddle—sat up suddenly in his bed. The lad was in trouble!

Merlyn slid on his boots, snatched up his cloak, his staff, his pack, and made a mad dash for the stables. He was in luck. The stable boy was still on hand.

"Saddle the black!" Merlyn roared at him. "I must away at once!"

The black was dancing as Merlyn leapt into the saddle. The beast was as excited as the man. Had the beast and the man shared the same premonition?

Needing no urging from his rider, the stallion shot off down the road. With no instructions from Merlyn, the magnificent horse appeared to know where his rider wanted to go. The man and the horse seemed of one mind.

After ten miles of hard riding, Merlyn and the black found themselves moving quickly down the same road Lute had traveled perhaps eight hours earlier. Merlyn sensed that they were getting close to the place they wanted to find, though he wasn't sure precisely where or what that was.

It was the horse who knew. He suddenly swerved off the road and headed straight for the coppice of alders.

Merlyn dismounted and walked into the trees, the horse following close behind him. The old man noticed the signs of a scuffle. When he saw the blood, his heart sank. Had he failed the lad? Was Lute now *dead?*

The black's nostrils flared and quivered—it was as if he was scenting the air. The creature moved to a small hollow filled with leaves, raised his head, and sniffed the air again. Merlyn came over and stood beside him, not sure what to make of the horse's actions as it pawed at the leaves.

Merlyn bent down at the spot where the black was pawing and began clearing away the leaves with his hands. Then he froze. Beneath these leaves, he knew without a doubt, was a body. "Oh, Lute," he said to himself disconsolately. "I failed you, lad, I failed you miserably."

Steeling himself, Merlyn began removing the leaves once more. And then a bloody face stared up at him. A face the old wizard didn't recognize.

Merlyn uncovered the body more fully. He didn't know who this man was, but he hadn't fogotten the trio of riders he'd seen pursuing Lute two days earlier. This man, he suspected, was one of them. What had happened here? Had the man's companions turned on him? Or had *Lute* done this? He hoped it wasn't Lute. In any case, it was a huge relief that the body he'd discovered wasn't the lad's.

Merlyn quickly re-covered the body and left it as he'd found it.

The black whinnied loudly, just as if he was telling Merlyn it was time for the two of them to be getting on their way.

"All right, all right," Merlyn muttered. "You can just keep your socks on, all right?"

"You accursed horse," he said, once he'd remounted the stallion. "What right do you have to be so much smarter than I am, hmm? Tell me that, you silly creature." The horse responded with a loud snort.

Merlyn and the black returned to the road and set off in the direction of a small hamlet that lay a mile or so away. Merlyn, now more hopeful about Lute's safety, knew he still couldn't afford to relax until he had more answers. And he could tell that the black's sense of urgency hadn't diminished one bit—which proved to be hugely important.

For from out of the darkness, two riders came suddenly charging—one from the right, one from the left. As the riders converged on them, the black put on an unexpected spurt of speed, nearly unhorsing his inexperienced rider. But once he was well out ahead of them, the black began to slacken his pace, allowing the riders to close the gap. Merlyn knew the black could outdistance them easily if he wanted to. Yet for some reason, the headstrong beast didn't want to.

Merlyn urged the black for another burst of speed, but the horse did just the opposite, slowing down to make things easier for Merlyn's attackers.

"You accursed creature!" Merlyn barked out. "Determined to make *me* do all the hard work, are you?"

Now all three horses, nearly side by side, had slowed to little more than a fast trot. The rider to the left of Merlyn drew even with him and raised his weapon, preparing to strike at Merlyn's unprotected neck. With a sudden flick of his wrist, Merlyn twirled his oaken staff. The stout stick caught the fellow smack in the throat, unhorsing him before he even knew what had happened.

In the next moment, the rider on Merlyn's right side leapt from the back of his horse onto Merlyn's and clasped his arm around Merlyn's waist. But the black, feeling the sudden addition of weight, shot his hind legs skyward. Merlyn's attacker clutched at the empty air, then landed hard on the gravel road. Merlyn let loose of his staff and flung both his arms around the horse's neck.

As Merlyn held on for dear life, the black spun about and rushed back to where the two men lay groaning on the roadway. With demonic glee, the horse began stomping and trampling on them mercilessly.

"Stop!" Merlyn shouted. "What are you *doing?*"

The black's battle fury was upon him, and he didn't stop—not until their two attackers had been pounded and pummeled into bloody masses of lifelessness. The black's three white socks were no longer white.

"Oh, lord in heaven, what have I got myself into?" Merlyn muttered.

Finally satisfied, the black paused for a moment to catch his breath, his battle fury now subsiding.

"You blasted, witless thing!" Merlyn cried out. "Did you enjoy that? You certainly *seemed* to. Is that why you've been visited upon me, to do vicious and cruel things such as *that?*"

As if in reply, the black snorted loudly.

"Well, you vile demon, I'll tell you one thing. I am not going anywhere without my staff! So you just turn your black arse right about and help me find it, all right?" Merlyn was quite vexed.

His precious staff having been duly retrieved, Merlyn and the black set off once more along the dark road. And as they did, the mind of the old wizard was all a-muddle. Apparently Lute was all right after all, at least for the moment. That was a great relief to the old man. And as horrific as all these events had been, at least now they had three fewer adversaries than they'd had before. But most perplexing to Merlyn was this startlingly violent and independent creature he was mounted on. Was he truly a friend? Or was he something else?

"I'd thought that beneath our skins you and I might share a lot in common," he muttered into the black's ear. "All I can say now, you accursed beast, is that I really *hope* not! I may be no prizewinner myself, but you, my friend, are the one who really takes the biscuit."

The black let out another great snort.

❖

After leaving the coppice, the distraught Lute decided to give the nearby hamlet a wide berth. He wanted to get as much distance as possible from the coppice and what had happened there, and he wanted to avoid encountering other people. He would complete his journey, he decided, by sticking entirely to the fields and woodlands and avoiding all roads and even the small trackways. He knew he was now quite close to his destination. With another three or four hours of riding, he might reach the hut of his uncle's friend before sunrise. Arriving under the cover of darkness, he reflected, might be a very wise plan.

As he rode he tried to concentrate his thoughts on the here and now, trying to block from his mind all that had occurred back in the grove.

He was disappointed in himself for having been taken unawares like that. Even more, he was aghast at what he had done. The moment the knife had left his fingers he'd regretted it. And when he'd seen the consequences of his actions, he'd regretted it even more. He hardly had any recollection of anything he'd done in the ensuing minutes.

It came home to Lute that this was the first time in his young life he'd ever violated one of the Commandments—and that the one he'd broken was probably the worst one. He would need to go to confession as soon as he could—though the idea of confessing such a terrible thing to the priest sent shudders running through him.

The moon was down by the time the lad arrived at the bank of a narrow river, which was probably the River Teamm. He'd been told to cross it at the village of Teammsford, and that once he'd done that, his destination, the small cottage and farmstead of an elderly herdsman named Wat, would lie just a few miles beyond. Wat, his uncle told him, was an old and much beloved family friend, a man who many years before had introduced Lute's uncle to the joys of the fields and forest and taught him the woodsman's skills. Wat was quite old now, Lute's uncle said, but he would still know all that had been happening in Sanham. Earl Thomas, Lute knew, trusted old Wat like a dearly beloved kinsman.

Although the sun was still an hour from rising, the dawn chorus resounded through the woodlands as Lute approached the little farmstead. The cacophony of the birds was soon joined by the barking of dogs, for Wat and his Welsh herddogs were already up and doing. As the dogs ran to investigate, the old man stood and watched, leaning upon a stout cane. Lute and the gelding seemed to pass muster with the dogs, for they wagged their tails as they began trotting along beside them.

"Shep! Em!" the man called out. "Come, dogs," and they quickly responded to his signal.

"I'm Lute," the young man said in a loud voice as he approached. "I'm looking for a man named Wat. Might you be he?"

"I might," said the old man. "Yes, I believe I might, though the name my mother once gave me was Walter." His eyes crinkled as he smiled at the young man on the horse. "So Lute," he said knowingly, "perhaps you're ready to break your fast? I was about to eat, myself."

"I wouldn't say no to breaking my fast," Lute replied. "My stomach has been growling for the last two hours." The lad slipped from the saddle and looped the horse's reins about a railing.

In only a few minutes' time, Lute and Wat were noshing on thick slabs of dark bread spread with butter and honey, and drinking large mugs of cool fresh milk.

"This tastes quite wonderful," the lad said.

"There be eggs, if you'll be wanting them," Wat said. "Or a venison pasty left over from last night?"

"No, thank you. But might I have one more piece of the bread and honey?"

"You should probably have two. And another mug of milk."

"Sir, I won't say no."

After they'd breakfasted, Lute listened carefully as the old man began telling him all that had been going on in Sanham.

"The reeve here is a man named Oswald," he said. "He's served your uncle for donkey's years, Lute, ever since the old earl, your uncle's father, passed away. Earl Thomas always had great faith in the man, and all the time your uncle lived here, Oswald seemed to serve him faithfully. But when your uncle was injured and had to remain down there in the old king's great city, well, that's when everything began to change.

"With the earl so far away, it began to dawn on Oswald that he could do pretty much any blessed thing he wanted with the lands and the crops. Before long, he'd even moved into a wing of the manor house, saying he could keep better track of things from there. *Ha.* Oh yes, he's surely been a-takin' better care of some things—especially *hisself*—though p'haps not such good care of your uncle's granges.

"For some time now he's been lording it over all of us, and until recently, he'd little fear of anything your uncle might do. Then he heard about you. Don't know how. All along he'd believed your uncle had no heir, but then he got wind of you. Shook him good, it did.

"The rumor is, Lute, that he's gone and hired some vile rogues who mean to harm you, rogues who've come all the way from Cornwall. They're saying these horrid fellows are capable of doing just about anything you'd want 'em to do. Some friend o' his down there made the arrangements.

"He's a-feared of you, lad, terribly a-feared. There's no doubt he's hired these ruffians with the goal of knocking you on the head. I hafta confess that until I heard Em 'n Shep a-barkin' at ya, I was a-feared it'd already happened. Their barking was music to my ears. Then there ya was, a-ridin' right up to my hut." The old man beamed at the young man. "I sure was relieved ta see you safe 'n sound."

"Well, sir, I did have one rather serious scrap along the way," Lute said, not sure how much he should tell the old man about the events of the previous night. "I had a bit of a set-to with a man who attacked me. Maybe one of those ruffians you were talking about."

"Well, I surely hope you settled that fellow's hash! Them rogues Oswald's brought in, they mean to finish you good 'n all. Now listen, lad, what you 'n me've got to do is do for them afore they do for you! I plan ta help ya, son. And if you think I'm not like ta be much help ta you, then you'd be wrong!"

The old man was getting himself quite worked up, and as Lute sat there looking at him in wide-eyed wonder, the old man nodded his head several times and said, "Yeh, you're right, son, you're right. I need ta calm down a bit. Gettin' a bit too excited, I am. Still and all, Lute, I've been a-wantin' ta settle that villain's hash for many a year now. Yes, Oswald's been a-stealin' from all of us, a-treatin' us in ways that just ain't right. Ways your uncle woulda never treated us. No one's had the guts ta stand up to 'im. Now we will, lad, you 'n me. Now we will!"

CHAPTER 12

Rain pouring off the high lead roofs, rushing through the gutters, downspouts, gargoyles; rain flooding the fields and woodlands, filling the moats and raising the city's encircling river to a dangerous level; rain pelting down on the city's open squares and anyone daring to move about them.

"Lord in heaven, how it does rain!" said the young man standing beside Mordred. The two of them were looking out of a high window in a room on the second floor of the citadel's great central keep, the room where the fencers' gallery was located. Windy gusts occasionally brought the rain in upon their faces. "It will be days till we can ride again," the lad complained. "And when we do, it will be nothing but slop up to our fetlocks. Ugh. How I hate that."

"And so in the meantime we work on our secret thrusts, our riposts, the deftness of our footwork and our parrying," Mordred replied.

"As if you need to!" the young man, whose name was Colgrevaunce, shot back. "Lord in heaven, how did you get so skillful? Even Sir Ascamour isn't a patch on you, Mordred. Before long you'll be able to handle Launcelot himself!"

Mordred just smiled. There was no reason to deny Cole's claims. They both knew they weren't far from the truth.

In through the door of the hall strode the tall lean figure of Sir Ascamour, their mentor in swordsmanship. He had six of them under his wing—Mordred, his friend Colgrevaunce, and four other young knight-aspirants. All six were highly promising youths, though none more promising than Mordred.

"Today, something a bit different," Sir Ascamour said cheerily. "Today, you won't be squaring off against each other. Today you'll be challenging the very same young men who were recently knighted at the Feast of Pentecost. Oh yes, lads, these fellows are sure to give you a very stiff test, one you may not be ready for. Still, I don't believe all of you will end up winless. Some of you are likely to win a bout or two. And even if you lose them all, there's no shame in that. These fellows are well ahead of you in training and experience. If they weren't, they wouldn't now be knights. Indeed, amongst them are one or two who may well end up becoming Round Table knights. But lads, that may be true for you, too. "

As Sir Ascamour was speaking, another group of young men entered the gallery. There were six of them, all wearing their protective cuirasses and carrying their long swords and helmets. They were strapping young fellows, and one of them was considerably larger than the others. Mordred knew who he was—his name was Lamorak. Amongst the king's new-fledged knights, he was the one everyone was talking about. As the saying goes, he was the one who "bore the bell."

Mordred eyed Sir Lamorak warily. He was the only one amongst the group who caused Mordred any trepidation.

They soon paired off and began their bouts. In that first round, only Mordred bested his foe. His friend Colgrevaunce, after a brave fight, fell victim to the mighty Sir Lamorak. But Colgrevaunce soon acquitted himself better, winning his second bout against another highly touted young knight. Mordred also won his second bout, and when the pair of lads looked over at each other, they exchanged grins.

After five of the six rounds of bouts, only Lamorak and

Mordred were still undefeated. That being the case, Sir Ascamour suggested that the final round for all the others be suspended so that they could observe the contest between the pair of undefeateds—Mordred and Lamorak.

Lamorak fought with a heavy longsword. He held it with both hands close together mid-way up its lengthy hilt, the conventional method of the time. Mordred favored a lighter, slightly longer sword, one that could be held with just one hand. That allowed him the possibility of making longer thrusts. Although Mordred was above middle height, Lamorak was a good three inches taller and far broader in thigh, chest, and shoulder.

"It will be the sinister lad versus the dexterous one," one wag remarked, playing on the literal meanings of the Latin words. Mordred, being left-handed, was the sinister lad, while the right-handed Lamorak was the dexterous one.

Though large and powerful, Lamorak was indeed dexterous. He was quick, agile, and guileful, and also quite skilled at analyzing his opponent. Indeed, after each of his first four bouts had been over—and they'd been over quickly—he'd kept a watchful eye on Mordred. He already had a good idea of the fellow's favorite tricks, of his cunning, and of his penchant for making daring and unexpected moves. Lamorak was too smart to be overconfident about this fight. He knew he faced a young opponent with special skills.

As the match began, both men proceeded with caution—thrusting, parrying, checking, riposting, getting a feel for their opponent's abilities and preferences. The contrast in styles was evident, both to the fighters and to those watching. Mordred's one-handed, left-handed thrusts posed a real danger; and dodging them and parrying them posed a serious challenge.

As did Mordred's darting, snake-like moves. But Lamorak was nearly as quick as Mordred, and he was far more powerful. If the match became an extended one, Lamorak had quite a good chance of wearing down his smaller foe, who'd already had five lengthy bouts against highly skilled opponents.

The longsword is not revered for subtlety. A strong and heavy weapon, it is best used for simple bashing and slashing, blows intended to disarm or disable. Still, in the hand of a strong and able swordsman some subtlety and deftness is possible. Lamorak was an able swordsman.

Mordred also had the ability to wield his lighter and slightly longer weapon with deftness and subtlety. Ironically, it was that ability which led to his undoing. For when he tried one of his more devious maneuvers, one Lamorak had seen him use in an earlier bout, the young knight adroitly avoided Mordred's blow, then brought his own heavy weapon crashing down upon Mordred's. For all his suppleness and unexpected strength, Mordred couldn't maintain his grip. His weapon flew from his hand and clattered onto the cold stone floor.

The watchers cheered the pair of fighters in full appreciation of having witnessed a stirring combat between two skillful young men. Lamorak graciously raised his own weapon in salute to Mordred, acknowledging the fine bout the lad had given him, far the most challenging of the day.

Mordred, too, dipped his head to his opponent, honoring his victory. But his impassive face concealed the terrible turmoil that roiled inside of him. He'd known all along that he might lose this match. But now that he had, it was all he could do to control his inner demons, demons which were battling to take control of him.

For Mordred found himself *despising* this man whom

he felt had humiliated him before his companions and his mentor. It was a public shaming the like of which he had never experienced. He *hated* it; and even more, he hated the man who'd given it to him.

"This Lamorak," a voice inside him said, "will pay dearly for the events of this day. Where, when, or how, I do not know. But pay he will. Oh yes, pay he will—and with the dearest thing he has to pay. No one shall ever humiliate Mordred, the Earl of Oakdon, and remain unscathed—*no one.*"

As the rain was finally slackening, Tib kept watch outside the Willows for the lad's return. But he waited in vain. So too did Colgrevaunce, who searched for Mordred all throughout the great citadel but to no avail. He and Mordred had planned to go out and dine together—and also to see what they might scare up in the way of willing women. But Mordred had disappeared. Colgrevaunce shrugged and set off on his own. Tib continued to keep watch, though eventually he, too, gave it up.

When Mordred left the keep, he didn't take the usual path from the citadel but instead went out to a place he knew in the woodlands not far from the jousting field. He remained there for a time, licking his mental wounds, thinking evil thoughts about Sir Lamorak.

Mordred wanted no company. What he wanted was to *hurt* someone. As he thought about it, the someone he wanted to hurt was Rafe, the ironmonger's apprentice. There was no logic to it, but yes, Rafe was the one Mordred wanted to hurt. He wanted to hurt the thick, rude bastard so bad that maybe . . . just maybe . . . he would actually *kill* him. Mordred wasn't entirely sure. But he knew that he wanted to thrust his sword into living human flesh. He wanted to watch as the blood and gore welled forth. *That* would give him immense satisfaction.

By late afternoon, when the sun had finally returned, Mordred left his retreat and wandered down to the lowest level of the city. The wet cobblestones were steaming as he walked across the open square. Relieved by the change in the weather, people were now quickly moving about the square, getting back to the activities they'd avoided during the heavy downpours. Mordred wandered amongst them aimlessly for a while, and then he began to think once more about the lad named Rafe and what he might do to him.

Suddenly, from atop the city gates, trumpets rang out. Someone was about to enter the city—someone of great importance. Everyone stopped right where they were and waited, including Mordred.

Through the gates came two pairs of riders, followed by a coach and four, which was followed by two more pairs of riders. The garb of the riders, as well as that of their horses, was beautiful and costly, but even so, it paled in comparison to the elegant coach. Mordred could see that inside the coach sat a regal woman with her attendants. In addition to the coach drivers, two liveried coachmen rode perched on small platforms on each side of the coach.

"It's Queen Margause!" people began whispering. "Queen Margause, the queen of Lothian." "The most beautiful woman in the kingdom . . . well, after our *own* queen, that is."

Mordred edged closer for a better look at this famous—indeed, infamous—woman. And suddenly, in his heart, something spoke to him. Something deep inside him created a feeling of greater joy than he had ever experienced before. "What does this mean?" he asked himself.

And then without realizing what was happening, his lips

began moving as he lapsed into one of his reveries:

A darkened room, a man, a woman.
Passionate desires,
Passionate desires.
Cries of joy, cries of woe;
Sounds of merriment, tears of grief.
Passionate desires,
Passionate desires.
A woman, a man, a darkened room.

When Mordred came out of his reverie, all thoughts of malice toward Rafe, the ironmonger's helper, had flown right out of his head.

CHAPTER 13

Lying in Wat's own small bed, Lute slept for most of the day. While he slept, the old man tended to Lute's horse, prepared a special stew for their evening meal, and began sharpening and polishing their weapons. Wat was spoiling for a fight. The safe arrival of the young man had breathed fresh vim and vigor into his tired old bones. Tomorrow, he hoped, the two of them would confront Oswald the Reeve. They would insist upon full recompense to Earl Thomas; insist that he swear an oath on the Four Evangelists to change his ways. If it came to a fight, a fight it would be. And in his heart, old Wat hoped it would be a fight.

Late in the day Lute awoke to the smells of cooking—freshly baked bread and a savory mutton stew spiced with garlic and leeks. When the lad sniffed the air, he realized just how famished he was. He sat up, stretched his long arms, then quickly pulled on his boots. "Yumm," he said, licking his lips, "yumm."

"Back in the land of the living, hey?" said the old man. Wat's two dogs came over to Lute and sniffed him good, both of them wagging their tails. Lute reached out and ruffled the fur around each of their necks. The dogs rubbed themselves against his legs and panted cheerfully.

"If Shep and Em likes ya, laddie, then ya can't be all bad," the old man said, grinning from ear to ear.

All bad? For a second the thought of the man he'd killed

rampaged through Lute's head. No, perhaps he wasn't *all* bad. But if there was any way he could undo his actions of the night before, he would undo them in a heartbeat.

"Not all bad?" Lute said, with a serious look on his face. "No . . . perhaps not *all* bad."

"Laddie, don't know what ya done that's a-troublin' ya, but don't go frettin' yourself. Ain't none of us neither all bad nor all good. As for Oswald the Reeve, now he's one fella who comes pretty near ta bein' all bad. You 'n me, Lute, we're gonna put an end to his chicanery right soon, ya hear me?"

"I hear you, sir. Indeed we are."

Lute went over to the water bucket by the door and splashed handfuls of cool water over his face. "C'mon, laddy, time we was tuckin' in!" the old man sang out.

That's what they did, and during their meal Lute refilled his large wooden bowl more than once with Wat's piping hot stew. He devoured four thick slices of bread covered with fresh butter and gooseberry jam and drank most of the milk in a large earthen jug. The old man couldn't keep pace with the lad, though he did his best.

Their evening repast over, the two of them, along with Shep and Em, strolled out into the woods.

"It were in these woods I first taught your uncle to track and hunt, to brittle a deer, and to appreciate the Lord's bountiful beneficence. He 'n me once killed a boar in these woods—with some bold, brave help from Shep's grandam Queenie. She were a gem, she were, old Queenie. Do you remember her, Shep?" he said, patting the dog's side. Shep tilted his head as if in thought.

"I've spent quite a lot of time in the woods myself," Lute said, "back home where my mother lives."

"I knew your mother when she were a girl, back before that

terrible battle, back before she and your grandfather, the Old Earl, went off to Uther's new city to celebrate the king's victory. I guess you know it were in that great battle your uncle Thomas took his terrible wound. He were so crippled up after that he never did come back. Nor did your mother or her father, the Old Earl. It weren't so long after that the Old Earl died.

"I went to that great city once, I did, to visit your uncle. It were like nothing I'd ever seen. Magnificent, it were. But it weren't my kind of place, neither. All the time I was there visitin' your uncle, I was just a-longin' to be back here. He knew it, too, and told me he would miss me but I'd best go home. He knowed this was where I belonged. Gwilym, the old sourpuss, he stuck with Earl Thomas to look after 'im." Lute chuckled, hearing Wat call Gwilym an old sourpuss.

"Your uncle and I, we kept in touch regular-like, and I let him know how Oswald was a-doin' overseein' things here. And for the first couple of years, he were doin' just fine. But then, sure as anything, that old devil Greed started sneakin' up on him. He started in ta cheatin' and stealin'. At first just a little, then more and more. That was when he gathered a pack of rogues about him ta do all his bidding.

"That's when he started in a-throwin' his weight around like he were lord of the manor hisself. And now it's gone way past the point of bein' tolerable. Lute, you 'n me, we's the ones have got to settle his hash, once and for all!"

"Tomorrow?"

"Aye, lad, it'll be tomorrow."

"Will it be just the two of us?"

"Two other lads'll be comin' with us, Lute, two sturdy farm lads who're tired as me o' seein' theirselves cheated out o' the fruits of their labors. And don't go forgettin' Shep and Em.

They'll be with us, too." Hearing their names, the two dogs glanced up eagerly at the old man.

❖

Merlyn's mind was all a-muddle. He didn't know where Lute was or what had happened to him back in the grove. Had he reached his destination safely? And now, worse luck, Merlyn seemed stuck with this unpredictable and enigmatic creature.

With those thoughts and others swirling in his head, he concluded that the best plan now would be to head straight for the Earl's manor house in Sanham. There was another matter he'd wanted to deal with first, but he'd best let it go for now.

After riding for most of an hour, Merlyn came to a riverbank. He slid from the saddle and led the horse straight into the water.

"Come on, you," he said to the horse, "can't have you walking about in dirty socks." While the horse bent his long neck down to drink, Merlyn ran his hands up and down on the creature's three white socks, trying to remove as much of the dried blood as he could.

"Best I can do for now," Merlyn said. "We do make a rather slovenly pair, you and me." The horse tossed his head, seeming to express the view that between the two of them he was certainly not the slovenly one.

As Merlyn was relieving himself against a tree, the horse came up behind him and nudged his shoulder affectionately. "Oh, so now you're trying to get on my good side, are you? The least you could do is wait till I'm done here!"

When the horse nudged him again, despite himself Merlyn reached out and patted his neck.

"I don't know who or what you are," he said softly, "and I don't know why you are here. One thing I do know, though, is that you aren't the one who's going to destroy me. Someone else will have that honor. Well, are you going to tell me who you are or not?" The horse made no response to Merlyn's question.

"Mum's the word, eh? Well, my dear, at the least we should be finding a name for you. Or do you have one already? Ah, you do, don't you. And I suppose you want me to guess what it is! Ha. Perhaps you think I'm some sort of mind reader." The horse gave a small snort.

"Your name," Merlyn mused aloud, "hmm, what might it be? . . . Iblis? . . . Ashtoreth? . . . Flibbertijibbet?" For a moment the horse's eye seemed to glow. "Don't get excited. I was just kidding about Flibbertijibbet. Where's your sense of humor?

"Let me see . . . what might it be? Don't be impatient, I'll come up with it. Not as quick as I used to be. Well, how about Marjodo? . . . Moloch? . . . Asmodeus? *Aha!* I've got it. Your name, my dear, is it *Raguel?*" The horse's eye gleamed brightly, and then he bobbed his head, almost as if he were nodding.

"That's it, isn't it," Merlyn said, "it's Raguel!" The horse gave a snort.

"Hmm. Doesn't come trippingly off the tongue. Are you sure?" Again the horse snorted.

"All right then, Raguel it is. I myself would have preferred Flibbertijibbet." The horse snorted, probably in derision.

❖

The earl's manor stood atop a low hill behind which rose a higher ridge crested with trees. As Lute, Wat, and the two sturdy farm lads made their slow approach, Lute could see that the manor house, though not truly a small castle, possessed some modest defensive fortifications. An outer wall enclosed the entire compound, and within the main building itself another structure, not unlike a keep, rose to a considerable height.

All around the outside of the main building ran a roofed gallery; various rooms apparently opened off of the gallery. The entrance to the main structure was through a large arched doorway with portcullises at each end. Beyond it, Lute could see, there was a small inner courtyard.

There was a gate in the wall of the outer enclosure, but it stood wide open. Even from a distance it seemed to be in disrepair, and when Lute and Wat reached it, they saw that one of its thick, heavy doors hung halfway off its hinges. Wat eyed the broken doorway in disgust.

"Things've got to change," he muttered. "No time like the present."

The four men, along with Shep and Em, passed through the gateway and walked up the hill, stopping just a few paces before the main building. It was already moving toward mid-morning, yet there were few signs of activity.

"Oswald!" bellowed Wat, shattering the silence. As if echoing his loud outcry, Shep and Em chipped in several loud barks.

Doors opened up on the gallery. Four men stepped through them and stood there looking down. Standing side by side were a mismatched pair of men, one hugely obese and one skinny as a beanpole—two fellows hardly likely to strike fear in one's heart. The other two, though, looked more like men who knew how to handle themselves. It was one of them who spoke.

"Wat! What in blazes do you mean, old man, coming round here in the morning, crying out loud enough to wake the dead?" He glared down at Wat and the two farm lads, all of whom he knew, before shifting his gaze to Lute.

"And who might this lad be, eh? Some fellow ya figured ya might bring along ta back ya up? Laddie," he said, addressing Lute, "don't know who you are. But you and the others had best turn around and take yourselves right on out of here."

"Oswald!" Wat bellowed again. "Where are you, you slug! We got business with you, ya stinkin' piece o' filth!"

"You just shut up, old man." Now the speaker was the man who was vastly overweight. "Oswald's gettin' sick and tired of all your bellyaching. You just shut up, you hear me?"

"Shut up?" Wat replied. "Why don't you come and make me?—ya fat pig!"

"What the hell's going on?" The new speaker, a tall man who looked to be in late middle-age, was standing beneath the arched entranceway only a few feet in front of Lute and Wat. He was flanked by two more men—a pair of hulking fellows who were probably his personal bodyguards. They both held unsheathed swords. The bearing and attire of the man in the middle suggested a person of authority. Lute knew that he must be Oswald the Reeve.

Oswald glared at Lute. As he did, the thought came to him that this young man might be the one he'd been warned would be coming; and if so, then the men he'd hired to deal with the lad must've failed. Well, if that was the case, then he and his own men would just have to handle the matter themselves.

"What is it now, Wat?" Oswald said. "Come to do more grousing about how we do things around here? Well, we're *tired* of it. We know Earl Thomas always had a soft spot for you. That's why we've left you be. But enough is enough. Go on back home now and hoe your bean rows. We don't need you telling us how to do our jobs. We know far better than you how they should be done."

"Oswald, you're right. Enough *is* enough. The time for cheatin' 'n stealin' 'n lyin' is over 'n done with. Lute here's come for Earl Thomas's money, the money you been stashin' away in your coffers. Time ta cough it up, Oswald. If you cough it up now and swear an oath to mend your ways, maybe Earl Thomas will allow you to stay on. I can't speak for him, but you know as well as me he be a very fair man."

"There is no money, Wat. I haven't stashed away a single ha'penny."

"That, you poxed son of a whore, is a bold-faced lie!"

"Wat, I've reached the end of my tether. Go now. If you do, I'll leave you be. If you don't . . . then be it on your head."

"Sir," said Lute, speaking for the first time, "I have seen the fields. The crops grow well. If I looked into your barns and granaries, would they be full? The sheep are thriving. Where have you stored their wool? Have you already sold it? There can be little doubt, sir, that those sheep have brought you quite a pretty return. But you've not sent any of it to my uncle. So where is it?"

"Your *uncle?* That's a laugh. Thomas had no brothers and just one sister, a little lass who disappeared years ago."

"She is my mother, sir—speak of her with respect! Wat and I are offering you one last chance to make recompense. Do it, sir. Or be it on *your* head."

"Fine words, laddie, fine words. Now get the hell out of here!"

When Lute, Wat, and the two farm lads showed no sign of doing anything of the kind, Oswald barked out his orders to his lackeys. "Okay, lads, time to be sending these miscreants on their way!"

The four men from the gallery now joined the trio already beneath the archway. While the other six men advanced slowly, their weapons drawn, Oswald remained behind.

"C'mon, lads, let's get the buggers!" Wat cried out. "Time ta settle their hash!"

And then the melee erupted.

A thick-bodied brawler of a man rushed at Lute. Holding his ancient broadsword in both hands high above his right shoulder, he intended to deliver a slashing blow. The ruffian was no weakling, and when his sword crashed against Lute's, it nearly knocked it from his hand. The shock of the impact ran up Lute's arm. The brawler's second blow came from the opposite direction, but Lute spun sideways and dodged it. The fellow's mighty swing at empty air nearly toppled him, and before he could right himself, Lute was on him. Lute's weapon flashed downward, and the finely honed blade found the ruffian's two wrists at the same time.

The man rolled on the ground, clutching his arms to his chest. His screams resounded throughout the enclosure.

A lot of wild fighting was going on all about Lute, but he had only the vaguest impression of the rest of it, for his attention was now focused solely on Oswald.

When Oswald saw the look in Lute's eye, he spun on his heel and fled. He sprinted back through the archway seeking safety inside the central tower. Lute was only ten feet behind him as the two of them dashed across the inner courtyard. Oswald pelted through the open tower doorway and tried to slam it shut, but Lute's shoulder reached the door before Oswald could shoot the bolt.

Lute pushed his way inside the room. When he heard footsteps echoing above him on the stone stairway, he charged up the stair two steps at a time. He was breathing heavily when he reached the top, but with hardly a pause he shouldered his way through the doorway. As Lute entered the high chamber, Oswald lunged at him with a pike. When Lute felt the tip of its iron spike penetrate his left biceps, he cried out in agony.

Oswald pulled the weapon free and surged forward again, this time aiming straight for Lute's chest. With cat-quickness, Lute's left hand shot up. Exerting all his will to ignore the pain shooting down his arm, Lute grabbed the shaft of the pike behind the sharp metal blade and managed to prevent it from impaling him. Its lethal point had passed through the lad's shirt and penetrated the brawn of his chest. But he held firm and saved his life.

Lute felt a wave of burning pain, but then realizing that his right hand still clutched his sword, he swung it hard against the shaft of the pike. The blow freed the pike from his chest and drove it toward the floor. As it moved downward, its blade plowed a shallow furrow across Lute's chest and abdomen.

Still grasping the pike, Oswald retreated across the room. He took up his position at a spot where two walls angled out from one of the chamber's high windows. With the walls protecting his flanks, he could use the pike to fend off his enraged pursuer.

Blood welled from Lute's wounds. But seeing that his prey was now cornered like the vermin he was, Lute intended to get this business over and done with. When Oswald jabbed toward his face, the lad dropped his sword and darted beneath the weapon's lethal blade. Lute grasped the pike's shaft with both hands and then using every ounce of strength he still possessed, he rammed the pike back into Oswald's chest.

The sudden impact of the weapon's blunt end drove Oswald toward the window. He took one desperate step backward, trying to maintain his balance. It was a fateful step. His thighs were now pressed hard up against the edge of the stone ledge of the window seat. Above the window seat there was nothing to stop the momentum of his upper body.

Oswald tumbled backward. As his body passed through the opening, one hand clutched frantically at the window frame. The tips of his fingers just barely brushed against it, then slipped on by.

Wat and the others, who by then had subdued the rest of Oswald's men, heard a terrified scream. And then a thud.

Lute heard those sounds also. For a moment he stood stock still, staring toward the empty window. With reluctance, he willed himself to go over and look down.

What he saw below him was what he'd hoped not to see.

"You all right, lad?" came Wat's powerful voice.

"Yes," Lute finally managed to call back to the old man. He felt lightheaded. His tongue felt thick in his mouth. "Yes . . . at least . . . mostly. Looks like I may need a bandage or two."

Ten minutes later, as Wat and the farmers' sons were still staunching Lute's bleeding wounds, there came the rapid drumbeat of a horse's hooves. As they looked toward the outer gateway, they saw a horse and rider come galloping through. The men snatched up their weapons, but there was no need. It was Merlyn and the black.

"Am I in time?" Merlyn shouted. "Do you need help?"

"Help?" Wat shouted back at Merlyn. "Don't be daft, old fellow. Why should we be needin' any bloody help from the likes of you?"

CHAPTER 14

It was June 24th, the feast day of Saint John the Baptist. And it was also one day after the unexpected and still unexplained arrival of Queen Margause of Lothian.

At mid-morning the nobles of the city all attended high mass in the minster. Following the service, they processioned back up to the castle's great hall where they joined the king and queen in celebrating the saint's special day.

Mordred and the other young knight-aspirants were included in these activities, the first time Mordred attended one of the king's great banquets. All throughout the day, though, even including the banquet, there was no sign of Queen Margause of Lothian. Folks had anticipated her presence with great eagerness, for there was little doubt that the woman would add a special piquancy to the celebration. But where was she keeping herself?

It wasn't until the feast was winding down that the door to the great hall flung open, and into the hall trooped Margause's several attendants. They crossed the tiled floor in a slow and stately procession. Behind them came Queen Margause stepping gracefully. The woman was swathed from neck to toe in a wine-colored gown trimmed with ermine's fur. The gown's hood was tossed back to display her lustrous red hair, hair that shimmered in the torch light.

When they had nearly reached the dais, her attendants parted and assumed positions to the right and left of the high table. The Queen of Lothian strode regally across the colorful tiled floor, then stopped and stood tall and silent before the king.

The king leapt up from his seat and hurried down from the dais to greet her.

"Madam," he said, bending slightly at the waist, "I am pleased to welcome you. It has been quite some time since you've honored us with your presence."

When the woman proffered her hand, he reached out and held it, once more dipping his head in greeting. Margause, however, offered no obeisance to the king. For a lengthy moment she gazed at him with a cold, haughty stare. At last she spoke.

"My liege," she said, in a harsh and accusatory voice, "what have you *done* with him? Is all that I've heard really *true?* Sir, how could you treat the dear boy in such a vile and shabby fashion!"

"Queen Margause," the king replied, looking perplexed, "pardon my ignorance, my lady, but I am all at sea. I do not know to whom or what you are referring."

"I am referring to *Gareth*, of course! Are you really so obtuse? Who *else* would I be referring to? Have you really, truly, turned him into a kitchen knave? How could you do such a shameful and insulting thing?"

The king still looked baffled. "Gareth? Little Gareth?" He held out his hand, his palm flat, a little above his waist as if measuring the height of a child. "Madam, I haven't seen Gareth in a good many years, not since he was quite a young lad."

"My lord," said a voice, "if you will allow me to explain." The new speaker was Sir Launcelot. "Sire, I believe the lad she means is the one whom we have known for the past year as

Beaumains. My liege, you may recall that when that young man first came to court and you asked him his name, his reply was that he couldn't say. We assumed that meant he didn't know his name. That was when Kay bestowed the epithet Beaumains upon him."

"Beaumains is *Gareth?*"

"How could you be so obtuse! Gareth was here more than a twelvemonth, and you didn't even know who he was! How could you be so obtuse?"

"Alas, Mother," Gawain said, joining in, "we knew him not. He chose not to reveal himself to us."

"You, my son, are even more obtuse than the king. How could you not recognize your own brother? You've brought great shame upon yourselves, all of you, lodging little Gareth amongst the kitchen knaves! Treating him like a servant!"

"Madam," said the king, "it wasn't our choice, it was what he himself insisted upon."

"And you happily allowed him to do it!"

"We must find him!" Gawain proclaimed. "My own dear brother! We have insulted him terribly. My liege, we must make amends as soon possible."

"Does anyone know what's become of him?" the king asked. "Or where he might be now? I know that I myself haven't heard a single word about him since he departed with that young maiden, the one who addressed us so rudely." The king's questioning eyes ran over the entire assembly. "Is there anyone here who knows what has happened to Beaumains?"

The king's question was greeted by silence. None of his knights, apparently, did know, including Launcelot, who had knighted the lad and then tested his strength against him.

After the long silence it was Mordred who stepped forward,

though he did so with a diffident air.

"My gracious liege," he said, dipping his head to the king, "and my gracious lady," again dipping his head. "Please pardon me if I am speaking out of turn."

The king gestured for the youth to continue.

"The young apprentices in the city, Sire, they have much to say of Beaumains. Besides singing his praises, every day they are a-buzz with the latest rumors of his successes. The most recent report, Sire, a report sent by means of Beaumains's dwarf, is that he has recently defeated the Red Knight of the Red Laundes. And thus, my liege, he has succeeded in rescuing the sister of the Savage Damsel."

At Mordred's words, a murmur swept through the room.

"And you *credit* such gossip and such rumors?" Now the speaker was Sir Kay. "Surely you aren't so naïve as that!"

"You are quite right, sir," Mordred said respectfully to Kay. "Those lads do love to exaggerate when it comes to the prowess of their beloved hero; and yet, sir, I have found many of their reports to be quite accurate. Only this morning three brothers—Sir Perimones, Sir Pertelope, and Sir Persaunte—entered the city. Beaumains had defeated each of them in turn, and they've been sent by him to swear homage and fealty to the king. I'm quite sure you will see them here at court before the day is out.

"Madam," Mordred said, now addressing Margause, "you may rest assured that your son has acquitted himself most nobly in his adventures. You may also be relieved to learn that he has suffered no major injuries."

"Of course he has performed nobly," she shot back. "Gareth has few equals—and certainly none amongst those I see assembled here."

"Madam," said the king, sidestepping her intended affront,

"far be it from me to dispute your words."

The king turned his attention back to Mordred and studied this young man for several seconds. "I believe you and I met a week or two ago," he said at last. "Remind me who you are."

"I am Mordred, Sire. We met by the jousting field."

"Yes, I remember. Well, Mordred, thank you for telling us this." He nodded at the lad as if to say, we need to hear nothing further from you at this time.

Mordred stepped back into the midst of the crowd of aspiring youths. But as he did, several pairs of eyes remained upon him—Launcelot's, Gawain's, and Queen Margause's, among others.

It was shortly after that that the three brothers, the ones Mordred had mentioned, did indeed appear at court to do homage to the king. Without shame they told their stories, singing the praises of the man who had bested them in honest combat. Gareth, it appeared, was truly proving himself a young knight of remarkable prowess.

The following morning, Mordred went down amongst the market stalls on the city's lowest level, ostensibly to run various errands but really because he was hoping to encounter the young woman named Gwendolyn. He'd had glimpses of her a few times in recent days but hadn't spoken to her since the day he'd arrived in the city. She'd been in his thoughts quite a bit since then, and he was eager to work his charms on her. Mordred suspected that the ironmonger's apprentice, the lad named Rafe, was her beau, and if that was so, he relished the prospect of dashing that lad's hopes. It shouldn't be so hard to do, he thought, and yet the very notion of doing it amused him.

After meandering for awhile and not catching any sight of

her, Mordred decided to pay a visit to the ironmonger's smithy. He remembered telling Rafe how much he admired the kinds of tasks he performed and how much it would please him to watch him at work. But as Mordred approached the entrance, Gwendolyn emerged from it and started walking off.

"Hello, miss," he called out to her back. She spun about to see who was hailing her. Mordred hurried up to her.

"You probably don't remember me," he said, taking off his hat and holding it with both hands before him, "but we met a week or two ago. I'm Mordred."

"Yes," she said, "I do remember. I hope I see you well, sir?"

"I'm doing all right now, miss . . . now that I've seen you again," he replied, looking wistful.

"Have you been ill?"

"Oh no, just terribly busy. I've been training up at the castle, and the king's taskmasters do rather put us through our paces. Believe me, miss, I could show you bumps and bruises that you wouldn't believe."

"Oh, I think I would believe them," she said.

"Miss, it would please me greatly if you would be willing to walk with me for a little while. Just being near you fills me with much pleasure."

Gwendolyn took a good, hard look at this earnest young man who stood before her, a young man who, she felt, was trying hard to look the picture of innocence—his eyes hopeful and beseeching, his hat held before him in his hands.

"Perhaps another time," she said. "I'm afraid I've already been away from my chores for too long."

"Of course, miss, of course. Perhaps another time." Mordred's eyes were not looking at her but down toward the cobblestone pavement.

"It's goodbye then, young sir," she said.

"Yes, miss, goodbye to you, too—until we meet again."

As Gwendolyn strode quickly away, Mordred kept his eyes upon her, admiring what he saw. His face still looked just a little bit woebegone, but on the inside the lad was laughing at himself. Actually *courting* a young maid was a completely novel experience for him, and he found the playing of this role quite to his liking. "Rafe," he said to himself, "I shall quite enjoy watching you squirm as I steal her away from you. It will please me almost as much as watching you squirm after I've impaled you with a steel blade, something I still intend doing."

Mador de la Port had worked his young charges even longer than the usual two hours, and he was immensely pleased with their progress. This was one of the most promising groups he'd ever worked with. The lad named Colgrevaunce was already highly skilled with shield and lance, and his powerful thighs made him almost impossible to unhorse. But even superior to Colgrevaunce, Mador thought, was the lad named Mordred. Mador had yet to see a young man his age so skilled at maneuvering his steed, so confident of his horsemanship, and so cunning in his tactics. Indeed, he found the lad rather scary. He himself, widely considered one of the king's ten best men on horseback, wouldn't relish facing the lad one-on-one.

Their afternoon session completed, the tired, sweaty lads turned their horses over to the grooms and gave their weapons into the care of their own serving men, which in Mordred's case was the man named Grim. Grim always enjoyed staying and watching the practice sessions in their entirety, and it pleased him that his young man was obviously superior to all the others. And yet to Grim, Mordred remained a mystery.

By now he was used to Mordred's unpredictable moods and sudden impulses, but he knew he'd never be able to completely fathom Mordred's mind.

As he often did, Mordred chose to be alone after the long practice session. The truth was, the company he most enjoyed was his own. And so it was only a few minutes later that he'd found his way to his own special place, a sylvan spot tucked away amongst the trees not far from the king and queen's own private castle.

But he'd only been there for a short time before his solace was pierced by a strident voice.

"Who *are* you?" it said.

The voice Mordred heard was a woman's. The lad had thought he was alone in his secret spot among the trees not far from the jousting grounds—but obviously he wasn't. He spun about and found himself looking straight into the face of Queen Margause. Quickly he dipped his head in respect to the woman.

"Who *are* you?" she repeated.

"Madam . . . I am not anybody, really. Nobody of any importance, that is."

"I doubt that," she replied. "I saw you offering your little speech at court yesterday. You were acting so humble, so modest, trying so hard not to call special attention to yourself. And yet, you weren't really humble at all. It was all an act. Oh yes, don't deny it. After that I kept my eye on you, and I watched how you were carefully taking everything in. I couldn't help wondering about you. And I've come to the conclusion that you are not nobody, despite your intention to make people believe that." Mordred didn't deny her assertions. Instead, his thin lips formed a small smile. Or was it a smirk?

Margause spent the next few moments looking the young man over thoroughly, studying his slim and handsome face; his lithe, athletic body; his simple, unostentatious clothing. As she was doing that, he was looking her over in return.

What Mordred saw was a striking young matron whose hair was a brighter shade of red than his own, her eyes a darker shade of blue, and her complexion a bit less pale than his own. And yet as he studied her face, he was suddenly struck by a startling fact—the face he was staring at was remarkably, indeed undeniably, similar to the one he saw every time he gazed at himself in a looking glass, something he did quite often.

Margause reached out and took the lad's right hand. She pulled it up close to her face. She was studying a thin golden ring he wore on his last finger. It was a ring she was certain she knew. She knew it, because it was a ring she'd hung on a slender gold chain some fifteen years ago, on the day when her youngest child had been snatched away from her.

She looked up at the lad. "Where did you get this?" she said quite softly.

He looked into the depths of her deep-blue eyes. "I have always had it. It is my special talisman. When I was only a tiny child, I wore it on my middle finger. Later, when I was a boy, on my third finger. Now it only fits on my smallest finger."

"Do you know what is inscribed on the inside?"

"Do *you?*"

"*Dominus est scutum, Dominus est praesidium,*" she said.

" 'The Lord is my shield, the Lord is my fortress.' "

For several seconds they both remained silent. It was Mordred who finally spoke. "Why do I have this ring?"

"Because I gave it to you."

"Why did you give it to me?"

"In the hope that it would keep you safe. It appears that it worked."

"Madam," said Mordred, " . . . are you my mother?"

" . . . yes . . . it appears that I am."

Mordred remained silent. He was doing his best to process this startling information. Finally he said, "Then Gawain and Agravaine are my brothers?"

"Yes, that is so."

"And so my real father was King Lot of Lothian?"

Margause paused for just the briefest moment before replying, "Yes, that, too, is so."

From her very brief hesitation, Mordred knew that she was lying. King Lot of Lothian, he knew, was *not* his true father.

CHAPTER 15

Lute hurried along on the old roan, eager to get back to the city. He had much to tell his uncle. The bags strapped on behind his saddle contained more than enough money to relieve his uncle's penury; and there was much more where it came from.

As the lad rode, many different thoughts crowded his head: thoughts about Merlyn and the strange black horse; about Wat and the reliable fellow he'd persuaded to oversee things temporarily in Sanham; about Lute's own deeds during his adventures, deeds he was mostly proud of but some that he deeply regretted; about Lute's own future, which now might not be as one of the king's knights; and also about the young woman named Gwendolyn. Her bright face and slender body had much intruded themselves into his thoughts.

Where Merlyn and the black had gone off to, heaven only knew. When Lute asked him where he might be going next, Merlyn had merely replied, "That would be telling, wouldn't it?" At Merlyn's remark, the black had snorted.

So Lute had bid goodbye to Merlyn and to Wat and set out on his return journey to the city, knowing he had a good three days of riding ahead of him. But throughout those days the late June weather remained dry and warm, and Lute's old horse moved along as steadily as his advanced years would allow. Lute didn't push him too hard, but the animal seemed happy to push himself. He seemed as eager to reach their destination as his rider.

It was already early evening as Lute and the roan entered the city after their three days on the road. At that hour there was little activity in the city's lowest square, for a good many of the stalls and shops had closed down for the night. But Lute, who'd had nothing to eat since early morning, stopped at one of the few remaining stalls to buy a hot pasty and a mug of cider. He ate and drank standing close beside his old horse, breathing in the smell of sweat and leather. "I'll attend to you soon, old friend," Lute said. "Don't begrudge me a moment's respite."

As he ate, Lute's eyes drifted upward toward the citadel and the king's great dragon banner above it. Those sights, which he'd always found so uplifting to his spirit, now produced in the lad a more somber mood. For Lute knew he would soon face a terrible conflict between the desires of his heart and the duty he owed to his uncle and to the little earldom of Sanham. If it came to making a choice—and it appeared that it soon would— Lute knew that he would put his duty ahead of his personal wishes.

It won't be so bad, he kept telling himself. You'll be serving your uncle well, and you should be able to do much good for the people of Sanham. Sanham is a fruitful earldom. You'll be able to live a fine life there, in peace and prosperity; in time you will marry and raise your family there. You may have sons, one who will succeed you as earl; and others, perhaps, one of whom may achieve the things you would like to achieve yourself. Those were some of Lute's thoughts. Yet in the end, none of them did much to raise his spirits.

But something did raise his spirits. Hearing the sound of someone skipping down the central stairsteps, Lute looked up to see who it was. It was the young woman named Gwendolyn, perhaps returning from an errand she'd completed on one of the city's upper levels. The sight of the young woman quickly dispelled Lute's gloomy thoughts.

Catching sight of Lute and his horse, she hurried over to them, her face rosy from her exertions. "Lute, you've returned at last!" she exclaimed, then blushed even more at the silliness of her words.

"Hello, miss," the lad replied. "I hope you've managed the city well in my absence."

"I've done my very best," she said.

"Then I'm sure things here are just as fine as they could possibly be."

Gwendolyn reached out her hands to Lute, and he took them eagerly. He felt their softness and warmth. It was the most intimate contact he'd ever had with a member of the opposite sex. He'd had quite a lot of new experiences lately, some not much to his liking. This one he liked.

As they stood there delighting in the moment, life continued going on about them. But Lute and Gwendolyn were largely oblivious to that fact.

High up on the central stairs, however, stood another young man who was hardly oblivious. Mordred had been on his way to meet Colgrevaunce for an evening of revels when his eye fell upon the two figures standing close to each other in the lower square.

Who the devil was *this* fellow Gwendolyn was speaking to? He wasn't anyone Mordred had seen before. From his appearance and the appearance of his horse—his rather *pathetic*-looking horse—he must have just entered the city.

Mordred moved slowly down the steps, wanting to get a better look. As he drew nearer, he could just make out the faint sound of their laughter.

Feelings of jealousy suffused his mind and body. Mordred had no doubt that this young fellow, whoever he was, represented a more serious rival to him than the ironmonger's apprentice. And yet, he reasoned, if she really preferred this lad to him, then she probably wasn't worthy of his interest anyway. Still and all, Mordred hated to be bested in anything. If this young fellow was going to best him with the maiden named Gwendolyn, then he would have to pay a price.

When Gwendolyn stepped quickly away, the youth stood for a moment and watched her go. Then, leading his old horse, he started toward the twisty road that would take him up to the higher levels. Mordred allowed him time to get a head start, and then began striding along behind him.

Mordred followed Lute up to the third level. From behind a tree he watched as the lad knocked on the wooden doorway to one of the finer dwellings. Someone came and spoke to him through a small panel in the door, and then the lad took his horse all the way around to the back of the building. Mordred continued spying on Lute as he was let in through another gateway.

Mordred spent the next few minutes looking the place over. Whoever lived there was surely a person of some prominence. Mordred would have to find out who that was. Perhaps the lad was his son. Whoever the young man was, he would require watching. And more than just watching. Eventually, this lad would need to receive his just deserts.

❖

As Lute rubbed down the old horse, he managed to push all the thoughts that had troubled him earlier to the back of his mind. At the forefront of his mind was the little encounter he'd just experienced with Gwendolyn. He ran over it again and again, especially the feelings he'd had when he'd reached out and taken her hands in his. Despite his inexperience with such things, the lad sensed that she'd thrilled to his touch as much as he had to hers.

And on top of that, he'd brought back news he knew would greatly relieve his uncle. For the moment, a local man much trusted by Wat had taken charge of things back in Sanham. It was only a temporary arrangement and it wouldn't do for very long, but Lute felt sure his uncle would be pleased by all he had to tell him.

In the meantime, anyway, the money in Lute's bags would make life a lot more pleasant for Thomas and Julianna. Why, it might even bring a smile to the sour face of old Gwilym, Lute thought with a grin. But on second thought, no, that was probably too much to expect.

Lute gave the old roan a hug and a pat, then headed up the garden pathway toward his uncle's dwelling. He was eager to see everyone there; even Gwilym.

CHAPTER 16

Merlyn and the black moved quickly through the Welsh Marches. Merlyn was going home, home to a place of solitude where he could think. Lute had handled his first great challenges quite well. Now Merlyn needed to reflect upon what he should do next and what he hoped Lute would do. At the moment, he wasn't quite sure what those things were.

Raguel, as Merlyn now called the black, trotted steadily up the muddy trail that ran beside the swiftly flowing waters of the River Wye. Merlyn's home, such as it was, was several miles upstream, well concealed behind a thick coppice of laurels high up the side of a steep hill. Curiously, Raguel seemed to know the way without any guidance from Merlyn.

Not quite a true cave, Merlyn's secret abode lay beneath a jutting ledge of rock. Someone—eons ago, perhaps—had delved deeply enough into the hillside to carve out a small chamber. At the back of the chamber was a ledge wide enough to serve as a bed; close by it were several large holes that Merlyn used for storage. He'd first discovered this place many years ago, having stumbled on it by chance. He was a young boy then, a young boy fleeing from the malicious intentions of his so-called playmates, the leader of whom he'd bested in a tree-climbing competition. Throughout the years, whenever he needed a place of refuge, it was here he'd always come to be alone with his thoughts.

Merlyn tended to the black as best he could, a new experience because he'd never come here before with a horse.

Then he laid a small fire in the fire circle, more for the sake of the comforting smell than from a need for warmth. Although he wasn't especially hungry, he gnawed on a dried-up turnip while he sat and thought. The black stood behind him, almost as if standing guard over his master. Raguel could certainly be an exasperating creature; but in the short time the two had been together, they'd formed a curious bond. Was it truly a bond of friendship? That remained to be seen.

Merlyn found himself thinking about the heirless king, the man he loved more than life itself, the man he'd gone to great lengths to shield from the corrupting influence of his father, King Uther Pendragon. Merlyn had compromised his own integrity to do it. But he believed it had been worth it. What he'd done to the gentle, trusting Igraine—creating the circumstance that permitted King Uther to satisfy his lust for her—had, of course, been deplorable. He'd long wondered whether he had actually fallen a little in love with Igraine himself, that what he'd done for Uther had held for him a strong element of vicarious pleasure.

In any event, the consequence of those dubious actions had certainly justified them. Or so Merlyn repeatedly told himself. He'd done it for the sake of the land he loved, for the sake of Albion, a land now called Logres by some and Britain by others. And it had worked. The child of Uther and Igraine had been everything Merlyn had hoped he would be. Now he reigned supreme, the finest leader imaginable. The finest leader Logres had ever had. And yet . . . and yet.

For the king and queen remained childless. After twelve years of marriage, they were still childless. *They* were childless —but the king wasn't. For in the years preceding his marriage to the queen, he had fathered two sons. One of them was the product of a liaison as deplorable as it is possible to be. That son was not only a child conceived in adultery, he was also a child of incest. Fortunately, the wee babe had been disposed of before any terrible consequences might ensue.

Now, sitting cross-legged before the small fire, his arms wrapped about his torso, his chin down upon his chest, these were just some of the things that crowded Merlyn's mind. It wasn't so long before the old man slowly began to enter the trance-like state he sought, a state hovering between consciousness and unconsciousness. It was in that state that the spirit that spoke to him would come—if it chose to come.

❖

After seeing Lute again and hearing all about his successful exploits—or about *most* of his exploits, since there were a few things Lute kept back—there was great joyousness in Thomas's household. Although now they could afford to bring back some of the household helpers they'd had to dismiss, Lute threw himself once again into all the necessary domestic chores. It was partly because he enjoyed those things, and partly because they helped to occupy his mind and keep him from agonizing about things he didn't want to think about. In particular, the two men whose lives he'd ended.

There was one thing he did want to think about, however, and that was the young woman who'd begun to occupy so many of his thoughts. He found himself thinking about Gwendolyn's eyes, her smile, and the soft feel of her hands in his. Lute had had very little experience with young women, and no prior experience of young love. However ephemeral it would probably prove to be—as most initial infatuations do—for Lute it was something new and exciting.

Thomas and Julianna, recognizing the tell-tale signs of first love, often exchanged knowing looks and smiles. Julianna went out of her way to create errands for the lad, just to get him out into the city, and Lute, oblivious to her not very subtle stratagems, eagerly complied.

So in the days that followed, Lute had several chance encounters with Gwendolyn, usually out in the open of the market square. Sometimes she accompanied him on his round of errands, and sometimes they just stood beside the central fountain and made small talk. Lute liked it that she was quick and intelligent; and he liked looking at the narrow band of freckles that arched across her nose.

But Lute didn't know that several of his meetings with Gwendolyn had been closely observed. Unbeknownst to him, he now had a serious antagonist. Mordred had been watching and waiting, waiting for a propitious moment to strike.

❖

Mordred stood atop the highest tower of the citadel, staring down at a great expanse of whiteness. Everything below him was invisible. The city was blanketed in fog. Only the top portion of the tallest tower upon which he stood rose above it. From time to time Mordred heard the muffled sounds of the bells of the city's churches as they called their flocks to Sunday morning services.

Off in the far distance above the fog, though, Mordred could see a line of high green hills. Between the tower and the hills was nothing but an opaque ocean of whiteness, a whiteness not even pierced by a single tall spire. As Mordred gazed upon this sea of fog, he lapsed into a reverie:

> *Ahead, a whiteness, a blankness, a nothingness.*
> *Far off, a hilltop, a green eminence.*
> *Is it too far, too far across the nothingness?*
> *Too horribly far?*
> *Give me a ship, a horse, a pair of wings:*
> *I shall sail, ride, fly. Or I shall sink and perish*
> *In a sea of whiteness, of nothingness.*

"Mordred! There you are. Found you at last, you scoundrel."

The voice belonged to Colgrevaunce, Mordred's sole close friend. He seemed excited. As it turned out, with good reason.

"Cole?" Mordred said, startled from his reverie. "Oh . . . yes . . . hello."

"Listen, my friend, I have news that will astonish you, delight you, make you cream your pants!" Colgrevaunce chuckled at his own vulgar remark.

"News?" Mordred said, his brain still a bit muzzy as he slowly awakened from his reverie.

"Double news, my friend. News that few people know, that I know, and that now you shall know."

"This had better be good, Cole."

"Oh, it's good, it's good. Comes from Sir Ascamour, it does. As solid a source as any. Mordred, listen, he told me that three of the fellows in our group are going to be knighted! Knighted at Lammas. That's less than a month from now."

"Knighted? Three of us? So that would be you, me, . . . and Melleas de Lyle?"

"Of course it would. Well, hell, Melleas is *almost* as good as we are, isn't he?"

"No, not really, though quite a bit better than the others."

"Just a month from now, Mordred—a month from now and we will be knights! Think of that, my friend! Sir Ascamour is terribly pleased, too, since under his tutelage we'll have completed our training faster than it's ever been done."

Colgrevaunce's news did please Mordred. While it didn't come as any huge surprise, it still pleased him a great deal.

"And here's my other news. There's going to be a great tournament. Way off some place or other, I forget where. But it's going to be held right around the Feast of the Assumption. Mordred, that's two weeks after you and me will be knighted. You and me, you scoundrel, we'll be able to be in it! So what do you think of that, you fornicating sodomite?"

His senses fully restored at last, Mordred smiled at his friend. "Did you just call me a fornicating sodomite? Where in the world did you learn such a vile and vulgar phrase?"

"Umm . . . I think it was from you."

On the day before she planned to set off on the long journey to her home in the north, Margause sent for Mordred. Before she departed, there were important things she wanted the young man to know. At the same time—her motives never being pure—there was much she wished to learn from him.

The sudden revelation that Mordred was her child—a child who'd been snatched away from her fifteen years ago—had produced in her a storm of emotions. Long ago she'd become reconciled to the loss of the baby boy. And not long after the child's disappearance, when she'd learned to her dismay that she and the king were half-siblings, both the children of Queen Igraine—knowledge she hadn't possessed when she'd so ably seduced the eager young king—she'd convinced herself that the loss of the child had been a blessing. But now, with the lad's reappearance, things were considerably altered.

"Mordred," she called out, hearing the soft knock on the door of her private chamber, "do come in."

The youth poked his head in first, then shyly entered, adopting his usual diffidence in the presence of his betters.

"No, Mordred, you needn't put on an act with me," she said. "We have too much in common for me not to see you for what you are." She motioned for him to sit down across from her on an ornately carved and softly cushioned seat.

"Madam," the lad replied innocently, "whatever do you mean?" He sat with his hands clasped atop his pressed-together thighs.

"You've played the innocent so long it's become second nature," she said, smirking at him. Mordred, abandoning his mask of innocence, returned her smirk.

"Madam," Mordred said, "would you mind if I called you mother?"

She gave the youth a long hard stare. Finally she said, "You may call me 'Queen Margause.' You may call me 'my lady.' Or you may call me 'madam.' But yes, if you really want to, you may call me 'mother.'

"However," she went on, "for the next few moments I would like you to sit quietly and listen while I speak. There are things you need to know. Listen carefully. I'll let you know when it's your time to speak. For just as there are things you need to know, there are things I wish to know also.

"So, Mordred, it appears you truly are my son. And that being so, you aren't an only son as you've always supposed, but one of five brothers. You are the youngest, though Gareth is only thirteen months older. Gawain, Agravaine, and Gaheris, who were born close together, are quite a bit older; six years elapsed between the births of Gaheris and Gareth; you were born just a year and a month after Gareth. So now I find that I have five living sons rather than four. Your eldest brothers are already Round Table knights. Gareth, no doubt, will soon join their ranks. And then, Mordred, there is you . . . .

"You, my mysterious youngest son—who was less than a month old when he was whisked away, never to be heard of again. Always assumed to be dead. Until now."

"Why was I whisked away, mother?"

"Hush. I'm still speaking!"

As Mordred stared at his mother, the look in her eye reminded him of a wild peregrine falcon he'd once caught, a spirited creature who'd put the goshawks in the mews to shame by its beauty, grace, and smug superiority—and also its flashes of viciousness. This woman, he had no doubt, was both beautiful and dangerous.

"Why was that, you ask?" she said, after a lengthy pause. "A question not so simply answered. In part, no doubt, because of an ancient prophecy which was being widely bruited about. It declared that a boy born on Beltaine—the old name for May Day—was fated to bring down the kingdom. It was a very simple little prophecy that went something like this:

> 'When a star falls on Beltaine Eve,
> So the Sybil once did say,
> A leopard born of a lion,
> Will Albion lead astray.'

"The year you were born, a star fell on Beltaine Eve. It flashed brilliantly across the western sky and plummeted into the sea. It was a sight seen by many, a fiery portent it was widely believed. Yes, the foolish, superstitious people put great stock in it. It would be a boy born the very next day who was destined to bring about the nation's destruction. You, my son, were born the very next day."

"As were a great many others."

"Oh, yes. And all of you were quickly gathered up and taken away."

"By whom, mother?"

"Now, *that* is quite a good question."

"By the king?" A look of anger flared in Mordred's eye.

"Perhaps. But I don't actually think so. He learned of it later, but I don't think he instigated it."

"Then who?"

"Some say it was the doing of Merlyn."

"Merlyn?"

"So you haven't met him as yet?"

"No, I know nothing of any Merlyn."

"Well, you will."

"He will be a danger to me?"

"He is a danger to all of us. But yes, Mordred, he will be an especial danger to you."

"Who is this man, mother? You must tell me about him—why he is important and why he will be a danger to me."

"He is the king's special friend and advisor"—for a moment the sight of a tall man mounted on great black stallion flashed through Mordred's head—"but who he truly is, that's something no one really knows, for his origins are shrouded in mystery. It's certain that he was a friend to Uther Pendragon. It is rumored that he played a major part in the destruction of the tyrant Vortigern, the event that allowed Uther's brother—the brother Uther succeeded—to become king. And it is rumored that he played a role in the birthing of the present king. Oh yes, there are many rumors about Merlyn—including that he was fathered by a demon."

Mordred remained silent, pondering his mother's words. The thought of the man on the black horse still lurked inside his brain. Finally he said, "If this man was involved in the snatching up of the baby boys, then we can't let him find out who I am. Or where or when I was born."

"This *man*, if that's what he is, has a knack for finding things out. But you are certainly right that we should keep him in the dark as long as possible."

Through Mordred's mind flitted the thought that the best remedy to his predicament would be to put this dangerous man in the dark *permanently*.

"Now, my son, since I can't seem to keep you quiet despite my attempts, perhaps it is time for you to speak. Mordred, I would like you to reach as far back in your mind as you can. Take me back to your earliest memories."

"My earliest memories? Hmm. All right, mother, I shall try. Yes, I remember that I was on the back of a pony. Perhaps I was about two. I believe it was my father, the Earl of Oakdon, who'd set me there. He was holding the reins with one arm and the other was about my waist, and as he walked slowly beside the pony, I suddenly snatched the reins from him and dug my heels into the pony's sides. The startled little creature took off running. As the wind rushed into my face I could hear people shouting and running after us. After a very brief moment of fright, I realized I was having the most fun I'd ever had. I was thrilled. By the ride itself, but even more by the fact that I'd astonished everyone. The folks chasing behind me feared for my life, the fools, but I had everything under control. From that time on, I took great pleasure in shocking people, in doing the unexpected.

"No one had ever seen a child who could ride like I could. I was soon given riding lessons, but who needed lessons? Within a few years I could ride circles around my instructors. Give me a fine mount sixteen hands high and I could jump fences and hedge rows that no one had ever jumped."

"Tell me about your parents." The woman's chin rested on her fist, her forearm propped against the armrest of her chair, as she awaited her son's reply.

"The earl and his wife were kindly folks, always well-intentioned. But it wasn't long before I began to think of them as weaklings. From the beginning they doted on me. Told me I'd been sent by the angels. At first I didn't know what they meant by that, but of course now I do. They gave me everything I wanted, and they did their best to tolerate all the things I did—even when they greatly disapproved. I learned early on that I could do pretty much anything I wanted. They suffered me. They suffered me because they loved me."

"And you loved them?"

"Loved them? . . . oh, I don't really know. I've never thought much about it. Probably not, I suppose. Actually, I'm not quite sure what it means to love someone. I liked them for what they could do for me. At the same time, I scorned them for their weakness. Since they'd wanted children for so long, I had a terribly unfair advantage. For suddenly, there I was. I was never especially mean to them or intentionally hurtful. I even made some efforts to be a dutiful son. But I knew there was no limit to what I could get away with. It might've been better for me if they'd tried harder to rein me in. But they never did."

"So you are the heir to the earldom?" Now her chin rested on both of her fists.

"Oh, yes," Mordred said, his hands stroking the sides of his face.

"But now, having tasted life here, you will never go back and take it, will you?"

"Now? Now that I've seen the great city? Now that I'm about to become a knight with the future entirely before me? Why would I ever go back?"

"Because it's your rightful place?"

"Me? A foundling washed up on the seashore? My rightful place? My rightful place would be more with you, dear mother, than with them. But no, my rightful place isn't with them or with you. My rightful place is here. It's my destiny to be here. That is why I was saved."

Mordred fingered the small gold ring on the last finger of his right hand. "I think it was because of you, mother, that I was saved. This talisman which you gave me. It was you who saved me, Queen Margause of Lothian—for better or for worse." Mordred laughed gleefully.

And despite herself, Margause did also.

CHAPTER 17

*T*he city was in flames. Uther Pendragon's great city, the greatest achievement of his reign, was entirely ablaze. The fire, which originated in the smithy, spread quickly to the nearby half-timbered structures, structures that flared up like matchwood. Towering plumes of smoke arose from their oak-shingled roofs. The western breezes fanned the flames. Now they swept upward toward the city's second and third levels.

Panicked people ran in all directions. Some rushed toward the city gates, some leapt off the high walls in the encircling river, a few immersed themselves in the water of the fountains. Most perished in the inferno.

On the second level of the city, no buildings were spared, not even the great stone minster, the city's largest church. The mortar between its huge blocks of stone cracked in the heat of the inferno; its heavy leaden roof sagged and then crashed down upon the high altar and smoldering choir stalls; intense heat cracked the elegant tiles of the nave.

The ravenous flames leapt ever upward. On the third level, the great conflagration consumed every manse and mansion of the city's most esteemed noblemen and women.

Then tongues of flames licked and scorched the magnficent structures on the city's highest level. King Uther's great citadel and all its surrounding structures soon succumbed to the raging inferno.

As wreaths of smoke swirled about it, the soaring tower crowning the citadel swayed and teetered. Down it came, crashing *upon the roof of the castle's great hall. When the heavy hewn stones smashed upon the roof which was supported by the hall's massive oaken beams, the structure imploded upon itself.*

Last to succumb was the private dwelling of the king and queen. The small moat that separated it from the main citadel did little to thwart the ravening flames of the great conflagration. The palace's stained glass windows cracked, the ceiling beams flared up, the tapestries and wall hangings smoldered and fell.

In the bleak evening rain, all that remained were jumbles of broken stones and cracked masonry, and gray-black piles of ashes. Scattered amongst the ashes were the charred bones of the once-proud city's citizens.

Merlyn awoke in a sweat. His head was totty, reeling in uncertainty. Where was he? Then it all came back to him. But what had just happened? What was this vision—this *nightmare!*—that he'd just experienced? What had just percolated up from the depths of his unconscious mind?

Merlyn was rarely frightened. Now he was.

He didn't know how long he'd been in his state of semiconsciousness, but he knew he must get back to the city as quickly as possible. Lute was probably there by now, and Merlyn felt sure that some ill-defined evil threatened the lad.

In fact, it was Raguel who'd nudged him awake. Apparently the horse was just as concerned as his master.

"Yes, Rags, it's time for us to get moving. I hope you didn't have to fend for yourself for too long. Did you find some proper nourishment?"

The creature stamped one foreleg impatiently. "All right, all right," Merlyn muttered, "keep your socks on."

Only a few minutes later the two of them were making their

way on up the Wye Valley. When they'd reached the top, the landscape leveled out. Broad green plains stretched off to the left in the direction Merlyn intended to go.

Raguel came quickly to full stride—a long, smooth canter that even a novice like Merlyn could take pleasure in. And when Merlyn gave the creature his head, Raguel took off like he'd been shot from a trebuchet. Reaching a gallop, he ran freely and fluidly, going faster than Merlyn had ever gone. The old wizard's heart was filled with joy as the wind streamed against his cheeks and through his beard. They were moving at breakneck speed. The man had never imagined that being on a horse's back could be so delightful, so wonderfully exhilarating.

Eventually Merlyn gently reined in the horse. "Now, now, my dear, perhaps that's enough excitement for one day."

The horse whinnied loudly. To his rider's astonishment, the beast was scarcely breathing hard.

"Yes, my dear, you are a remarkable creature. I only wish there was some way for me to siphon off a bit of your vitality. You seem to have more than enough for the both of us."

The horse tossed his magnificent head and tugged impatiently at his reins.

"All right then, perhaps we could run just a little bit more, since you insist on it."

As the glossy-black creature raced across the sward, its elderly rider clutched fiercely to its mane. Fearing for his life, the man found himself muttering imprecations to the God of all creation.

❖

On the morning after Lute's return, a messenger arrived from the king summoning Earl Thomas to a meeting of the king's council. The messenger said the king especially desired the earl's presence. So once more Gwilym rigged out Lute's gentle old gelding so Lute could assist the earl in making the short trek up to the citadel.

"What do you suppose is happening?" Lute asked his uncle, as he led the old horse slowly. "Do you think there's some kind of crisis? That messenger made it sound like this is quite an urgent meeting." In fact, as the old earl well knew, to be given only two hours' notice of a meeting of the king's council was highly unusual.

"We'll soon find out, Lute," his uncle replied, "but until we do, there's little point in speculating."

Earl Thomas was as curious as Lute, and he was mightily pleased to be asked to sit once more amongst the king's most intimate advisors. Earl Thomas's vitality had been much restored by Lute's presence and generous actions. Now being asked to rejoin the king's council created in him an even greater sense of renewed zest for life.

"Come back in an hour, Lute. If discussions are still going on, I'll send someone to tell you."

Lute helped his uncle dismount, and watched as he walked by himself, with the help of his canes, through the door and into the king's private council chamber.

Lute had deep affection for the old earl. Even though he'd only known him for a short time, Lute knew he owed his uncle a great deal. And he knew that if it came to it, as it probably would, he would return to Sanham and take up the family responsibilities there. And yet, as those thoughts passed through his head, he couldn't help emitting a small sigh.

Leading the old roan through the passages of the citadel, Lute moved on foot in the direction of the athletic fields, where, he suspected, the young men aspiring to knighthood might now be practicing their horsemanship. He had only gone there a few times before—times he judged no one else would be around—but now he just hoped to watch.

He was in luck, for two different groups were just then engaging in their exercises. As Lute stood watching, he found himself longing to join in. But as things presently stood, that was out of the question.

The young men he watched were quite accomplished riders. Lute guessed they must be nearing the end of their training. Their mounts were splendid creatures, and despite himself, Lute couldn't help feeling ashamed of his own humble mount. But at the same time, out of loyalty he patted his horse's neck affectionately.

As he studied the riders, Lute couldn't help taking note of a slender young man riding a sleek bay stallion. This lad's skillfulness clearly surpassed that of the others. He guided his horse with such grace and finesse that the animal's movements belied the deadliness of his rider's tactics. The lad unhorsed three riders in rapid succession before splintering his lance on the shield of a fourth. One of the downed men remained down. Apparently he'd been seriously injured.

"Lad!" the slender youth suddenly shouted at Lute, "Come and ride."

"*Me?*" Lute said, pointing at his own chest.

"Yes, why not? Come and take Aglovale's sorrel. He's one of the best horses here. Leap up into the saddle and I'll show you a few things."

When Mordred had noticed Lute watching them, he'd immediately recognized him as the same young man against whom his mind had been swirling with malice. Maybe,

Mordred thought, his brain moving as swiftly as ever, he might first befriend the young man, win his trust, and make him feel comfortable about being in his company. Then, when the right moment came, he would exact whatever retribution he'd finally decided upon. Mordred chuckled to himself. He knew he was a devious bastard. He prided himself in being that.

"Mordred, what are you doing?" The speaker was Mador de la Porte, their riding instructor.

"All right if I show this lad a few things? We're almost done here anyway."

The older man, looking hesitant, rode over to Lute and said, "Son, do you have much riding experience? We can't have you putting yourself at risk if you don't."

Lute was uncertain what he should say or do. At the same time, he certainly didn't want these men thinking he was faint of heart.

"Actually, sir, I'm quite an experienced rider, though I admit I know little about mounted combat. Sir, if it's all right with you, it would be wonderful to learn a few of the basics."

The older man studied Lute a moment longer. He was reluctant to allow a completely unknown young fellow join in, despite his claim that he was a proficient rider. Still, judging from his overall appearance, the young man looked like someone who might be quite capable.

"I'm Earl Thomas's nephew," Lute said. "I'll be starting my chivalric training next month."

"Well," the older man finally said, "all right, then. But only for five minutes. And do be careful, eh? And as for you, Mordred, we'll have none of your wise tricks, or I'll see that you are not knighted come Lammas. Is that clear?" Then Mador turned his horse's head and rode back to where Aglovale was being attended to.

"Well, come on, my young friend," Mordred said. "No more dillydallying, eh? You and that sorrel look made for each other." Lute looped the reins of his old roan around a post and soon settled himself in the saddle of Aglovale's prancing sorrel.

To Lute, it felt like he'd just entered heaven.

❖

Merlyn and Raguel clip-clopped across the high wooden bridge and passed through the gate and into the city. It was just past dusk, still a few hours before curfew. The horse, he knew, presented a bit of a problem. Judging from the previous reactions to the creature, he doubted if it would be welcomed by the grooms in the king's stables. Lute's old roan, though, seemed to like the black. Perhaps he could be stabled with Earl Thomas.

Skirting the city square, Merlyn moved slowly up the left-hand lane that circled around behind the buildings. He and the horse ascended to the second level and then on up to the third, where most of the nobles lived. It was only another few moments before he was rapping on the outer doorway to the earl's habitation. The little wooden panel slid back, and there was Gwilym's beaky face peering out at the old wizard.

"You, huh?" he grunted.

"Yes, Gwilym, me. Would it be all right if I were to leave this creature in the earl's stables for a few days? I doubt if Earl Thomas would mind."

Gwilym gave Merlyn a squinty-eyed stare. Then he grumped, "Come on 'round to the back, then. Don't suppose it can do no harm."

It was Lute who opened the back gate for Merlyn. The lad

was beaming. He was delighted to see Merlyn, and also to see the black, and he had exciting things to tell the older man.

"I'll put the black in the same stall as my old horse," Lute said. "They seem to get on well with each other. Oh, Merlyn, if only I'd had the black to ride earlier today, then I would've shown those fellows what I'm really capable of. Aglovale's horse was good—but not like the black."

Merlyn raised his eyebrows at Lute's remark but didn't comment. He supposed that Lute would explain later. He'd certainly better.

In the earl's cozy sitting room they found Thomas and Dame Julianna seated close together. On the table before them stood a pitcher of wine and four small goblets.

"My lady," Merlyn said, "you are more lovely than ever." Julianna's eyes smiled brightly. "And you, Thomas," Merlyn continued, "look at you. You look like your old self."

"No, not quite my old self, though I'm doing better than I have in a great long while. Sit, Merlyn. Share a glass with us."

"I believe I shall."

"Stay with us, too," Julianna said, "if you wish to. You would be welcome to use our guest chamber."

Merlyn tilted his head in thought. Perhaps he just might do that. He normally stayed in a small private chamber reserved for him in the king's private residence, being one of the few allowed that privilege. But, it might make sense for him to lie low a day or two while he found out where things stood. He'd certainly not forgotten the dark and terrifying vision he'd experienced back at his cave.

"Do stay, Merlyn," said Lute. "During our adventures out on the road, we were hardly together long enough to have any proper conversations."

"Well, perhaps I'll stay tonight, at any rate," he said.

"Wonderful." Dame Julianna poured wine for each of them, and when she handed a goblet to Merlyn, he raised it in a silent toast, then sipped gratefully.

"Lute, it seems that something exciting has happened to you?"

"Today, Merlyn, I made a new friend."

"And who was that?"

"His name is Mordred." At the sound of that name—a name Merlyn had never heard before—a sharp chill suddenly shot through his body.

"He's been training for knighthood," Lute continued, "and he's nearly finished. He's one of the special few who'll be knighted at Lammas. I was watching them train while Uncle was at the king's council"—Merlyn cast a curious glance toward Earl Thomas—"and this lad invited me to join them for a bit. Sir Mador didn't seem happy about it, but because I acquitted myself so well, in the end I think he was mollified.

"Mordred and a fellow named Colgrevaunce welcomed me warmly, sir. They said they were impressed with my riding, and they invited me to join them for dinner. I had to decline, since I'd be helping Uncle return here after the meeting was concluded. They told me, sir, that Mador de la Porte and Sir Ascamour were the perfect knights to train with, should I ever plan to do that." His face wore a hopeful look.

Earl Thomas and Dame Julianna couldn't help smiling at the excited lad with deep affection. Merlyn, however, only looked pensive.

"I've heard of Colgrevaunce," he said. "But who is this *Mordred*? What do you know of him?" As the word "Mordred" passed through his lips, it gave the old wizard another chill.

"Nothing at all, sir, other than that he was very welcoming to me. And that he is one of the finest riders I have ever seen. All the fellows out there impressed me, but Mordred was head and shoulders above the rest. And they say he's flown through his training in record time. Not so surprising, seeing how skillful he is. I'm sure he's going to establish himself as a top knight in no time. Who knows, he might even be invited to join the Table Round before much longer."

"And Merlyn," Julianna said knowingly, "Mordred isn't the only new friend Lute has found recently."

"Oh yes?"

"Oh yes," replied Thomas. Lute, though, looked terribly embarrassed.

"A young woman?" asked Merlyn.

"Oh yes," replied Thomas.

Merlyn laughed. "Well, Lute," he said, "that's an experience most of us can remember having—and fondly, too."

After their evening meal, Lute went off to attend to the horses, and after that, to wander down to the lower square. His plan wasn't to rendezvous with Mordred and Colgrevaunce. What he hoped for was a chance encounter with Gwendolyn.

Merlyn, finally having Thomas to himself, intended to do some serious probing; he wished very much to know more about the urgent concerns of the king's council.

Initially, Thomas was hesitant to say much, and the two men did some cautious verbal fencing. But eventually, being mindful that Merlyn had long been one of the king's most trusted associates, and also feeling the need to confide in someone, Thomas came around to the view that there'd be no harm in putting the old wizard in the picture. Besides, the king would surely do it himself tomorrow.

"Frankly, Merlyn," he said, "the king is facing a bit of a dilemma. You see, King Ban and King Bors have sent urgent messages from across the water. Their circumstances are dire. They desperately need his help."

"That old tyrant King Claudas, is it?"

"Yes, it is."

Merlyn didn't need to be filled in on the background of this matter. He knew the great debt the king owed to Ban and Bors, men who had come to Logres with their armies and played a vital part in defeating the rebellious barons who'd nearly ended the young king's reign before it had begun. Indeed, it was in the climactic battle of that civil war, the Battle of Bedegraine Forest, that Thomas had sustained his horrible wounds.

"Well," said Merlyn, "I am sure he will do everything he can to aid them. So what's the dilemma?"

"Because a serious threat to Logres itself has also emerged."

"Oh dear. Not King Rience again?"

"Yes, that's who it is. He's brought all the kings of the western isles into an alliance, and reports are that at this moment they've amassed a large force on the island of Anglesey."

"What a bloody fool that man is!" Merlyn blurted out, shaking his head in disbelief. "He doesn't know when he's well off. So then, Thomas, what are the plans in regard to these two quite different threats?"

"You realize, of course, that the king would never let down Ban and Bors when their need is so great."

"Of course he wouldn't. And so . . . ?"

"And so the plan appears to be that the king and about fifty of his best knights will cross the sea and go to their aid. They'll take a troop of 250 horse soldiers and 1,000 foot soldiers.

Obviously, Launcelot and his kin will go since it's their fathers who are threatened." Launcelot and his brother Ector de Maris, as Merlyn well knew, were the sons of King Ban, while their cousins were the sons of King Bors.

"And the plan for dealing with King Rience and his confederates?"

"That, it seems, will be chiefly Gawain's responsibility. He and his brothers will go north, taking a large number of the best Round Table knights with them."

Thomas paused for a moment. Then he looked directly at his guest. "Merlyn, might you be willing to go with them?"

Merlyn grimaced. "Go with them? For the purpose of tempering Gawain's impulsiveness—or should I say hot-headedness?"

The two men grinned at each other knowingly. "I wouldn't put it *quite* like that," Earl Thomas said.

"No, but I would," Merlyn replied.

"In any event, I feel sure the king would be greatly relieved if you went along—just to be available to offer Gawain your sage advice, should the need arise."

"Gawain is a very capable knight, you know."

"Oh, yes, no question about that."

"Are none of the king's other advisors available to go?"

"Ulfin and Kay will remain in the city to keep an eye on things here. Sir Brastias has left us to become a churchman. Sir Jordan, sadly, is too ill to be of service to anyone. Merlyn, Gawain could use you. If you were willing to go, I'm sure it would be a great relief to the king."

Merlyn lifted his goblet and drained what wine remained. Then he set it down and looked across at Thomas.

"Oh, dear," he said. "Here I am, just returned from a trying and exhausting outing. I was quite looking forward to a few days of peace and quiet. Well, as the old saying goes, there's no rest for the weary."

"I thought the old saying was there's no rest for the wicked?"

"Yes, well . . . that too, I suspect."

CHAPTER 18

The July evening was delightfully warm and pleasant. Many of the city's ordinary citizens were enjoying the almost carnival-esque atmosphere of the main market square. Lute, seeing that some of the city's noble folk also mingled amongst the greater number of commoners, hoped his own intentionally modest attire didn't mark him out as one of them.

As he wandered, Lute remained on the lookout for Gwendolyn. They'd made no plan to rendezvous, and he'd come down merely on the off-chance of seeing her. Since his recent return to the city, he'd been fortunate enough to encounter her three different times, and as Thomas and Julianna suspected, he was now fully aware of her charms. Thoughts of her had been crowding out thoughts of other things, which was probably just as well, for some rather grim things still haunted his mind.

Lute knew that on such an evening several of the young knight-aspirants were likely to turn up here also, but he hoped he wouldn't run into them. His impressions of the two lads he'd met earlier in the day, Mordred and Colgrevaunce, had been mostly favorable. And yet from his brief acquaintance with them he'd sensed that they were wild young fellows with raging appetites. Lute, not being especially prudish himself, didn't mind that. But he did suspect that his interests and theirs were not well-matched.

Lute wandered about, keeping an eye out for Gwendolyn, and as he did, his eyes passed over many other young women, several of whom eyed him back unabashedly. None of them was the young woman he sought, though one older woman, her cheeks rouged to cherry-red perfection, boldly approached Lute and latched on to his arm.

"And what is it ye might be seeking, love?" she rasped in a throaty voice.

"I'm . . . I'm . . . looking for my sister . . . thank you kindly," he stammered back.

"Har, har. O'course ye are," she replied with a wink. "Too bad for ye that I ain't she. Were I ta be ten years younger, p'haps I would be she, hey?"

Mordred and Colgrevaunce were also on their way to the market square. As they hurried down the broad steps toward the lower city, Colgrevaunce gave voice to a banal little tune about going a-wenching. He'd sung it so many times it was getting on Mordred's nerves.

"Just *hush*, all right?" Mordred snapped at him. "That may be what we're doing, but there's no need to be announcing it to the world."

"Well, pardon me, milord. Anything you say, milord," Cole replied with mock deference. Then beneath his breath he muttered, "But I'm still going a-wenching."

For a while the two young fellows moved about the square aimlessly, eyeing every woman who looked even remotely promising. They stopped in one public house and then another, sampling the ale and looking over the clientele. With a long evening ahead of them, they were in no hurry, though Mordred could tell that Colgrevaunce was growing more and more eager to get on with his wenching.

By law, there were no bawdy houses in the city. But the two young men had quickly discovered that the pleasures of the flesh were readily available. And they knew that if they were cautious and selective, their keenly anticipated pleasures might be well worth the wait.

After making brief visits to a couple of the more high-class establishments, they wandered into the Fox & Grapes, the inn where Mordred, Grim, and Tib had stopped on their first evening in the city. As Mordred looked about, everything here seemed much as it had then—roughly the same clientele, the same banal topics of conversation, the same undertone of hostility toward folks belonging to the higher social classes. And what's more, it was the same ironmonger's apprentice, the lad named Rafe, who plopped himself down at their table right across from Colgrevaunce. Rafe shot Mordred a look of recognition and gave Colgrevaunce an indifferent nod.

"What's the news of that fellow Beaumains?" Mordred asked Rafe, hoping to stir him up.

"*Pah!*" came Raf's predicable reply.

"Beaumains?" said a voice from close by. "Ya wants ta know the news about Beaumains? Here ya go, then." The man dropped his oversized self down across from Mordred.

"What they're sayin' is the king sent Beaumains a message. Told him ta get right on back here. But that lad o' ours, ya know what he done? He sent a message right back sayin' he ain't ready ta be a-comin' back just yet. Still has business of his own ta be takin' care of. Har, har. So how does ya like *them* apples, eh? That lad o' ours, what a lad he be! Had the gumption ta stand up to the king hisself. That's Beaumains for ya. A lad after our hearts, he is."

"*Pah!*" said Rafe.

"Pah, nuthin'," said the other speaker. "He's our very own hero, that's what he be."

"Beaumains has done this, Beaumains has done that," Rafe said scornfully. "The next thing they'll be sayin' is he was born of the Virgin Mother. That's the next thing they'll be sayin'."

"Now you just shut your filthy gob, Rafe, you hear? Don't be blasphemin'. And don't be comin' round here belittlin' our Beaumains, neither. You just shut your gob."

"Shut my gob? Why don't you try 'n do that, Willikin? It's open, see," he said, pointing to his open mouth. "Try 'n shut it, eh Willikin?"

"Not in here, lads!" came the deep growl of the innkeeper. "You wanna have a go at each other, you take it outside."

"Come on, then!" Rafe shouted. "Let's just see if you're man enough to shut my gob—ya fat slug!"

The two men got to their feet and shambled toward the door, with almost everyone else in the Fox & Grapes trailing along behind them to watch the fun.

"Come on, Cole, this is going to be good," Mordred said with glee. He hadn't known what kind of trouble he might be able to stir up, but this looked like a promising start. Seeing these two lugs having a go at each other should be highly entertaining. Not likely to be a fight of real quality, Mordred knew, but that would be part of the fun.

Outside, most of the folks formed a ragged circle about the two would-be fighters. Most of them were hurling taunts and gibes at Rafe, whose skepticism regarding Beaumains didn't set well with them. Amongst the dozen or so men in that circle, Rafe didn't appear to have many allies.

Right away the two men began throwing awkward punches at each other, neither of them displaying much savvy or subtlety. But whenever Rafe found himself within reach of any of the encircling men, they too shoved and punched at him.

Seeing how terribly one-sided the affair threatened to become, Mordred found his gorge rising.

"Leave 'em be!" he shouted at the other men. "Ten against one is no fair fight."

"Stay out of this, your highness!" another fellow shouted back in derision. "No one invited *you* here."

Without even thinking about it, Mordred found himself standing right in front of the man, a look of pure spite on his face. When the fellow raised his hands in a boxer's stance, Mordred shot his left knee straight into the man's unprotected crotch. As the fellow doubled over in pain, Mordred brought his right knee up into the man's face. The cartilage crunched inside the fellow's nose, giving Mordred a sensation that vibrated all through his body. He cackled with glee.

"Ya bastard!" another fellow shouted. But before he could direct his upraised fist at Mordred, Colgrevaunce had seized his arm in a vise-like grip.

At that point all the other encircling men joined the fray. At almost the same time, seven or eight men had pounced upon Mordred, Rafe, and Colgrevaunce. The only ones who didn't were Rafe's two or three erstwhile supporters. Those bravos had taken to their heels. Now squirming and twisting and swarming on the cobblestones of the city's market square was a throbbing tangle of men who were indiscriminately gouging eyes, biting ears, grabbing and choking other men's throats.

The noisy, frantic hubbub attracted a large crowd of onlookers, and amongst them was Lute. When the lad realized that in the midst of the melee were his newly made friends, he had no doubt about what he should do. Grabbing one of the louts by his shirt neck and belt, Lute tossed him headfirst against the outer wall of the Fox & Grapes. Pulling another of the ruffians free of the pile, Lute punched him fiercely in the eye, the blow sending a stab of pain all down Lute's arm. The man fell in a heap, dazed or unconscious.

Lute had definitely changed the odds. And Mordred and Colgrevaunce, able and tenacious, were now doing more than just holding their own. Although Mordred didn't look like much of a brawler, when he went into action he fought with the ferocity of an uncaged panther: quick, agile, vicious. Colgrevaunce's greatest assets were his brute strength and his imperviousness to pain.

Seeing their numbers dwindling, the final few ruffians called it quits. And when the last man had slunk away, there stood Rafe, Mordred, Colgrevaunce, and Lute—battered and bruised, tattered and torn—but victorious. The large crowd of onlookers, disappointed that the fight was over, now dispersed. Perhaps they would encounter some other excitements before the evening was over.

Mordred gave Rafe a hefty whack on the back, nearly sending him sprawling. "I don't believe he shut your gob, my friend, no, I don't believe he did."

Rafe opened his mouth and moved his jaw in a circle. Most likely he was checking to see if he'd lost any teeth.

"Well, hello, Lute," Colgrevaunce said, a trickle of blood in the corner of his mouth. "Whose side were you on, anyway? Hope I didn't hurt you none. Just kidding ya, Lute, I knew you were with us. Hey, anybody around here fancy a drink?"

"Come on, lad," Mordred said to Rafe, his arm about his shoulder. "Come on and join us. I'm buying."

"Nah, nah, I'd best not. Thank ya, but I'd best be goin'." Rafe knew he'd already spent way too much time in the company of these wild young noblemen, the kind of fellows he so greatly despised. And he knew his other acquaintances would never let him forget it, either.

So the three young nobles settled themselves at another public house across the square, knowing they'd worn out their welcome at the Fox & Grapes.

"Cheers, lads!" Mordred cried out, as the three of them lifted their frothy mugs.

"My word, Lute," Cole said, "you're a handy fellow to have around. Thanks for coming to our aid." He licked one finger and rubbed it at the dried blood in the corner of his mouth.

"Cole's right," Mordred said. "My word, you were out there fighting like Duke Joshua before the walls of Jerico." Mordred chuckled. "I have to say, young sir, that you are a pearl among swine, a rose without a thorn."

Lute struggled to come up with a witty reply but he was stumped. At last he managed to say, "I think I probably have a thorn or two."

"Yes, well, don't we all," Mordred replied.

As he sat looking at Lute, Mordred savored the irony of celebrating their little victory and acting like he had the greatest goodwill in the world toward his new young acquaintance.

Yes, Mordred didn't doubt that Lute was a fine young fellow. But he'd long since determined that Lute was someone who would have to receive his proper comeuppance.

For Mordred felt sure that eventually he would have to give this young man exactly what he deserved. He wasn't sure what form Lute's comeuppance would take. But there was no rush. He would have to give the matter some thought. Then, when it happened, it would be a thing of beauty. And anyway, Mordred agreed with a dictum he'd learned long ago—that vengeance is a dish best served cold.

CHAPTER 19

"Your father did some things very well," Merlyn said. He and the king were standing alone atop the highest tower of the citadel looking down upon King Uther Pendragon's great city. They were standing at the same place where Mordred had stood two days earlier. Now the city wasn't blanketed in fog but was bathed in the glorious sunshine of mid-morning.

"He'd never been to Rome," the king said, "though the men who helped him design the city had. The high walls, the many sets of steps, the broad piazzas—they wanted it to evoke the greatest Christian city."

"Yes. And yet the city they created has more of a British feel than a Roman one, which I quite like. Your countrymen, my lord, while learning a very great deal from the Romans, never truly belonged to Rome. Not in their hearts. They never relinquished their ties to their ancient heritage."

"You would know far more about that than I."

"It is that heritage, one you share with your cousins in Armorica, which now takes you abroad, I believe."

"Ban and Bors have sore need of me, Merlyn. I must go."

"I wouldn't expect you to do anything else. Do you wish me to come with you?"

"There's nothing I would like better . . . but no. Merlyn, what I would wish, if you are willing, is for you to accompany Gawain. His dealings with King Rience are likely to present him with some difficult decisions."

"Is he ready to shoulder such responsibilities?"

"Mostly, I think. But having a sage advisor at his side, just as a precaution, mind you, strikes me as being quite a good idea."

Merlyn smiled. He was well aware of Gawain's tendency to fall prey to his emotions. Merlyn's job would be to save him from himself. "Yes, my lord, I shall do that, if it's what you wish."

The king reached out and placed his hand softly on the shoulder of his dear friend and mentor. Although they always spoke formally to each other, their relationship was one of great intimacy.

The two men stood there together in silence, leaning on the parapet and looking out at the lush green valley beyond the city and the high hills that rose beyond the valley. King Uther and his advisors had chosen the site well. As Merlyn had said, it truly combined the best of both worlds, of ancient Britain and of imperial Rome.

"Sire," Merlyn said after several minutes of companionable silence, "what can you tell me about a lad named Mordred?"

"Mordred?" The king face's bore a look of surprise. Merlyn's question was completely unexpected. "Ah, Mordred. Yes, now I remember who you mean, the young lad who's just begun making a name for himself. He arrived in the city a short time ago, and I've only met him in passing, though I know he's in training for knighthood. I've heard he's shown himself a lad of rare abilities and that he's flown through his training faster than anyone ever has. He's soon to be knighted, I believe. Merlyn, why do you ask about him?"

Merlyn didn't respond to the king's question. Instead he said, "And do you know Earl Thomas's nephew? The young lad they call Lute?"

"The shy young man who accompanies Earl Thomas to

events in the citadel? No, Merlyn, I don't know him at all, though I have had several glimpses of him. These are strange questions. Why do you ask them? Are there things I should know about these two young men?"

"My lord, I'm not entirely certain, but perhaps there are. I know a good bit about Lute, but nothing at all about this Mordred. My lord, you have asked me to go along with Gawain on his mission and I have agreed. Now, Sire, I should like to make a request of you. Could I ask you to make sure that the young man named Mordred also goes along with Gawain, once he's been knighted?"

"Merlyn, what are you up to?"

"This Mordred causes me some concern, Sire. I think I should be keeping an eye on him."

"Merlyn," the king said after a long pause, "has anyone ever told you that you are a very strange man?"

"Yes, my lord, I believe I've heard that a time or two."

Finally the king said, "All right, then, I will make sure that the small group of newly made knights shall be included amongst those who go with Gawain. That way we won't be calling special attention to Mordred by singling him out."

"A good plan, my lord," Merlyn replied.

"And so what are your wishes in regard to Thomas's nephew, this lad named Lute? I suspect you must have some, old friend."

"My lord, could you make sure that he stays here? I would very much like to keep him out of harm's way."

"And why is that, Merlyn?"

"He is still young and inexperienced, Sire. Though in time, perhaps, he may prove himself someone quite special."

"Merlyn," the king said, smiling at his old mentor, "has anyone ever told you that you are a very strange man?"

"*Me?* A very strange man? Why no, my lord, I don't believe I've ever heard that."

❖

Merlyn woke up with a start. Something seemed amiss. What could it be? He knew he'd better find out, and quick. He sat up and reached for his boots, then he leapt to his feet and snatched up his cloak.

Only a dim light shone through his small window, and he guessed it was very early in the morning. Merlyn moved swiftly through Earl Thomas's silent dwelling. He passed through the kitchen and went out into the back garden.

A heavy morning dew sat upon the tall grasses, and as Merlyn made his way toward the door to the stables, the lark's morning song greeted his ears.

The stable door creaked as Merlyn entered. Lute's old roan stared nervously at him as he approached the stall, and Merlyn snatched up a handful of hay and held it out to the horse. But the horse shied away, as horses always tended to do whenever Merlyn got too close to them. Every horse had always done that, every horse but one—Raguel.

But as Merlyn looked into the stall, no other horse was there.

"Rags?" Merlyn called out. "Where are you, you devil?"

Merlyn's words fell only on the ears of the trembling old roan. Merlyn's magnificent black stallion was gone.

CHAPTER 20

In addition to the main gateway into Uther Pendragon's city, there were three lesser entryways, small postern gates that were closely guarded. These private entrances could only be used by the nobles living on the highest levels of the city. It was through one of them that Lute exited that morning, riding the black.

The men stationed at the postern gate waved this young nobleman they didn't know to a halt and looked him over guardedly. Then, seeing nothing to alert suspicion, they opened the double set of doors and motioned him through.

Beyond the city wall Lute found himself on a steep, graveled pathway that led down to a short wooden bridge. The bridge spanned a narrow place in the flowing river from one high bank to another. It, too, was guarded at each end, though once more the guards paid the lad little heed. It was more the lad's mount they noticed, for they'd seen few horses so magnificent, even among those belonging to Round Table knights. This unknown lad, it seemed, was someone of importance.

The day before, when Lute had ridden on Aglovale's sorrel with the young knights-to-be, he'd found himself wishing he'd been mounted on Merlyn's horse instead. For Lute, the only day in which he'd actually ridden the horse—that day when the horse first turned up—was one he would never forget. Lute had never been a finders-keepers person, and yet he couldn't help feeling that his claim on the horse was as great as anyone's. Besides, he and Merlyn were the only two people who'd had any significant contact with the horse who didn't seem terrified by him. Lute couldn't help feeling a deep affection for the strange and mysterious creature.

Once out on the meadow Lute gently gave the horse his spurs. The black shot forth like a bolt from a crossbow. Lute stood up in the stirrups and bent his body forward into a horse-racer's crouch. The wind, whipping through his long brown hair and across his face, felt wonderful. As he dashed across the open meadow, Lute sensed that the powerful creature beneath him could easily ratchet up his speed several more notches, should Lute wish him to. But he didn't. He was loving it just the way it was.

Always lurking in the back of the lad's mind, though, was Merlyn's dire warning, his assertion that Lute must have nothing more to do with this creature. But Lute couldn't help scoffing at the foolishness of the old man's fears.

Riding with those knights-in-training yesterday had made Lute jealous. He wanted to proclaim to them that he had a horse as fine or finer than any of theirs, that he could ride just as well as the best of them. Well, all right, perhaps he wasn't yet the rider that Mordred was, though he believed he might become that good, given half a chance.

While Merlyn's advice continued to nag at him a little bit, Lute did his best to shove those thoughts far back into the recesses of his mind.

After half an hour of hard riding, Lute brought the noble steed to a standstill to give it a breather. As they stood in the shade of an elm, Lute loosened the reins so the horse could crop a few mouthfuls of grass.

While the black chomped away, Lute looked back toward the city perched high on its hill. He hadn't seen it from this vantage point before, and from here it looked even more magnificent than it had when he'd glimpsed it on that very first morning. He'd come to love this city, and the thought of having to leave it was one he hated to contemplate.

Now Lute saw that another rider was moving briskly along the same path he and the black had just taken. This rider was also mounted upon a most impressive horse, a great bay stallion of sixteen or seventeen hands. Lute recognized neither the horse nor the rider. But when they'd finally come within thirty or so yards, he did. The man on the horse was the king.

"Hello," the king called out, raising his hand in greeting. He rode up close to Lute and halted his towering steed. Then he, too, loosened his reins to allow his horse to crop at the tall grasses. The two magnificent horses eyed each other cautiously; it was almost as if they were wondering how they might stack up against each other.

"Sire," Lute stammered. "My most noble lord." He inclined his head in obeisance to the king.

"I think you are Lute," the king said, "Earl Thomas's nephew?"

Lute just nodded. He felt completely tongue-tied.

"Upon my word, Lute, that's an astonishing mount you're sitting on!"

The black raised his head and tossed it almost arrogantly. Then he looked directly at the king.

Again Lute nodded mutely. Summoning up his nerve at last he said, "Sire, the horse isn't mine. He belongs to Merlyn."

"*What?* The horse is *Merlyn's?* Now you've truly astonished me. In all my life I've never known Merlyn to have anything to do with horses—and I've known Merlyn for all of my life. Indeed, I've never seen any horse who wanted to have anything to do with him."

"This horse is rather unusual," Lute said.

"He certainly is. But Lute, if the horse is Merlyn's, how does it happen that you are riding him?"

"Umm, he's been stabled at my uncle's since Merlyn's return, along with my own horse. And when I was tending to them this morning, I could tell he was greatly in need of exercise, so I took it upon myself to do that." Lute was stretching the truth only a little.

"You sit him well. The two of you look as though you were made for each other. Tell me, how does it come about that Merlyn now owns this horse?"

"Well, Sire, it's through some rather odd circumstances, actually."

"With Merlyn," the king said with a smile, "I wouldn't have expected anything else."

"You see, Sire, during some recent travels of mine I encountered the horse alone and riderless in a meadow. I searched high and low for his owner but couldn't find him. Not knowing what to do and thinking I shouldn't just abandon him, I took him with me when I went to meet Merlyn. At the place we were staying, no one wanted to have anything to do with the horse. Indeed, they wanted the horse away from there as quickly as possible. But right away the horse attached itself to Merlyn."

"How *strange*," the king said with a wide grin. "Old Merlyn having his own horse. Merlyn, a man who doesn't know a hock from a fetlock! And strangest of all, a horse that isn't terrified of Merlyn. I've never known such a creature."

"Sire, that's just what Merlyn said himself. But the black here, he acts just the opposite."

"Don't tell me that Merlyn has actually learned to ride this beast?"

Now it was Lute's turn to grin. "Well, Sire, after a fashion. Only after a fashion."

The king laughed at Lute's comment. He'd now seen this youth four or five times, and he felt a distant memory tugging at him. He had a strong sense, not for the first time, that the lad reminded him of someone. But for the life of him, he couldn't quite put his finger on who that might be.

"Merlyn riding upon this magnificent beast," the king mused with a chuckle. "Now that's a sight I can't wait to see. Anyway lad, it's come time for me to be turning around and riding back to the city. It would give me pleasure if you would ride back with me."

"Sire, I would be honored."

"Then let's go!"

The king quickly brought his large bay steed to a gallop, but only a moment later Lute and the black had caught up to him. The two magnificent horses, matching each other stride for stride, streaked toward the city.

When the king and the youth passed back across the small bridge and went through the postern gate into the city, Lute couldn't help noticing the looks of great respect the various guards now gave him.

"Lute," the king said as they were about to part, "I may not see you again for several months. I will soon be going off on a mission of great importance. But I hope very much that when I've returned, the two of us can become better acquainted."

Lute blushed. He was overwhelmed by the king's kindness. "Sire . . ." he finally managed to say, "that would give me immense pleasure."

The king stared at Lute a moment longer. Who was it the lad reminded him of? Well, perhaps it would come to him later. He gave the lad a final nod and set off for the royal stables.

When Lute, now leading the black, came in through the back gate to Earl Thomas's garden, Merlyn was there awaiting him. He did not look pleased.

"What have you just done, you fool!" the old man blurted out. "Where have you been and what have you been doing? Didn't I tell you that you must never *ever* come in contact with the black?"

"Sir," Lute replied, "the black and I, we've been riding in the meadow. Your horse hadn't had any exercise since your arrival. Sir, he was greatly in need of it."

"Riding in the meadow. Riding in the meadow. And were you riding in the meadow alone? I hope to goodness you weren't riding with that fellow Mordred!"

"No, sir, I certainly was not. Sir . . . I was riding with the king. I was riding in the meadow, sir . . . with the king."

Merlyn gave Lute a wide-eyed stare, his mouth hanging partway open. "You were doing *what?*"

"I was riding with my friend the king."

Merlyn just stood there looking at Lute. For once in his life he didn't know what to say.

THE REBELS

CHAPTER 21

The king's two armies were gone—along with nearly every man in the city between the age of fifteen and forty.

The king's own army, the smaller of the two forces, was the first to depart. With him went his royal guard, a superlative group of one hundred knights. Also with him went select companies of archers and crossbowmen and a troop of foot—about a thousand men in all. These units had all gathered on the shores of the Sabrina Estuary where a flotilla of thirty ships awaited them—flat-bottomed cogs, carracks, stately galleys, and small, swift-sailing pinnaces—all displaying colorful banners and flags that snapped in the western breezes.

When the men, horses, and equipment were safely aboard, the fleet set sail, moving swiftly down the estuary propelled by their bellying sails and the flow of the river's powerful tidal currents.

In the days following the king's departure, Sir Gawain's larger, more unwieldy force slowly began to take shape in the great meadow below the city's high walls. It required more than a week to assemble and organize, as the leaders awaited the arrival of the small groups of men who straggled in from towns and villages, hamlets and small farm holdings ranging all across southern Britain. These men were conscripts, the so-called volunteers that every shire was required to provide. A great many of them were simple farmers and their sons, men with little experience of warfare. They would make up the bulk of Gawain's troop of foot.

Some who'd ridden in on horseback and who possessed a modicum of riding skills were given special duties; and a few of the more skilled riders amongst them were assigned to the irregular troop of horse, a cavalry unit consisting of lesser knights and younger noblemen who aspired to knighthood. That unit was designed to augment the more elite cavalry wings commanded by Sir Gawain's brothers, Sir Gaheris and Sir Agravaine.

Gradually the men in Gawain's sprawling army were formed and shaped into companies.

Then, the great troop of foot—numbering more than a thousand men—pushed off slowly on their long march toward North Wales. They would have a three-day head start on the cavalry, which would catch up with them by week's end.

Mordred, Colgrevaunce, and the three other newly made knights, all accomplished riders, were assigned to the elite cavalry units. Composed of Round Table knights and newer knights who'd shown themselves capable horsemen, this elite troop of horse was divided into two wings, each with about seventy-five men. Mordred and the other new knights rode in the wing commanded by Sir Gaheris.

Sir Gawain, the king's eldest nephew, his small clutch of personal advisors, and a few of the most elite of the Round Table knights, rode behind all the others; from them scouts and messengers were constantly riding to and fro.

Amongst Gawain's advisors rode his cousin and closest friend, Sir Uwain, and also a famed eastern knight named Sir Sagramour. With them, too, was the young knight Sir Lamorak, whose name had been on many tongues of late. He was the fellow who'd bested Mordred in a fencing contest a few weeks earlier, a minor event that had now slipped from the minds of most people. For Mordred, however, it remained a stinging humiliation, one he had no intention of ever forgetting.

Two especially important advisors to Gawain were Sir Bedivere and Sir Lucan, two of the king's closest friends and most trusted knights. Also with them, at the king's request, was Merlyn. He was well known to the other advisors and respected by most, though he tended to hold himself somewhat aloof. That was partly because it was his wont and, in this case, partly because of the apprehension his new horse was likely to cause even in the breasts of the steadiest and bravest men.

Merlyn, to his good fortune, had stumbled upon someone who was willing to come along and serve as his groom—an emaciated little lad who was truly a stray waif.

When the pathetic-looking lad had first appeared in the meadow below the city and offered his services as a soldier, he'd been rudely rebuffed.

"No free handouts here for the likes o' you laddie. Go find some bleeding-heart nuns who'll take pity on your miserable carcass. This here's an army, lad, so bugger off. No place here for starving urchins."

Merlyn had first noticed the boy when he saw him stroking Raguel's neck. Merlyn paused in what he was doing and watched. He saw the lad talking softly to the horse, and to his surprise, he saw the mysterious black stallion begin to nuzzle at the lad's face and neck affectionately. Aside from Lute, Merlyn had never seen any other person who'd wanted anything to do with Raguel.

"Hello," Merlyn called out to the lad.

The lad looked up apprehensively, as if he'd been caught out doing something he shouldn't.

"Sorry, sir. Weren't doin' no harm," he replied nervously.

"Just sayin' 'ello to your steed. A most beauteous creature, sir. Didn't mean no harm nor disrespect."

"What are you called, lad?"

"Tom, sir."

"Tom? Then your mother calls you Thomas?"

The lad blushed. "Ain't never had no mother, sir. And Tom ain't short for Thomas. It's short for . . . well . . . it's short for Tomfool. 'Go 'way, Tomfool, get away from here, Tomfool,' that's what they's always sayin' ta me, sir. So I shows 'em and took that name for meself. Took it with pride, sir, though I shortened it to Tom."

"You like horses, Tom?"

"Loves 'em, sir. And they seem ta like me. This here one, most beauteous he is. I knows why folks don't like 'im. But makes no matter to me. 'Sides, I can tell he likes me, too."

"Why do you think folks don't like Raguel, Tom?"

"With respect, sir, I don't need to tell you that. Anyone knows that."

"Then anyone knows a lot more than I do," Merlyn grumbled to himself.

The lad just cocked his head sideways and looked at the old man curiously.

"How old are you, Tom? Eleven, twelve?"

"Can't rightly say, sir," he replied, again looking embarrassed.

"Well then, Tom, how would you like a job?"

"A job? With the army?"

"Looking after Raguel for me when I'm tending to other things. You could come along as my groom. Would you like that?"

"Oh sir, I would like that more than anything. And I promise you, I won't cause you no trouble a-tall. I'll be good as gold, I will. You'll see, sir, I'll be good as gold." When the lad said that, Raguel nickered loudly.

"I think he's saying he wants you to come," Merlyn said. "Either that or he's saying I'm a bigger tomfool than you are."

"No, you ain't, sir. There ain't no bigger tomfool than me."

"Can you ride, Tom?"

"Oh, yes sir." Then he added with a sly smile, "With respect, sir, I think better than you."

"You've seen me ride?"

The lad couldn't keep from smiling. "Sir, I have."

"Then we'd best find you a mount."

"No need, sir. Already got one." The lad pointed behind him to where a little swayback mare of indeterminate age was grazing.

"I'm no judge of horseflesh, but . . ."

"Don't you worry a-tall, sir, she be serviceable enough."

"And how is it that you happen to have such a . . . umm . . . magnificent beast, Tom? Or maybe I don't want to know."

Tom just grinned and gave a little shrug.

❖

After three days of hard marching, Rafe, the ironmonger's apprentice, was weary and footsore. And he was making no bones about it.

"Walk, walk walk," Rafe groused. "Do this, do that, don't be a-sittin' down just yet, mister. Stop your bloody jabbering, mister. Pick up that weapon and shoulder it! Do it now! Jesu Crist, Perkyn, what have we got ourselves into?"

Perkyn, Rafe's friend and companion, a slender, gawky fellow, had grown tired of Rafe's constant griping. He was a quiet and long-suffering young man, but even he had his limits.

"Rafe," he said, "why don't you just stuff a rag in it, eh?"

Rafe and Perkyn were pikemen, two of the men who belonged to a unit of roughly six hundred foot soldiers. When it came time for the battle, they were the ones most likely to experience the full brunt of the enemy's attack. They knew it and weren't happy about it. They'd been marching for several days now in a rather shapeless mob behind a more elite unit of crossbowmen. In battle the crossbowmen would probably occupy the first rank, though once they'd loosed their quarrels, they would quickly retreat to safety behind the pikemen to re-arm their weapons, a slow process.

Behind Rafe and the other pikemen walked another large unit, this one composed of longbowmen, perhaps three hundred of them, men whose skills might well carry the day against King Rience's troops. For although Gawain's army, in the aggregate, was smaller than King Rience's, certain units—especially the various bowmen and cavalry wings—were more experienced and better trained.

King Rience's army, the scouts reported, had been hastily assembled from raw recruits and volunteers scraped up by the lesser kings of the Western Isles. It was an unwieldy force that mirrored the unwieldy alliance Rience had cobbled together from the tribes and clans of North Wales and the western isles of Britain.

As evening descended, a halt was called and the men in Rafe and Perkyn's troop of foot were allowed to sprawl out on the grass or seek shelter beneath the trees. Rafe and Perkyn pulled off their boots and bathed their tired feet in the cool water of a small rivulet not far from the old Roman road on which they'd been marching, a road still quite wondrously straight and firm, though also quite hard on their ill-shod feet.

Many of their fellow pikemen were doing the same as they awaited their evening meal, now simmering in gigantic pots. Hard bread and a meat-and-vegetable stew it would be, made from food stocks carried on the supply wagons and ox-carts that trailed in the wake of the walking men. The wagons contained enough food to see the army through their first few days, though foragers were already ranging far out ahead of the army, men responsible for gathering sheep and swine and kine to keep the men of Gawain's forces fit and able.

"Smells good," Perkyn declared hopefully. "Me mam was one bloody awful cook. This'll be better for sure. Leastways, couldn't be no worse."

"Just so's there enough of it, however it tastes," Rafe declared. "I'm hungry enough to eat your leather jerkin."

"When this fight's over and done with, Rafe, you be more'n welcome to eat my jerkin. Till then, I'd best keep it."

Both of the lads, like a great many of the pikemen, wore boiled leather vests in lieu of armor. Their thick tough jerkins could be pierced by arrows or pike thrusts, though it would take a strong man or a direct hit to do it. For the looming fight, their jerkins would serve them well. Proper head protection was another matter. Most of the men carried leather caps they would don when the time came, but a few possessed metal hats or helmets. Rafe and Perkyn were among those few, since Rafe was an apprentice in an ironmonger's smithy. Before leaving the city, he'd rummaged about behind the smithy in the reject pile and snatched up a couple of pieces deemed too poorly made to serve a nobleman properly.

The pikemen's food was ready, and one by one they advanced to the great pots where the cooks glopped the meat-and-vegetable burgoo into the wooden bowls they carried in their packs. The men also grabbed up large hunks of the hard bread to chew on or dip into their bowls.

Through the trees not far from Rafe and Perkyn came two figures on horses. They were Merlyn and his servant Tom, heading for the pavilion erected for Sir Gawain and his chief advisors.

"Look-a there," one man sang out, "a waif an' a warlock!"

"Careful what ya say, Lum, that there fella really is a warlock."

"That old geezer, Lum," another voice chimed in, "is nought but the devil's spawn. Leastways, that's what they say."

"I'll tell ya one thing," another man said, "he surely ain't no horseman! Looka him tryin' ta ride that monster."

"Monster is right," the first speaker said. "That there horse does give me the shivers."

"No, he surely ain't no horseman. That old feller'll never shit a horseman's turd!" The remark resulted in sniggers and guffaws.

Merlyn and Tom passed on by without paying the men any mind, though they'd overheard some of their gibes. Merlyn was used to being the object of the common man's levity, and Tom, in his short life, had already endured more scorn than Merlyn ever would.

Not far from where Rafe and Perkyn were sitting, a man had begun plucking at the strings of a lute.

"Sym," one of his friends called out, "why'n ya sing us the one 'bout the monk and the milkmaid, hey?"

"Yeh, Sym give us that one, why doncha?" several other voices chimed in.

And so Sym, after strumming a few introductory chords, launched into his ribald tale.

❖

Mordred and Colgrevaunce dined in greater comfort than Rafe and Perkyn. They ate and drank of the best in a splendid pavilion erected by Gaheris's yeomen. The seventy-five men belonging to Sir Gaheris's cavalry wing were all present and seated according to rank, which meant that Mordred and the other newly made knights were relegated to the far ends of the two long tables. Mordred didn't mind. As soon as he found the right moment to show his "betters" just how capable he was, he felt sure he would no longer be considered a lesser knight.

As the meal was finishing up, Sir Gaheris rose from his seat and stepped out between the two long tables. He walked slowly down to the far end of the tables, smiling and nodding at his men, then turned and walked back toward the other end.

Then he addressed them: "Friends, noble companions, valiant warriors—let me share with you information recently sent from my brother. He says that according to our scouts, the enemy forces are now a two-day's march to the northwest, moving slowly towards us. Our scouts estimate that the combined troops in King Rience's army outnumber us by two to one. So, my friends, it appears that this will be an unfair fight. I suggested to my brother that to make it fairer, we should send half our men home." Gaheris's men cheered.

"His response was that we should probably send two-thirds of them home." More cheers.

As Gaheris spoke, Mordred studied him. The man was not only the leader of Mordred's cavalry wing, he was also his brother, both of them being the sons of Queen Margause of Lothian. Like Mordred, Gaheris stood a little above middle height, though he wasn't as tall or as burly as their brother Sir

Gawain. He was more round-faced than his other brothers, and his wavy brown hair bore only a hint of a reddish tinge. He was confident and well-spoken and was reputed to be a brave and highly competent warrior. To Mordred he seemed a solid and able fellow. Mordred found himself liking this brother.

As he considered Gaheris, Mordred couldn't help reflecting on his third brother, Sir Agravaine, who commanded the other elite unit of the cavalry, a troop of men who were dining in a separate pavilion. Agravaine, to the extent that Mordred was familiar with him, seemed cut from different cloth. In physique he stood an inch or two taller than Gaheris but was more slender, with a long face that typically wore a frown. He seemed a quiet fellow, and, in contrast to Gaheris, by no means an open book. Though Agravaine was said to be a most capable warrior, Mordred sensed his potential for both deviousness and violence, traits he himself possessed. But with one important difference—Mordred prided himself on his ability to conceal his deviousness.

Mordred's conclusion about his three brothers was that Gawain and Gaheris were quite similar in temperament and abilities; and that he and Agravaine were also. Mordred smiled, thinking that they made an intriguing foursome, the four sons of Queen Margause. In any case, in coming days he would continue his close study of his brothers, who were as yet unaware of his very existence, let alone his relationship to them. But that would soon change. When it did, Mordred hoped he might someday use his knowledge of his siblings to his own advantage. He'd long since learned that if you know a person's passions and foibles, you are well on your way to being able to manipulate that person.

❖

Merlyn would have had few disagreements with Mordred's initial readings of his brothers. Although his knowledge of them exceeded Mordred's, it was particularly in regard to Gawain that Merlyn's assessment might be at slight variance with Mordred's. For Merlyn understood well why the king wanted him to be there in the midst of Gawain's advisors. He was a bright young man, fair-minded and generally good-natured, and he was a fearless and formidable warrior. But despite his virtues, Gawain had a key weakness, his tendency to allow his personal passions to overcome his reason. He was much beloved by the king and was surely the right man to be directing this military expedition—so long as he was surrounded by cooler heads.

After dining in the pavilion with Gawain and his advisors, Merlyn carried a small sack of food back to the grove where Tom, his young groom, had remained with Raguel and Tom's mare.

When Merlyn arrived, he found the lad curled up asleep against the belly of the snoring mare. Raguel stood guard over them. Merlyn stopped and took in the scene. The black, sensing Merlyn's presence, raised his head and stared at him. For just a brief moment Merlyn thought he saw a little glimmer of fire flare up in the creature's large amber eyes.

CHAPTER 22

With the two armies gone, the mood in Uther Pendragon's great city was somber and subdued. Only a small corps of guardsmen remained behind to stand watch. They manned the gateways and patrolled the high walls. Within the city itself, the only men now there were fellows who possessed special skills or responsibilities, or those few whose state of health prevented them from going.

To his embarrassment and pique, Lute was one of them. When he learned that he was supposed to remain behind and attend to his crippled uncle, he was both surprised and irked. It was especially irksome because it was his uncle who'd requested that favor. Lute didn't understand. His uncle hardly needed his help now. But he swallowed his disappointment and did as he was told.

What Lute wasn't told was that it was really Merlyn who'd wanted him to stay behind; Lute's uncle had merely acquiesced when he'd learned of the king's and Merlyn's wishes.

So on the morning following the departure of Gawain's final units, Lute, feeling at loose ends, trekked down to the lower market square armed with a list of tasks Julianna wished him to perform. But as he moved about through the stalls and shops, he was met with looks of suspicion and resentment by nearly everyone he encountered. Lute hated the position in which he found himself, a position he could do nothing about.

The most humiliating episode occurred an hour or so later when he chanced to encounter Gwendolyn. His errands finished, Lute was walking across the market square in the direction of the central stairsteps. That was when he heard Gwendolyn call out to him.

"Lute? Is that you? I was sure you'd gone with all the other knights." The look on her face mingled surprise, relief, and confusion. "I felt sure they would have assigned you to one of the cavalry wings."

"Hello, Gwendolyn. No, no, they didn't. So yes, I'm still here," he said, his eyes averting hers. "I wanted to go, but they didn't want me to. Told me I needed to stay here and attend to my uncle."

Reading the emotions in Lute's face, Gwendolyn reached out and took his hand. She exerted a soft pressure. It was the best thing that'd happened to him since the armies' departures.

"Oh, Lute," she said shyly, "I'm so very glad you will be safe. That's one less man I need worry about, one less man I need pray for."

"You would have prayed for me?"

"Of course, Lute. You were at the top of the list."

For a lengthy moment the two of them just stood there without speaking, each finding sustenance in the other's presence. But their happy moment was short-lived.

"Why's *you* here, then, eh?" grumped an old woman who was passing by. "All my sons be gone. And *you* still here? Why's that, eh? Why's that?"

Lute responded to her scowl with an apologetic shoulder shrug.

"He has important duties here, Mabely, that's why!" Gwendolyn flung at the back of the indignant woman. Gwendolyn's words stopped the old woman in her tracks. She spun around to face them.

"Important duties, *pah!*" came the woman's reply. "Able-bodied man like you. For shame, laddie, for shame!"

"That's not fair, Mabely!" Gwendolyn declared.

"*Pah!*" was Mabely's only reply. Then she stomped away without another word.

Lute's eyes remained directed toward the cobblestone pavement of the square. But his hand was still in Gwendolyn's, and she squeezed it tightly, expressing her loyalty to Lute.

Lute and his uncle sat out in the back garden enjoying the soft air of the August evening. Gwilym hovered nearby, as usual, but Julianna had stayed away, suspecting the two of them had things they wished to discuss in private.

"Sir," Lute began, "I was thinking about going away for a short while. Would you have any objection to my doing that?"

"Back to Sanham? To see how things have been going there since your fine handiwork six weeks ago?"

"No, sir, that wasn't what I was thinking."

"Then what were you thinking, Lute?'

"Sir . . . I've been thinking about my mother. I haven't seen her since early May when I first set out for the city. I thought I might go and visit her."

"My beautiful little sister," Thomas mused. Then he said with a smile, "You know, Lute, I would dearly love to see her again myself. How I wish that were possible. For now, of course, it isn't. But I am mending, I truly am. And you know, I have never once visited that little hamlet where you grew up, that place she fled to all those years ago."

"Would you mind if I did that, sir? I wouldn't be gone long. Probably no more than about two weeks. I know I was told to stay here and be with you, Uncle, but you have more support now than you did when I first arrived. I don't think you have any real need of me."

"And as for you, Lute, I'm guessing you don't find it so pleasant being seen here in the city when all the young men in the armies are off afar doing manly things."

"Yes, Uncle, you are right. But sir, it's also really true that I would like to see my mother. There are things I wish to tell her. And things I hope she'll be willing to tell me."

Earl Thomas remained silent for several seconds. "If you ask her the things I'm guessing, Lute," he said at last, "be gentle with her. It will not be easy for her to tell you what you wish to know."

"Uncle, I have always been gentle with my mother. Still, I do wish to ask her certain questions. When she hears them from her own son's lips, perhaps she will choose to answer them. I won't press her. If she wants to continue harboring her secrets, I will respect her wishes."

"Yes, Lute," Earl Thomas said, "I think you should go and do that. Your questions will eventually be answered anyway, whether or not it is your mother who answers them. When she thinks about that, she will probably talk to you. Your mother is no fool. She will see it's best that she be the one to tell you what you wish to know."

"Uncle, I would like to leave early tomorrow morning."

"That would be fine. If you wish, you could take one of our new horses, Molly or perhaps Trumpet."

"No, sir, but thank you. It seems more fitting to me that I ride back home with just my old gelding."

❖

The weather was warm and dry during the four long days that Lute rode toward the small hamlet, the place where he'd lived for the first sixteen years of his life. As he and the old roan plodded slowly along, many thoughts crowded the youth's mind. He thought about his mother and what her reaction would be at seeing him again. And he worried about what her reaction would be when she listened to the questions which he wanted her to answer.

He also thought about the young woman named Gwendolyn. He remembered the thrill that ran through him when she'd taken his hands in hers. He didn't really know what his true feelings toward her were, but it was certainly exciting to feel the touch of a young woman, a young woman who'd befriended him. Nothing like that had ever happened to him before.

He also thought about the king, who said he wanted to know him better; and about the strange man named Merlyn, whose advice had already profoundly affected Lute's life. And he thought about the young man named Mordred. He appreciated Mordred's kindness to him, though there were things about the fellow that made Lute quite uncomfortable. It wasn't just that Mordred and Colgrevaunce were given to bouts of wild behavior. There was something about Mordred that unsettled him. If truth be told, there was something about Mordred that frightened him.

For the four days that Lute traveled, all those thoughts swirled about inside his head. The old horse moved steadily onward, needing little direction from his rider. Indeed, when at last the roan intuited where they were going, his own excitement caused him to move along even more quickly. The hills and valleys through which they rode were now familiar to him. Never a creature to show strong emotion, his steps had become a little more spritely. For just as Lute was going home, so was the old roan.

When they topped a gentle rise, Lute and his mount halted a moment and looked down upon the fields of golden grain, fields ripe for the harvest. Not far beyond those fields lay the hamlet where Lute grew up. The roan gave a soft little whinny of joy, for he was returning to where he belonged.

"Yes," Lute whispered into the horse's ear, "we are almost home. We are almost back to *your* home, anyway. Whether it will ever again be my home is something I'm not sure about. I do love this place, and I always will. But in my heart, I do not think it is where I truly belong."

Chapter 23

King Rience's heralds, holding white flags atop tall staffs, advanced slowly toward the middle of the long open field. A third of the way down they stopped and waited. It was twenty minutes before Sir Gawain, accompanied by Sir Uwain and Sir Bedivere, reached them. The knights wore their swords, but when they arrived they saw that King Rience's heralds bore no weapons. They brought their mounts to a halt ten yards from the heralds.

"You wish to parley?" Bedivere said brusquely, serving as Sir Gawain's chief spokesman.

"Sir, that is of course what we wish. I am Sir Bersules," the man said, "chief herald to King Rience of the Outer Isles and Lord of Islay."

"And I am Sir Bedivere. If you wish to parley, sir herald, perhaps we could pass over the niceties and get on with it."

The man stared for a moment, then shrugged. Extracting a small piece of parchment from his scrip, he unrolled it and began to read: "Out of compassion for the lives of his men and yours, King Rience proposes that this conflict be resolved through single combats: the king himself and his two best champions offer to face any three knights you might wish to send forth. He offers combat either on horse or on foot. With lances or with swords. He and his champions will be here at this same spot two hours before sunset. It is the king's hope that three of your best will be here then to engage in single combats." Sir Bersules rolled up the parchment and put it back in his scrip.

Gawain, Uwain, and Bedivere sat upon their mounts in silence. Then Bedivere replied, "Sir herald, we will retire and consider what you've proposed."

"The time specified for the combats, Sir Bedivere, is just three hours hence," Sir Bersules stated. "Don't allow your consideration to be too lengthy."

"You needn't tell us our business, sir herald," Bedivere replied. "Your proposal shall be taken under advisement."

Then he and his companions wheeled their horses about and rode back to the British encampment.

"Not fight?" Gawain shouted. "Of course I shall fight!"

"Sir, it isn't that I doubt your abilities. Or those of Sir Lamorak and Sir Sagramour. I'm confident the three of you would prevail. With respect, sir, that isn't what concerns me."

The speaker was Sir Lucan, Sir Bedivere's sober and level-headed brother. "We don't need to defeat King Rience and his two best knights, we need to defeat his entire army. We need to do it decisively. We need to rout them completely."

"Cousin," Sir Uwain added, addressing Gawain, "it is most unfortunate, but what Lucan says is so. The sad truth is that we need them to suffer a catastrophic defeat—a defeat so calamitous it will eradicate future threats to the kingdom. Sir, we must kill as many of King Rience's men as we can. If we do, it will discourage further rebellions by their chieftains."

"So we let them think we are *cowards?* We let them impugn our honor and our courage by refusing their *challenge?* My dear sirs, that is unthinkable." Gawain was in a passion.

"Merlyn," Gawain finally said, calming down just slightly, "what do you think of my advisors' advice?"

"As for me," Sir Lamorak interjected, "I say we must fight!"

"And what say you, Merlyn?" Gawain asked again.

Merlyn, who was sitting alone in a far corner of the pavilion, slowly rose to his feet and ventured forward. His face bore a frown.

"Well," he finally said in a raspy voice, "my dear young friend, perhaps we should consider something else. What we should consider, I suggest, is what your uncle might counsel us to do in this situation. Do you think if the king were offered a challenge such as this that he would choose to accept it? If he were offered such a challenge, Gawain, would you *want* him to accept it?"

Gawain glared at Merlyn. "Trapped me, haven't you Merlyn? No, of course I wouldn't want him to accept it, though I know he would prevail."

"Yes, he would prevail," Merlyn replied, "as would you. But is it the wisest course?"

Gawain was silent a moment, then slowly nodded his head.

"Merlyn, you old devil, you are right. I'm sorry, Lamorak, but they are right. We shall not fight this afternoon. But tomorrow, we *shall*. And we shall rout them totally. We shall crush the very life out of them!"

"Hear him! Hear him!" Gawain's advisors all cried in unison.

Merlyn smiled at Gawain and nodded his approval. Gawain, in reply, nodded back and gave the old man a tight-lipped smile. Gawain, despite himself, was glad that Merlyn was here.

High on the long, sloping hill, three armed knights rode forth. For several hundred yards their horses trotted down toward the mid-point of the field, small puffs of dust rising from their hooves. Then they stopped and took up their positions.

From afar, the men in Gawain's army gazed upon them. It

was clear that the one in the middle was King Rience himself. It wasn't clear who the other two were, though they were surely his champions.

The men in Gawain's army now glanced toward their leader's pavilion, curious to see who would come forth to accept King Rience's challenge. It would be Gawain, no doubt, and perhaps Uwain and Sagramour, or maybe even that brash young knight named Lamorak.

The three riders and their horses out on the field remained stock still. After a few minutes of waiting, their horses began to fidget. Gawain's men were fidgeting also. What was the holdup? Where were their champions? Then it dawned on them—their leaders had decided *not* to accept the challenge!

When it finally dawned on the three riders also, they wheeled their horses and rode back up the hill. As they did, from their army came a great jeering shout. Gawain's knights had backed down. They'd been too afraid to fight!

Rafe and Perkyn had been taking all this in also.

"They're leaving it up to *us* blokes," Perkyn said grimly.

"No surprise there," Rafe scoffed, "the cowardly curs, the craven bastards. Let *us* be the ones who bleed and die. That's their idea of a battle. Leave it up to the scum. Don't want to dirty their own lily-white hands with men's work."

Outside the inner circle of Gawain's advisors, virtually everyone in the king's army was dismayed and displeased at this turn of events. Mordred, too, was quite shocked that King Rience's challenge had been refused. But unlike most of the others, he was also quite pleased. Had the challenge been accepted and had Gawain and his champions prevailed, then Mordred would have been left out of the heroics. He didn't know why the challenge hadn't been accepted, but he knew there had to be a reason. It surely wasn't from cowardice.

After finishing his evening meal, Mordred walked out into the woods behind their pavilion to the makeshift paddock where his unit's horses were attended by young grooms. Since Tib and Grimm, Mordred's regular manservants, now had taken places amongst the longbowmen, Mordred himself would make certain that all was well with his horses. Tomorrow, he very much hoped, he and his war horse would have a chance to distinguish themselves. If they did, he planned to exploit the opportunity to the fullest.

"Sir," said one of the young lads as Mordred approached, "your mount be in very fine fettle. He's one of the best, sir, one of the very best. I just fed 'im the finest fresh hay, sir, and he showed a wondrous appetite."

"Thank you," said Mordred. He handed the lad a tuppenny piece. "Now that I'm here, I'll just visit with him a few moments myself." The lad nodded his thanks and walked away.

Mordred took his time carefully inspecting all of his steed's hooves and shoes. No stones, no cracks, no loose shoes or missing nails. While the horse stood there patiently, Mordred felt up and down his firm, well-muscled legs. Finally he examined the horse's mouth and teeth.

"You great big beautiful bastard," Mordred whispered to him. "That lad is right. You are in very fine fettle. And I am too, you bastard. What a pair we make. Tomorrow, you and me, we're going to show the world what a couple of evil bastards like us can do." The horse's big eye gleamed as Mordred ran his hands up and down his neck and through the long, thick hair of his mane.

Mordred gave the horse a final pat, then turned back toward

the pavilion. But he didn't go there just yet. Instead, he walked out toward the edge of the great wide field. Tomorrow, Mordred knew, this field was likely to become not just a field of battle but a charnel house. Mordred turned and stared toward the far end of it, toward where he knew the enemy was encamped. He could see wisps of smoke from their fires but nothing more.

From deep within his subconscious mind a stark vision emerged:

A darkened sun, a darkened moon,
A croaking of ravens, a murder of crows,
A rabble of dogs, snarling and snapping, battling for bones.
Rottenness and putrefaction, death and desolation,
Crows croaking, dogs snarling, snapping,
A terrible stench, the odor of death rising to the heavens.

Like Mordred, Merlyn also left his pavilion after his evening meal to check on his horse and the young lad named Tom. He found them amongst the trees, keeping a good distance away from where other lads attended to the rest of the advisors' horses.

"Thought you might be hungry," Merlyn said as he approached them. He carried a small wicker basket covered by a cloth. Then he saw on the ground beside the boy the remains of the lad's own meal. Merlyn's stray waif had been dining on roast chicken, a meal as fine or finer than the one Merlyn had just finished.

"Saved you a chicken leg, sir," Tom said, holding it up. "Thought you might like it." The lad was grinning, chicken grease all over his hands and brightly shining face.

"Tom," Merlyn admonished, "how have you come by a meal as fine as that enjoyed by anyone in the king's whole army? Oh lad, you haven't gone and raided some local farmer's henhouse, have you?"

"*Me*, sir? Oh no, sir, I would never do such a thing. Found a big fat capon just a-wanderin' about in the woods all by hisself, sir. Feller must've strayed off from some local farmstead. Finders keepers, eh sir? Anyway, went ahead and cooked 'im up proper over my own little fire. Spiced 'im with wild leeks and onions. Right tasty, sir, if I say so myself. Saved a leg for you, sir. Thought you might like it."

Merlyn couldn't help being charmed by the lad's disingenuousness. "All right, Tom, let me say that I believe you—though I certainly don't. I will give you a coin that you can take and leave on the farmer's doorstep, just to pay him back for that big fat capon you happened to find wandering in the woods. If I give you the coin, you will take it to the farmer, won't you?"

"Oh, sir, if you were to give me a coin, I certainly wouldn't do anything else with it."

"Yes, I'm sure you wouldn't."

CHAPTER 24

The sun rose early and warm on the day of the battle—it was August 15th, the Feast of the Assumption—and many a man offered up his heartfelt orisons to the Virgin for her protection.

It soon became clear that Gawain intended to hold his forces on the lower reaches of the long field and await the enemy there. King Rience would have to bring the battle to them. And for Gawain's forces, the longer it took King Rience to arrive the better; for by mid-afternoon, the sun would be shining in the eyes of the rebel army.

As the morning drew on, very little happened, and so Gawain's men remained undeployed. There was no need for them to form ranks until the enemy came into view high up on the sloping hill. Once King Rience's men were sighted, it would take them most of an hour to come within striking distance; thus there would be ample time for Gawain's units to be properly positioned.

For now, they rested and waited. Perkyn and Rafe, like most of the others, found spots in the shade where they busied themselves honing their weapons. Although they were pikemen, they carried swords and knives for close-quarter combat. Perkyn's sword was a heavy falchion, and he labored most of the morning to bring its long, single-edged blade to razor-sharpness. It was a brute of a weapon, more suited to a cavalryman than a foot soldier.

"Good slicer, this," he remarked to Rafe. "Cleave a man in half, it will."

"Pah," Rafe scoffed. "Need a sharp sticker, not a meat cleaver. You ain't no butcher, Perkyn, though you got a face like a butcher's arse."

"You bury one o' these in a man's skull, Rafe, and it's like ta cool his ardor."

"Cool his *what?*"

"Means it's like ta discourage him."

"Way you been caressin' that meat cleaver o' yours, you'd think it was your lover. Too bad it ain't got no tits."

Since Perkyn was a lanky lad, his weapon might actually prove effective in battle—if he could bash his foeman's head in before the fellow'd reamed his guts. Rafe's weapon, on the other hand, was a more conventional two-edged sword. Hammered from the finest steel, Rafe had it on loan from his master the smith back in the city. The man had allowed him to take it if he swore his oath to bring it back. Rafe had promised on his life that he would. If he was still alive when the day was over, he might be able to make good on his promise.

It wasn't until it was drawing toward noon that a dark line finally appeared near the top of the field. It was the great mass of King Rience's army, advancing slowly, still some two miles distant. Gawain's men clambered to their feet, knowing it was time to assume their battle positions. Their commanders barked out their orders, and the various units began forming in their designated places.

Out before the others, in a single rank, crouched Gawain's unit of crossbowmen. About one hundred in all, their initial role in the battle would be brief, for when the enemy had come within fifty yards they would fire a salvo, then scurry back behind the ranks of pikemen to prepare a second round of shots.

With the crossbowmen out of the way, the wide ranks of pikemen would be the ones to absorb the full brunt of the enemy's attack. These men, numbering in the hundreds, were positioned in four tight ranks, each rank of about one hundred men standing shoulder to shoulder.

Rafe and Perkyn were positioned near the center of the first rank. Their long-handled weapons, twelve-foot shafts of ash capped by sharply pointed iron spearheads, especially effective against attacking horsemen, now lay flat on the ground beside them. If the enemy's cavalry attacked first, they would hold their pikes firmly anchored to the ground at forty-five degree angles in hopes of impaling the horses. If the footsoldiers came first, their pikes would be held horizontally in an effort to blunt the impact of the mass of charging men.

Gawain's longbowmen, numbering about three hundred, were positioned behind the pikemen, their ranks more widely spaced to give them ample room to work. Their bows were now strung, their many arrows stuck in the ground within easy reach. Their work would begin once the enemy was within four hundred yards, when they'd send their high-arching arrows skyward to come raining down on their foemen.

Gawain's irregular troop of horse had been moved to a position well behind the other units. They would be held there in reserve. If the battle reached a point of crisis, they would swarm forward to ride roughshod over the enemy's troop of foot, their horses' hooves inflicting as much damage as possible.

Gawain's pair of elite cavalry units, the troops of horse commanded by his brothers Sir Gaheris and Sir Agravaine, had not taken up positions on the field amongst the other units. In fact, they were nowhere to be seen.

Slowly, inexorably, King Rience's forces advanced down the field. As they drew nearer, Gawain's men could hear the rhythmic tattoo of the enemy's drums. Above the sound of the beating drums rose another sound—the shrill, discordant cacophony of King Rience's pipers.

Rafe and Perkyn watched nervously as the enemy's forces, a dark, slow-moving tide, flowed down the greensward. The nearer they drew, the louder the drumming and piping became. Now the individual figures of the men could be made out, the bright colors of their clothing, the shining weapons they brandished. They moved in a slow, seething mass.

Fear churned in Rafe's and his fellow pikemen's bellies, men who knew that many of them were about to die. Most tried to mask their fears with brave, sober faces; some succeeded. Off to his left Rafe heard the sound of retching, then smelled the stench of vomit. To his right, someone was mumbling a prayer or reciting one of the psalms.

"Don't none o' you bastards be crappin' your pants!" a voice rang out, causing the men to snicker nervously all down the line.

"Look a' all them buggers!" Perkyn muttered, mostly to himself. "Like ta give us a bloody thrashin', they are."

"Jesu Crist," came Rafe's soft reply, more an oath than a prayer.

When the advancing army had come within a quarter mile, Gawain's longbowmen began launching their arrows in successive waves. For a moment the sky turned dark as the arrows rose and then fell violently upon their victims. They must have been inflicting harm, but even so, they had little visible effect upon the approaching army.

"Where be their horsemen?" Rafe whispered to Perkyn.

"Word is they ain't got so many. So they prob'ly don't wanna be riskin' 'em at this point in the fight. Question is, Rafe, where be *our* horsemen?"

"No doubt run home ta their mams," Rafe said. He spat out a big glob of mucus in front of him. "King Rience challenges 'em ta single combat and all they does is piss their pants and run home ta their mams."

When the initial ranks of King Rience's army had closed to within 250 yards, a loud voice suddenly shouted out an order to Rafe and his companions: "Pikemen!—to the rear! Fourth rank, to the rear now! Third rank, you next."

This sudden order caught the men in the four ranks of pikemen completely off guard. What the hell was *this* all about? It took a moment for most of them to realize just what they were being ordered to do. "Carefully now, carefully!" the voice rang out. "Don't be stabbin' none o' your own fellows with them pikes!"

The pikemen in the fourth rank raised their weapons to a vertical position, spun about, then quickly threaded their way through the bowmen behind them. When they were clear, the third rank did the same, then the second, then the first.

"Thank you, sweet Jesu!" Rafe murmured to himself, making the sign of the cross on his chest with his free hand. He and Perkyn, amongst the last to retreat, stepped gingerly through the bowmen to the relative safety of the rear.

The men in the front ranks of King Rience's army, now less than two hundred yards away, could see that something very strange was occurring before them. It appeared that the enemy was retreating! Seeing what they were seeing, the men let out a great roar—the enemy was falling back! The cowardly vermin were fleeing! Rush them now, they thought, overwhelm them! Smash the bastards to a bloody pulp!

With such thoughts surging through their heads, quite a few of them couldn't restrain themselves. They began making a headlong rush toward the fleeing enemy. A great many others, seeing what their compatriots were doing, couldn't help doing the same.

"Hold your lines! Hold your lines!" their commanders screamed at them.

But the sight of their foemen turning tail was too tempting to resist; they couldn't hold back. Now the fleetest of the men were out ahead of the others. They had almost reached Gawain's line; they couldn't wait to begin the piercing and the hacking. Right on their heels came hundreds more.

With Gawain's pikemen in retreat, his crossbowmen were now his first line of defense, as originally planned. Down on one knee, each of them waited patiently until the first of the enemy attackers was within thirty yards. Then they loosed their bolts. Their volley tore into the lead runners, bringing several down. But now the mass of charging men was just yards away. From the throats of the attackers rose a hair-raising ululation, yells that brought terror to the stoutest hearts.

The crossbowmen retreated swiftly, leaving the more loosely arranged ranks of longbowmen to face the onslaught. Dropping their bows, they unsheathed their swords and prepared to receive the full force of the enemy's charge.

King Rience's men crashed upon them like a sea wave, piercing with spears and slashing with long swords.

The first two lines of bowmen stood their ground valiantly. But they were all alone. The men behind them had retreated in search of greater safety. With no one supporting them, those brave fellows were doomed.

Suddenly, from off to the left and also the right, trumpets rang out. And bursting from the trees on each side of the wide field came two troops of riders—the cavalry units led by Sir Gaheris and Sir Agravaine. 150 knights in all, they spurred their steeds straight into the midst of the onrushing men.

Gaheris's troop rode straight at the foremost men, while at the same time Agravaine's troop had begun wreaking havoc amongst the attackers a hundred yards behind them.

Because of their mad, headlong rush toward the retreating enemy, King Rience's men had spread themselves too widely across the length and breadth of the field of battle. In such disarray, they'd rendered themselves easy prey for the highly skilled cavalry units. Those units now crashed upon them in a blur of hooves, bright helmets, and deadly lance points.

Most of the cavalrymen bore lances, though several swung long swords and a few wielded falchions, battle axes, or maces. The cavalry smashed upon them like the hammer upon the anvil.

In seconds the field had become a whirl of horses, dust, gleaming weapons, and dying men. The horse soldiers hacked, pierced, gouged, and lunged. Blades chopped down, lances impaled, and the charging horses trampled upon the bodies of King Rience's men. It was a cavalryman's dream, attacking a broken enemy on foot and with no place to retreat. It was a slaughter, pure and simple.

Higher up on the hill, King Rience's men who had yet to reach the killing field could see the disaster unfolding below them. Stunned, they watched in horror. And then, as the fight began to move toward them, they turned and fled.

Agravaine's horsemen pursued them for several hundred

yards, but when a phalanx of King Rience's pikemen finally formed up and confronted them, the mounted men swerved away from the sharp points of the threatening weapons and returned to the killing field. Thus far in the affray they had lost very few men or horses.

As the slaughter began to abate, Gawain's irregular troop of horse finally entered the fray to perform mop-up duties. Since the wounded foe still out on the field posed real dangers, there was no reason to endanger the elite cavalry units any further. Those fine men had carried the day. Their losses had been remarkably light—only five men killed, two by falls, and only a dozen or so seriously wounded. Eighteen crippled horses had to be put down.

As dusk fell, both armies pulled back. The tattered remains of King Rience's forces retreated to a position at the top of the long sloping hill. No sounds came from their encampment. The men in Gawain's could be heard celebrating. The ordinary men were drinking, singing, and dancing around their victory fires. The noble units were dining in splendor.

The long field of battle between the distant camps was bestrewn with the bodies of the dead, and in some cases the bodies of men not yet dead.

As night descended, the groans of dying men were audible to those close by. It wasn't long before dark shapes could be seen moving swiftly about on the field amongst the corpses. They were the dark shapes of the pillagers and the robbers, folks who'd come to scavenge what they could from the bodies of the fallen men. They were snatching up the spoils of war.

Merlyn slipped away from the celebrating and went in search of Tom. He feared he wouldn't find him. The lad, he felt sure, would be out on the field with all the pillagers, stuffing his pockets with rings, armlets, and neck torques.

As he neared the place where their two horses were normally picketed, he saw the dark shapes of the animals, first Raguel's tall stately silhouette, and then the lower, dumpier outline of Tom's swayback mare.

"Tom?" Merlyn called out. He got no response.

Then Merlyn heard a movement in the bushes.

"Sir?" came the lad's answer. "Just relieving myself, sir."

Merlyn smiled at his own unwarranted skepticism. He was pleased that he'd been wrong about the lad. Tom, resisting temptation, hadn't abandoned his post.

"Everything all right here?" Merlyn asked.

"Oh, yes sir. Fed and curried the horses. That black o' yours, sir, he sure did want to be out there on the field of battle with all the others. Had to fight like the devil to keep 'im from running off."

"Like the devil? You had to fight like the devil?"

"Oh, yes sir, like the very devil hisself."

CHAPTER 25

The sun rose upon a grisly sight. The field of battle was now rife with raucous birds—magpies, crows, ravens, and griffon vultures—hissing and cawing as they fought over the corpses of the slain.

And yet, despite the gruesomeness of it all, the men in Gawain's army remained joyful, for few of those bodies were theirs. The first round of the battle had gone decisively to them. King Rience's army might still have some fight left in it, but everyone now expected their enemy to sue for peace. They surely would if they were wise. But, they weren't wise.

High up on the hill a small group of horsemen trotted forth in the mid-morning sunlight. There were five of them. Two were standard bearers, three were armed knights. As they advanced down the sloping hill, it became evident from their appearance that the three men were King Rience himself and his two greatest champions. They hadn't come to sue for peace. They'd come to offer single combat. They were making an appeal to Gawain's sense of honor, hoping he would grant them a chance at redemption on the field of combat.

"Bit late for that, eh?" grumped Rafe to Perkyn.

"Not by me it ain't," his companion replied. "Not if it means that them knights can be the ones to finish up the fightin' and us poor blokes don't hafta go marchin' up that bleedin' hill and polish off the rest o' them evil buggers."

"You don't want ta be bloodyin' your blade? You come all this way to fight a battle an' yor willin' to go back home without even bloodyin' your blade?"

"I can think o' better uses for me blade," Perkyn replied, lowering his hand to his crotch and giving it a squeeze. Rafe chuckled at his friend's ribald remark.

Mordred, sitting atop his steed, also watched the men advancing down the hill. And then he knew. Here was his chance, the very thing he'd hoped for. This was his moment. He fewtered his lance and loosened his sword in its scabbard. Then he spurred his horse forward out onto the field.

Mordred had sized up the situation quickly, but another rider had been quicker. That man was already on the field, his horse now trotting toward the five men higher up. This rider was unknown to Mordred. Mordred felt sure he wasn't a member of Gaheris's cavalry wing or Agravaine's. This unknown man's horse was bedecked with golden trappings, and the early morning sun sparkled upon the man's bright helmet.

Mordred brought his mount to a canter in order to catch up to the man. As he did, he saw that another rider was doing the same, a man who'd appeared from the other side of the field. It was Agravaine, Mordred's brother.

With the unknown knight riding in between Mordred and Agravaine, the three of them advanced up the slope toward the king and his champions. This trio of men had *not* been selected to represent Gawain's army. They had simply taken advantage of an opportunity that had presented itself. Simply put, they were glory-seekers. Would their impulsive actions prove disastrous?

As King Rience watched the trio of riders approach, he felt a huge sense of relief. He'd feared that his challenge wouldn't be taken up, but his fear had proved ill-founded. The man spoke a few words softly to his standard bearers, who wheeled their horses and rode to opposite sides of the field. That left three warriors to face three warriors.

King Rience nodded his welcome to the three men but eschewed any further ceremony. The two sets of riders readied themselves for action. Then the combats began.

Without any fancy maneuvering, the unknown knight and King Rience charged straight at each other, each of them wielding their long swords. As the horses nearly collided, there came a fierce clash of weapons. The clang of metal meeting metal rang out across the field.

Mordred and his foe sat upon their steeds for a moment longer, each one eyeing the other cautiously. King Rience's champion was mounted upon a huge sorrel. His left arm bore his shield, his right cradled his lance. The man was garbed in a red hauberk, and his shield bore a pair of slanting golden bands across a field of red. Mordred was dressed all in black, his black shield displaying the image of a fierce silver falcon with talons flaring.

His opponent raised his lance and Mordred raised his in response—it would be a jousting match. Mordred, however, being left-handed, cradled his lance in his left arm, a fact that may have led to his foe's hesitation. Mordred was pleased to see that this man, like most of the men he'd fought before, was flustered to find himself facing such a foe. Beneath his visor Mordred smiled his thin-lipped smile.

The two men charged. Their horses nearly collided, and at the same moment each man's lance crashed home upon the other's shield. Both lances splintered against the shields. Mordred felt himself being rocked back violently in his saddle; but he hadn't been unhorsed. His foe turned a somersault in the air and landed in the dirt.

Mordred dropped his useless lance and leapt down from his charger. His opponent rose groggily to his feet and drew his sword. Mordred rushed upon him, and the man parried Mordred's thrust just as it neared his throat. He was a large man, a strong man, and though shaken by his fall, he fended off Mordred's blows with consummate skill. The man fought well on the defensive, and for several moments Mordred felt thwarted. The thought crossed his mind that today he might have met his match.

Then his foeman tried shifting his tactics. Rather than continuing his strategy of fighting defensively and wearing Mordred down, he suddenly went on the offensive. It proved a fatal blunder. He lunged at Mordred but tripped over one of the broken lances. His tumble left him sprawling at Mordred's feet. Then he felt the point of Mordred's sword pricking at his throat. Knowing he was doomed, he dropped his weapon and held his hands out at his sides. He'd capitulated.

Off to the left a loud, angry voice boomed. It was Agravaine. "*Mercy?* You're begging for *mercy?* If it's mercy you want, sir, you've come to the wrong man!" Mordred heard a cry and knew that his brother had just dispatched his opponent. All the while he listened to those words, Mordred eyes hadn't strayed from the face of his own vanquished foe.

"Would *you* like mercy?" he said softly to the man. The man merely nodded. "Say the word," Mordred whispered to him, "say the word."

"Mercy," the man whispered back.

"I thought you might say that," Mordred replied. Then he rammed his sword straight through the man's neck. Eight inches of blade extruded out the back.

Mordred looked beside him and saw that the unknown

knight now had his blade at the throat of King Rience. King Rience lay still, his eyes staring at the tall man in the golden trappings who had bested him. He said nothing. His arms and chest were bleeding. His weapon lay several feet away.

"Arise, sir king," the man said. "You may keep your sword. But you must come with us and explain yourself to Sir Gawain. He and his council will determine what punishment befits a rebel king. It isn't for me to determine that."

"Well hello, Gareth," said Agravaine. "You seem to be in quite a generous mood today, dear brother." Holding his horse's reins, Agravaine walked up close beside the knight in gold and the vanquished king.

"Gareth? You know who I am?"

"I'm not wrong, am I? Or would you prefer that I call you Beaumains? Dear brother, today you don't look so much like a kitchen knave. Oh yes, Gareth, I know who you are. Our dear mother came looking for you. 'What have you done with my baby boy? Turned him into a scullion?' My word, brother, our dear mother was more than a little bit irked."

"She does tend to get irked," the young man replied with a knowing smile. "But Agravaine, who is this noble companion of ours?" Gareth asked, gesturing toward Mordred, who'd remained standing a few feet apart.

Agravaine and Gareth both looked expectantly at the young knight dressed in black. And King Rience, now on his feet, couldn't help doing that, too.

"Um, sir," Mordred said, looking down shyly, "I'm called Mordred. And actually, sir"—now Mordred raised his eyes and looked straight at Gareth—"I too am your brother, although Agravaine doesn't know it either."

"*What?*" said Gareth and Agravaine in unison.

"How can *that* be?" Gareth asked.

"You're the little boy who disappeared?" said Agravaine, his eyes wide with astonishment.

"Yes," Mordred replied, giving a little shoulder shrug. "At least, that's what our mother has told me."

"The little boy who disappeared?" Gareth asked. "I don't have any idea what are you talking about."

"That's because you were too young to know about it, and because it soon became such a painful topic that no one ever dared talk about it. Yes, Gareth, when you were hardly a year old yourself, you had a baby brother—a baby brother who simply disappeared when he was only a few days old. No one knew what happened to him. I wasn't old enough to see how terribly distraught our mother was, but Gawain was. No, Gareth, it's something no one talks about. Frankly, except for Gawain, who was greatly affected by it, the rest of us had pretty much forgotten about it. Well, not anymore, I guess."

Both Gareth and Agravaine stared for a moment at Mordred—the little boy who had disappeared. Then a broad smile swept all across Gareth's face.

"Well, brother," he declared, stepping over to Mordred, "I think we have some catching up to do." He embraced Mordred with both of his muscular arms.

When Gareth released the young man, Mordred smiled and said, "Well, sirs, I guess that makes me the youngest of the pack. I promise you both that I will do all I can to be worthy to be called your brother."

"You acquitted yourself rather well just now," Agravaine remarked.

"My dear sirs!" King Rience blurted out, "could you please stop your blathering and get on with whatever it is you have in mind? The wounds you so kindly inflicted on me, sir, continue to bleed freely." The brothers, who'd been so caught up in the their unexpected discovery, had nearly forgotten their central purpose for being there.

"Sir king, please accept our apologies," Gareth said. "If you will mount your steed and ride on before us toward Sir Gawain's camp, we'll see that your wounds are attended to. We shall ride behind you—trying to refrain from blathering."

The four riders set forth, leaving behind them the bodies of King Rience's two champions.

Having given the brothers his parole, King Rience preceded them as they made the ride down through the scene of battle to where Sir Gawain's pavilion was pitched near the bottom of the long field.

As they rode past all the men who'd come forth to cheer them on, the pikemen suddenly began chanting: "Beau-mains, Beau-mains! Beau-mains, Beau-mains!"

The lad still remained the hero of the people. To them, he was still the kitchen knave who'd worked humbly right alongside them. He'd never shown them any superior airs. He would always occupy a place in their hearts.

Gareth couldn't help grinning. He lifted one hand to acknowledge the men's adulation.

Agravaine and Mordred also basked in the glow of victory, though they knew that Gareth was the real hero of the day.

Today is Gareth's day, Mordred reflected. But my day is coming. Oh yes, it is. Soon the name those people will be chanting won't be Gareth's. It will be *mine*.

CHAPTER 26

As the late afternoon sun dipped toward the horizon, Lute and the old roan moved down the narrow, rutted road. They went past the abbey's great tithe barn and on into the small village, a handful of low structures clustered about a village green. On the green a raucous game of football was in progress. As Lute rode by, he recognized every player. Some were nearly his own age, some were as young as six or seven.

Spotting him, several lads shouted out greetings to the best-liked lad of the village. "Lute! Come and play." "Lute, we want you on our side." "These teams aren't fair, Lute, we need you in goal!"

The year before Lute had led this motley assortment of youngsters all the way to the final game of the shire championship where they'd lost to a side from Hexham. In the waning moments of the game, the diving Lute hadn't been able to block the winning goal, scored off a deflected kick.

"I can't just now," Lute called back to them. "But I'll play tomorrow, I promise you."

"Play *now*, Lute! We need you *now!*" came the high-pitched cry of the smallest lad on the pitch.

"Neely, that's what you always say. Really, I can't just now. Tomorrow, Neely."

"Oh, all right then," the little lad reluctantly agreed.

As Lute approached the Green Man Inn, the village's only public house, he saw a pair of old men seated on a bench outside the front door. This was where they sat every late afternoon when the weather was fine, nursing their mugs of ale.

"Where ya been, lad?" one of them called out to Lute. "Ain't seen ya in a goodly spell."

"Oh, he's been off to that city, don't you know. I told you that months ago."

"Off to the city? Why'd he want to do a thing like that?"

"Youngsters get their notions, don't you know."

" 'Ello there, Lute," the first speaker called out. "How're ya findin' yourself, laddy?"

"Hello there yourself, Gaffer," Lute called back. "How're you two doing this fine day?"

"Doing good, Lute," the other man called back.

"And how's Mistress Tolson's ale today?"

"Oh, it's all right, I s'pose," Gaffer replied.

"It's good as ever," the other man avered. "Don't mind the gaffer. He always be complainin' 'bout this nor the other."

"Goin' ta see your mam, Lute?" the old gaffer called out. "Prettiest lass in the whole blame shire, that little mam o' yours."

"Oh hush, Gaffer, you say that about all the young lasses— even if it's surely true in the case o' Lute's mam."

"Don't be drinking up all Mistress Tolson's ale now," Lute said. "I'll be needing a jar or two myself after a bit."

"We'll try n' save a little for you. Just cuz it's you, mind."

As Lute continued on his way, the two old men watched him go.

"Fine lad, that," the second man said.

"Too bad he never had no father," the gaffer murmured. "But he done pretty good without none."

Two others, a young man and a young woman, had also been watching Lute as he came through the small village. The young man now remarked to his companion, "Is it the prodigal son a-coming back home?"

"It's the son, certainly, though I don't think he's got a prodigal bone in his body," she replied.

"Well, if anyone knows about his body, I guess it would be you." The young woman gave him a sharp elbow to the ribs. "Ouch. You don't have to take it out on *my* body!"

"Jill!" Lute shouted at them. "Rob!"

Lute leapt down from his mount and dashed over to them. He and Robin clapped each other on their shoulders, and then Lute and Jill hugged delightedly.

"Couldn't stay away, eh?" Robin said. "Had to come back and see how the simple folk are getting on?"

"It's wonderful to see you, Lute," Jill said, her dark eyes sparkling with joy.

Lute grinned at his two closest childhood friends with warmth and affection. He and Robin had learned to ride together, had scythed the fields of wheat and barley together, and were the two biggest heroes on the village football team. At times they'd led the lads of the village in the turf wars they waged against the rude, vile ruffians from the next village over.

Lute and Jill had gone through catechism together, and together they'd sung in the chapel choir. They'd learned to read and write Latin under the stern tutelage of the local curate. Jill had learned the seamstress's craft from the hand of Lute's own mother. She was the closest thing Lute had to a sister, Robin the closest thing to a brother.

"Well, Lute," Robin said, "I do call this good timing, for tomorrow's the final day of the harvest. We'll be scything those last few ripe and waving fields of barley you just came past. Must be why you're here. Knew we needed your strong back."

"What time do we start, Rob?" Lute asked.

"Same as always. Or have you already forgotten? Be ready by prime, my friend." By prime Robin meant the period from six to nine, the first three-hour division of the natural day.

"That late?" Lute said. "Guess I get to sleep in a bit."

"Will we see you at the Green Man later this evening?"

"Couldn't keep me away. Though I won't be making a late night of it. Not if I have to be up by prime."

For a moment Lute's eyes held Jill's. He couldn't help seeing the warmth in them, and for the briefest moment an image of Gwendolyn flitted through his mind.

Still holding the reins of his horse, Lute led the old roan the short distance to the turnoff toward home. Lute knew that his patient old gelding was ready for his evening feed and yearning to be back in his familiar stall. Lute felt much the same.

Lute's mother's cottage—the daub and wattle dwelling in which he'd lived until three and a half months ago—lay halfway down a short lane bordered by low-clipped hawthorn hedges. Separate from the thatched-roofed, half-timbered cottage were two other small outbuildings, a storage shed and a small stable that opened onto a wood-fenced stable yard.

As Lute walked between the hedgerows leading his horse, the old gelding suddenly whinnied loudly—and his cry was answered by the whinnies of two other horses. What in the world? Lute wondered. Did his mother have visitors?

Nearing the entrance gate, Lute spotted a scarfed head poking up just beyond the thorny tangle of eglantine that grew wild in the low hedge. His mother was tending her little patch of vegetables—radishes, carrots, onions, pole beans, turnips— as she did every evening during the growing months.

"Mother?" he called out.

"Lute?"

Her smiling face appeared through a small gap in the hedge, her cheeks as pink as the blossoms of eglantine. Lute saw her bright blue eyes, her gamine face, and the few stray bits of honey-brown hair that poked out from beneath her faded blue scarf.

Lute led his horse through the open gate and into the graveled yard. He and the roan were home.

"Look at you," his mother said, admiring her tall, strapping son. "Grown another inch since I last saw you." She came and latched one arm about Lute's waist and pulled him against her side. As Lute smiled down at her, he realized that his mother's head now just barely reached his shoulder.

"Might you be able to find your son a bit of nourishment?" Lute asked hopefully. "That growing lad of yours is one famished young fellow."

"If that famished young fellow can survive for half an hour, he might be in luck. Do you think you could do that, Lute?"

"I'll make an effort," Lute said, rubbing his free hand over his tummy. "But Mother, those horses in the paddock? When I heard them whinnying, I thought you might have guests."

"No, no guests. I'll tell you about the horses over supper."

"Well, then I'd best attend to this old beast, and to the others also, if there's a need. This old creature of ours, I can tell, is very glad to be home again."

"Lute, I'm glad you are home again. I'm oh so very glad."

"I'm glad also, Mother. As I rode through the village just now, it struck me how much I'd missed things here."

His mother smiled hopefully at her son's words.

Lute gazed upon the two horses in the paddock—a sleek

young filly with a shiny chestnut coat, and a powerful bay
stallion of sixteen hands—as fine a pair as any two horses
possessed by Round Table knights. As he led his old roan into
the paddock, the others came over to investigate. It appeared
to be a case of the more the merrier, as is often true among
herd animals. Standing next to the two stellar creatures, Lute's
old horse looked tired and pitiful. But it didn't diminish Lute's
affection for the stalwart creature who'd served him so loyally.

All three horses followed him into the stable, and Lute
fed them liberally from the large sack of oats he found there.
Grain-fed horses, he'd been told, had more stamina than grass-
fed ones, so whenever possible he fed his mounts with oats and
barley.

While the old roan ate, Lute carefully toweled him dry. The
other two didn't need any further attention, but Lute couldn't
keep his eyes off of them. What were they doing here? How in
the world had his mother come by them?

The air inside the cottage was filled with the smell of baking
pasties. Lute hadn't eaten any since he'd left home, and the
aroma caused his mouth to water. As he waited for the meal to
be ready, he took in the familiar sights of the room—the low
sideboard, the rude oaken table, the pair of three-legged stools,
the several beautiful wall-hangings his mother had made, and
her weaving frame in the corner of the room.

Lute's mother was a talented cloth-maker, seamstress,
weaver, and tapestry-maker whose talents were admired
throughout the shire. As Lute studied the partially completed
tapestry on her weaving frame, it was obvious she was well along
on some major endeavor. Lute was struck by the complexity of
the designs and the subtle pattern of their colors.

"Are you making this for the old earl?"

"No, Lute, for the new earl," she called back from the kitchen.

"Athelstan has died?'

"A fortnight ago." Lute's mother walked back into the room and set her wooden tray with two large pasties down on the darkened wood of the old oak table, a table whose every scar and stain was familiar to Lute—many of them having been caused by him. Then she fetched a clay pitcher filled with chilled elderberry wine. Lute pulled up one stool for his mother and the other for himself.

Without needing to be told, Lute bowed his head for a moment in silent prayer. "Amen," said Lute's mother. She looked across at Lute and smiled. "It's wonderful having you home again, my son."

Lute smiled back and nodded. Then he sliced apart the steaming pasty on the plate before him and inhaled the rich smell of onions and turnips. With the tip of the knife he speared a morsel and popped it in his mouth. His mother watched him, still smiling.

"So now Aldhelm is the new earl?" Lute said after he'd chewed several bites. Lute had grown up with the young man, who was only a few years older than he was. Not so long ago they'd played football together on the village green.

"He is, yes. The tapestry is for the coming celebration a fortnight hence. Will you still be here?"

"No, probably not. I told Uncle I'd be back before then." His mother looked disappointed.

"How is Thomas doing?" she finally asked. "I can't tell you how long it's been since I've seen my big brother."

"He's doing quite remarkably, considering that just three months ago he was nearly incapacitated. Now he can get about by himself with the aid of his canes. He hadn't been up to the castle in years, but not long after I got there we managed to do that with the help of the old roan. Since then we've done it several more times, for banquets and meetings.

"Mother, they were so terribly pleased to see him. Uncle Thomas is much admired by everyone there. Even the king thinks highly of your brother."

She stared across at Lute without replying, her face betraying no emotions.

Lute went on talking about the life he'd been living in the city—about his first meeting with his uncle and Julianna; about his developing friendship with Merlyn and about the great black stallion he'd found; and also about Merlyn's warnings that the horse might pose some danger to him. Lute laughed when he said that, but at the same time two frown lines appeared between his mother's eyes, though the lad didn't notice.

He blushed when he described his growing friendship with the young lass named Gwendolyn. At that his mother's frown lines were replaced by a smile. The lines reappeared when he described his acquaintance with a pair of wild young knights named Mordred and Colgrevaunce. To mask her concern, she sipped from her cup of elderberry wine. She didn't know why the names of the two young men should make her uneasy. They weren't names she'd ever heard before. But for some reason, they did.

"Have you been to Sanham yet," his mother asked, setting the wooden cup back down on the table, "where your uncle and I grew up?" Lute thought his mother looked a bit flustered.

"I have, Mother. I was there for several days in June." Lute wasn't sure how much he should tell her about his adventures in Sanham. There were parts of them that still grieved him deeply—two parts in particular.

"Some serious problems had cropped up there involving the overseer's stewardship. Uncle wanted me to go and see what I might be able to do about them. It wasn't an easy thing, actually, but with the help of old Wat we managed to get the problems sorted out. Do you remember Wat? He spoke quite fondly of you."

"Wat," she said smiling broadly, "the one person in Sanham I truly miss. He was a dear and loyal friend to Father, and he spent hours and hours teaching Thomas a whole host of useful things, especially about woodsmanship and hunting. Wat was always kind and generous to me. The wooden bowl beside you on the sideboard was something he made for my twelfth birthday. He carved all the little images around the rim, the twelve signs of the zodiac. Since my birth sign is Virgo, he took special care to make that one the loveliest of all."

Lute's mother wasn't telling him anything he didn't already know, but, for old time's sake, he reached over and picked up the bowl. He turned it slowly in his hands, studying each of the little carved figures, just as he'd done many, many times over the years. It had always amused him that Wat had given several of the figures—the ram, the lion, the goat, the fish—human faces.

"Mother," Lute said, setting the bowl back in its place, "you said you would tell me about the horses."

"Ah yes, the horses. The horses are gifts from the old earl. It was his earnest desire that we accept them. He offered me a great many things in recent years, and I always refused them. So this time he told me firmly that these gifts were *not* for me, but for you. Clever man. He knew I couldn't refuse gifts intended for someone else. Besides, Lute, I couldn't have said no, not when I knew it was one of his dying wishes."

"Gifts for *us?*"

"No, Lute, for *you.*"

Lute sat there in stunned silence. Those splendid horses were for him? He remembered how thrilling he'd found it to go tearing across the fields on the back of Merlyn's great black stallion. And he remembered how terribly excited he was that day on the sports field beside the castle when he'd climbed up onto the back of the injured knight's horse and had his first real taste of chivalric training. Now he would possess horses nearly as fine as those, horses that would put him on an equal footing with almost any other knight.

"Mother," Lute finally said, no longer able to contain his curiosity about his mother's relationship to the old earl, "was the man perhaps in love with you?" For the last five years the earl had been a widower, and Lute knew that, following the death of his wife, he'd lavished a good bit of attention on Lute's mother.

"He was always very kind to me, Lute. So yes, perhaps in a way he was. He never actually said as much to me, though I suppose we both knew what was in his heart and mind. But he came to understand that, while I had real affection for him, my feelings were not of the kind he wished them to be. That may have caused him some hurt, though I always treated him with as much kindness as I could."

"He wasn't the only man who has taken an interest in you, Mother. I feel sure there have been others."

She sighed. "Yes, Lute, I suppose that's true."

"You were never able to find someone you could love?"

Lute's mother didn't answer. She sat looking down at the wooden cup she cradled in her two hands.

"No," she said at last, "I guess I never did. Once, a very long time ago, there was a man I believed I could love. And for a little while I believed that he could love me, too." Again she was silent for another long moment. "But," she said with a sigh, "I was probably wrong on both counts."

Now it was Lute's turn to look pensive. He stared at his mother, who continued looking down into her wine cup.

Eventually, though, Lute returned to telling his mother about life with his uncle and about his various activities and his new acquaintances in the city. His mother remembered old Gwilym, his uncle's manservant, and hearing Lute's description of the cantankerous old fellow resurrected her smile. He told her about Julianna, whom she had never met, about her devotion to Earl Thomas, and how gracious she'd been to Lute.

"Mother," Lute said after eating his final bite of pasty, "I have kept the best surprise for last. You will never guess who has now befriended me."

Lute sat there looking very smug. He raised his cup and took a sip, his eyes looking over the rim at his mother's face.

"Well, Lute," she said, "since I haven't any idea who that might be, I suppose you had better go ahead and tell me."

Lute placed his cup back down on the plank table. "Mother," he said, "I have met the king himself. One day, just a few weeks ago, I went out riding on Merlyn's horse in the meadow beside the city, and there was the king, riding there also. He remembered having seen me before, Mother, and he spoke to me so very kindly. We rode together for a few hours before returning together to the city. Mother, he is such a fine, fine man. Imagine that, me and the king riding together—just the two of us! Mother, the unimaginable is really true. The king has called me his friend."

Lute, who'd been completely caught up in his own happy recollections, failed to notice that his mother's face had turned pale and that a small vein in her throat began to throb. He also didn't notice that the hand holding her cup was trembling slightly. When she tried to set it back down on the table, it tipped over on its side and wine spilled across the width of the table.

"Oh dear," she said, "I'd better wipe that up."

"No, mother, you sit still. I shall take care of it."

Lute dashed to the kitchen for a damp cloth. His mother raised one trembling hand and covered her eyes.

CHAPTER 27

Lute was startled from his dreams by the raucous cries of a cockerel. The dratted bird was perched atop the stable only a few feet from his window. The lad lifted his muzzy head, trying to get his bearings. Why was a rude bird crowing outside his window? He hadn't heard a rooster the whole time he'd been in the city.

Then it came to him where he was. *Argh.* It was time to be getting a move on it. There were fields to be scythed. If he were late joining up with the other workers, he'd never hear the end of it from Robin. Lute rolled out from beneath his covers and quickly pulled on his shirt and breeches.

The aroma of breakfast filled the little dwelling. His mother wasn't going to let him go off to the fields without having a hearty meal. In addition to the eggs and ham she'd fried for him, she'd packed him a lunch. It was wrapped in a cloth, ready to go into his knapsack. Lute wolfed down his meal, hugged his mother, and dashed off to rendezvous with the other workers. City boy or not, Lute intended to prove to his friends he hadn't forgotten where he'd come from.

Every man and lad from the village and surrounding farmsteads had come to help in the harvesting. Among the large party of workers were quite a few sturdy women. It would be a long day in the fields, and they hoped to complete their work by evening, for as the old saying went, it's best to make hay while the sun is shining. The day would be dry and sunny, but who knew what the weather would be tomorrow?

Throughout the long morning of scything, Robin made frequent gibes about Lute's lily-white hands. Lute suffered the good-natured abuse patiently, though, in fact, his hands were well calloused from all the sword and lance practice he'd been doing for the last several weeks on the sports field near the castle.

Jill didn't work alongside the others. She was the niece of the old earl and the cousin of the new one; as a highborn young woman, it wouldn't be fitting. But she remained in the fields with the workers throughout the day, serving them fresh water from the wooden bucket she constantly refilled.

When she held out the dipper to Lute, his two hands partially overlapped with hers as he held it. Jill's long-fingered hands were warm to the touch; Lute found himself relishing the inadvertent contact. On the backs of her pale hands he noticed delicate, bluish veins. As he drank gratefully, his eyes met Jill's and Lute suddenly felt confused. He'd always had the deepest affection for Jill. But until that moment, it was the affection one felt toward a beloved sister. Had something changed?

All through the long day the work progressed slowly but steadily. Finally, toward the late afternoon hours, the grain was gathered into sheaves and the sheaves loaded onto carts and wagons to be hauled off to the various barns and granaries. The first tenth was taken directly to the abbey tithe barn. Then, as the many other wagons and ox carts were loaded up, they began heading off to their assigned destinations. A goodly number went to the earl's own granary, and others were dispersed amongst the tenant farmers whose modest farmsteads were scattered about the surrounding area.

As the last of the carts rumbled off, the workers took turns splashing handfuls of cold water over their faces and arms.

"Come on, Lute," cried the young lad named Neely. "You 'member you promised to play with us today, doncha? Ya ain't too tired to do it, is ya?"

Other voices chimed in on the razzing and cajoling. Lute and Robin exchanged looks, shrugged, then set off toward the village green along with all the other lads.

In the gloaming the tired and sweaty youths straggled back to the village. There was still enough light, for those who had the energy, to work in a short game of football. With Robin choosing the players for one side and Lute those for the other, the players were divided up as evenly as possible. Little Neely, chosen early on by Robin, could barely restrain his tears. He'd so very badly wanted to be on Lute's side.

During the first part of the match Lute and Robin went head to head, engaging in some fierce tackling and a good bit of rude jawing. Neither team was able to score, and with the match still tied at nil-nil, Lute moved back into goal. As dusk descended, it appeared that the match would end a scoreless tie. But then, in the very final moments, Robin intercepted a pass and broke for Lute's goal. In his mad dash, his footwork displayed the consummate skill he'd always possessed.

Lute knew his friend well and anticipated his move. He knew that at the last moment Robin would shift the ball from his right foot to his left, and then, when Lute made his dive, he wouldn't boot it toward the left post but instead would try to sneak it past Lute toward the right post.

Just as Robin flicked the ball from one foot to the other, Lute made his dive. But rather than taking the shot, Robin flicked the ball back to a tiny figure that had streaked up behind him. Lute saw the maneuver but reacted too slowly. Neely caught the ball on his right foot, gave it one soft dribble, then booted it cleanly with his left foot straight between the posts—the winning goal.

The cheerful lads on Robin's side hoisted Neely onto their shoulders and marched off the green, their voices united in lusty song. The exhausted, grass-stained Lute leapt to his feet and reached his hand up to the young lad. Neely shook Lute's hand and squeezed it tight, grinning from ear to ear. The little lad who'd begun the match holding back his tears was no longer anywhere close to being tearful.

Amongst the several onlookers were the two old gents sitting on their bench outside the Green Man.

"Year or two ago," the gaffer said, "Lute'd stopped that one easy. Lost his touch, the laddie has."

"Oh, well, I'm not so sure about that," his companion replied. "No, I don't really think Lute has lost his touch."

"No? Sure looked that way ta me."

"I kinda suspect things ended up just the way Lute wanted 'em to end up."

"Ended up the way Lute wanted 'em to? Well, p'haps ya be right."

In the morning Lute was awakened by women's voices coming from the next room. The hour wasn't early. Not like the previous day. When Lute opened his eyes and glanced out the window, he saw that the sun was already well up. He'd slept long and deep. Even the raucous cries of the dratted cockerel hadn't intruded upon his sleep. The previous day had been arduous in a way Lute was no longer accustomed to. And after their long day's labors in the fields and their evening football match, he and the lads had spent several more hours in the Green Man.

It had been quite late when Lute finally dragged himself back home, a bit worse for wear.

The voices Lute heard in the next room belonged to his mother and Jill. As Lute listened, he realized his mother was giving Jill advice about a needlework project. When Lute opened his door and looked out, they were sitting at the old oak table, examining Jill's handiwork. Lute mumbled his greetings to them, shambled through the room, and went outside to wash himself from the well bucket beside the paddock.

When he came back in he said a more proper "good morning" to them.

"I hoped you would have a good sleep-in today, Lute," his mother said, smiling at him, "after the hard day's work you turned in yesterday."

"And the hard night's work, too," Jill said with a chuckle. "And all of that on top of that football match you and the lads enjoyed."

"Life in the city is rarely so arduous, I admit. Though all those flights of steps in the city do serve to keep one fit."

"When your mother and I are finished here, Lute, perhaps you could tell me more about King Uther's fair city?" Jill asked. "I would love to hear about it. And about all those knightly things you've been doing there."

"Could we put that off for another day, Jill? I was planning to take out the two new horses today and give them a good workout. I'm eager to see what they're made of. That's likely to take most of the day, especially as it's already mid-morning."

"Why don't you and Jill ride out together, Lute? I could pack you a picnic lunch. Then as you're eating, you could regale the lass with tales of your knightly exploits."

"No, mother, I don't think so. Jill's not dressed for riding, and besides, I was planning on really exercising those two creatures most vigorously."

"Lute, I ride nearly as well as you. I'm perfectly capable of giving that palfrey a vigorous workout. As for my clothing, it will hardly take any time at all to go home and change. I could be back in ten minutes."

"That's settled then," Lute's mother said. "Let's us finish up here, Jilly. Then you go change while I get some breakfast down this lad and make a lunch the two of you can take with you."

Lute had the feeling there was a lot of decision-making going on in which he was having no say.

Jill was truly an excellent rider, and when Lute brought the stallion to a gallop out on the grassy lea that stretched for several miles east of the village, she and the smooth-gaited filly were matching them stride for stride.

Lute proceeded to put his powerful steed through a series of maneuvers that he'd learned on the field near the castle. Although the horse wasn't familiar with them, he was an intelligent creature who quickly grasped what was expected of him. Lute sensed the creature's remarkable athleticism and exulted in the quickness of his mind. The wondrous steed was exactly the kind of mount Lute had dreamed about possessing.

Jill's elegant palfrey was nearly as fine. She was perfectly suited for long hours in the saddle when comfort was the chief thing, not power. A knight's charger was his warhorse, but as a general rule he spent more time atop his riding horse than his mighty steed. Both were essential. Lute was certain he'd been hugely fortunate with these horses the old earl had given him.

To the east of the lea where they'd been riding there arose a long, high ridge of hill. Known as Barham's Edge, it was part of a rugged ridge of upland that extended many miles toward the north of Britain. Footpaths and trails twisted upward toward the top of the hill, and Lute, ready to give the horses a break from their exertions, now rode up one of them to where he and his friends had often gone in past times. It was a place which provided superb views in all directions.

Off to the west they could see the mountains of Wales; to the east the great forests and farmlands of the flatter plains of Britain; to the north the long line of hills that stretched far off into the distance. South of where they stood, a four or five-day ride, lay the great city of Uther Pendragon.

While the horses busied themselves cropping grass, he and Jill stood close together in companionable silence, taking in the impressive sights. "Jill, off there to the east," Lute finally said, pointing, "there's a place called Sanham. It's maybe a three-day ride from here. My Uncle Thomas is the earl there."

"Your mother's brother?"

"Yes, her older brother. I've been staying with him in the city. He's a fine man and one of the king's most trusted advisors. My uncle is crippled, Jill. From a terrible wound he received in the Battle of Bedegrain Forest."

"I've heard of that battle," she said.

"Jill, he's never had any children. He wants to make me his heir. He wants me to be the next Earl of Sanham."

"That's wonderful, Lute." She linked her arm through his and squeezed it, sending a thrill of excitement through him.

"Yes," he replied distractedly, not quite sure what he was feeling, "I suppose it is."

"Why wouldn't it be?"

Lute breathed a big sigh. "Well, . . . I'm not really sure it's what I want, Jilly."

"What is it you want, Lute?"

Lute remained silent for several seconds before saying, "Jill, the truth is, I'm not really *sure* what I want. Nor am I sure what I don't."

She stepped around in front of him and took both his hands in hers. She looked up into his face and held his eyes with hers. He'd never stared so deeply into her eyes before.

"You have many fine choices, Lute," she said, her hands softly kneading his. "But there isn't any rush. Take your time. When you know what it is you really want, I think you will hear bells sounding inside your head and inside your heart. When you hear them, then you will know. Wait and listen for the beautiful sound of those bells."

Lute couldn't help smiling at her words.

"Bells? You really think that one day soon I will hear bells? Jilly . . . um . . . that sounds just a little bit silly to me."

"Yes, of course I'm being silly. But Lute, you really don't know how fortunate you are. You have so many more choices before you than Robin or I will ever have."

Lute reflected on her words for a moment.

"I guess that's true, Jill. I never really thought about that."

"Take your time, Lute. You'll figure it all out. Whether or not you hear any silly bells."

"Right now, I guess, what I'd most like to do is spend as much time as I can being close to the king."

"To the *king?* Do you think that's possible?"

"I don't really know. But that's what my heart seems to be telling me."

Jill and Lute stood together on top of Barham's Edge several more minutes. And while they did, neither of them felt any great urgency to remove their hands from those of the other.

CHAPTER 28

In the days that followed, Lute continued to work the horses. He wanted to know them as intimately as he possible—their likes and dislikes, their liabilities and limitations, their quirks—which he knew every horse had. He continued to be mightily pleased with them. Many times he said a silent prayer of thanks to the old earl for his magnificent gift, even if it was a gift more intended to express gratitude to his mother than to him.

Lute also spent one entire day working side by side with Robin as the men and lads burned the stubble on the grain fields. They'd waited for another dry and windless day, and the thick, black smoke from the fires rose straight to the skies, its smell filling their nostrils. Afterward they all splashed about in the small stream that flowed through the woods beyond the fields. But when Lute went to bed that night, he could still smell the smoke in his hair.

The days flowed by until it was the last day before Lute intended to begin his return to the city. Part of that day he spent giving the horses another workout on the long grassy lea; he didn't push them too hard, wanting them to be fresh for the long ride. They were fit and strong, and by riding them in turns, he should make good time during his return trip, better time than if he were riding his stalwart old roan. Lute would miss that loyal beast who'd served him so well. But in all fairness, it was time the gelding was put out to pasture.

As the youth trotted down the lane toward the gateway, Jill came through it. Lute hopped down from the back of the filly and looped the reins of the horses around the gatepost.

Jill carried the wicker basket containing her handiwork. The two stopped and looked at each other without speaking. They both knew this was likely to be their last chance to speak for a good, long time. Jill waited for Lute to speak first.

"So I'll be off again in the morning," he said.

"Yes, your mother told me."

"How's the project going?"

"Without your mother's help, I would be completely lost."

Lute felt tongue-tied and made no reply.

"Lute, could I ask a favor?"

"Of course, Jilly."

"Could I ride a ways with you tomorrow? Just for the first few hours? Just to have a last chance to share your company?"

"Oh, you don't want to be doing that, Jill. I'll be getting off to an early start and moving quickly, now that I'm not riding the old roan."

"I don't mind an early start. Lute, I'd just like to spend a few more hours with a young man I've known for most of my life. Who knows when we'll see each other again."

"You're probably right about that, Jill. The city's going to be quite a lively place once the armies return. I don't know exactly how I'm going to fit into things there, but I have my hopes."

"It won't be long, Lute, before those folks in the city recognize your true abilities. The king, his advisors, and Merlyn will soon discover what a treasure they have in you."

"I'm not even a knight yet, Jill. I have months of training ahead of me."

"Whatever happens, I know you will make us proud. If you decide to become a knight, you will be one of the best. If you decide to do what your uncle wants and become the Earl of

Sanham, that will make us proud, too. And if you conclude that knighthood and the king's court isn't what you want after all, you'll be most welcome right back here. Whatever you decide to do, Lute, it will turn out brilliantly."

Lute laughed at his childhood friend's well-meant words. He stepped over and pulled her to him in a warm embrace. "Jilly, you say they will discover what a treasure they have in me. Maybe they will and maybe they won't. But one thing I know for sure is that I have a wonderful treasure in you."

As he hugged her, he didn't notice the tears in her eyes.

When their evening meal was over, Lute told his mother to sit still while he did the clearing up. She went over to her loom and stared at the tapestry she'd been working on for the new earl. She knew she was nearly finished, and she felt pleased with how it was turning out.

"It's beautiful, Mother," Lute said. Standing beside her, he put his arm around her shoulders and she put hers around his waist. They remained that way, staring at the tapestry.

Lute studied the intricate design, which largely consisted of crisscrossing bands of red and russet colors, with just a very few purple and green threads mixed in. The subtle variations in both the shades of the colors and the width of the bands lent a shimmering quality to the work. Lute was entranced.

"If the earl doesn't like it, Mother, I would be pleased to take it and give it to a special friend of mine in the city."

"Would that be the young woman you told me about named?"

"Actually, no. I was thinking of someone else."

"And who might that be, Lute?"

"Mother," Lute said, abruptly changing the subject, "come

and sit down beside me for a while. There are things I wish to discuss with you."

His mother did as he requested, though as she sat on the little stool her right hand began to tremble just slightly.

"Mother, I don't know any other way to broach this subject, so I'm just going to plunge in." Lute's mother's face turned pale. "When we were talking a week or so ago, you told me that you once knew a man you thought you could love, a man you thought might also love you. Mother . . . was that man my father?"

At Lute's words, his mother seemed to freeze. She'd realized at the time she'd said far more than she'd ever intended to say to him. Afterward she'd found herself hoping the topic wouldn't ever come up again, though she knew it would. Now it had.

"That matter is personal and private, Lute. It was a long time ago, a time I've largely forgotten. I hope you can respect my wishes that we not talk about it."

Lute sat with his arms folded across his chest, one hand cradling his chin. He was torn between his desire to do as his mother wished and his need to discover the truth about things he'd every right to know. He sat quietly, hoping she would go ahead on her own and speak to him without his having to force her to. For a full minute they played a waiting game.

"Lute," she said, "dear son, can't you see that that is a terribly painful subject for me?"

Lute nodded slowly. But his arms remained folded on his chest, his lips compressed.

"Yes, dear son," she said at last, "you are right. That man was your father." She looked down at the table avoiding his eyes, and said nothing more.

"Mother," Lute said at last, "I would like to know more about him. It's only fair that you tell me about my father."

She sighed, still looking down. She raised her head, sighed again, and looked straight at her beloved son.

"Yes, you do have a right to know. I've been selfish in not telling you. But Lute, this is not easy for me."

"I know that, mother. Take your time and tell me only what you think I ought to know. I have no desire to hurt you."

"Lute, we were so young and foolish. It was right after the terrible battle. Father and I had gone to the city to join in the celebration. It was a time of great jubilation. We were the victors and the rebel kings were shamed and defeated.

"The city was filled with music and feasting and drinking. Everyone was giddy with joy, knights and noblemen alike. So, too, were all the young women. Father was as exuberant as everyone else. For several days I didn't even see him.

"One evening during this exciting time Merlyn came and found me. He asked me if I would be willing to come with him. I didn't know what he wanted."

"Merlyn?"

"Yes, Lute, your very own friend Merlyn. He told me that someone especially wanted to see me. I trusted Merlyn and so I went with him willingly.

"He led me along darkened passages through the back hallways of the castle until we reached a private chamber. He took me inside. There, inside, was the man I've already mentioned to you. A very beautiful young man. He smiled at me and told me that he'd much wanted to get to know me.

"We talked together quietly for several hours that evening, sipping wine and looking at each other shyly. He was kind and gentle, and I found myself being drawn to him. I could tell that he very much liked me, and I'll confess that I found his interest in me quite flattering. Lute, all the while I was there he never once touched me. After a few hours, Merlyn came back for me and took me away.

"The next night Merlyn came for me again. Once more the young man and I visited, laughed, and looked at each other. There was no doubt that we both were feeling a very strong mutual attraction. Before I left that night, he took me softly in his arms. He told me it was wonderful spending time with me.

"The nights that followed were different. We still talked and laughed and sipped wine together. But Lute, we also became lovers."

She stopped for a moment, lost in her thoughts. Lute could see tears glistening in her eyes. "After that, we had several more wondrous nights together. Lute, they were the happiest nights of my life." She dabbed at her eyes, her hand trembling visibly.

"At week's end the celebrating in the city finally began winding down. People were leaving. It was time for everyone to return to their normal lives.

"Father had reappeared, and now he was eager for us to return home to Sanham. Thomas was being treated by the finest physicians, and there was nothing more we could do for him. He would have to remain behind to be cared for. He would probably be crippled for the rest of his life, though it appeared he wouldn't have to lose either of his legs.

"I spent one last night in the chamber with my friend. He knew I was about to leave, and I could tell it saddened him. But he had a great many important responsibilities he needed to attend to. That last night was a beautiful night but also a woeful one. I'll admit I shed many tears. In the morning, he and I shared a last embrace. He told me he would always be thinking about me. Then Merlyn came and led me away.

"A few hours later, Father and I set off for Sanham. I have never been back to the city. And I have never seen my friend since the final night we shared together in his chamber."

Lute got up, stepped over to his mother, and put his arm around her shoulders. He squeezed her gently. He knelt down and crouched beside her, holding his arm about her.

"So you went back to live in Sanham?"

"Only for a few months. When I realized I was with child, arrangements needed to be made. Old Wat was the one who came to my rescue. His widowed sister lived here in this little house, Lute. He sent me here to stay with her. Then, only half a year after you were born, she died. All of this she left to me. You and I have lived here ever since."

"Mother . . . did he know?"

"No, Lute, as far as I know he never did."

"Did he ever try to find you?"

"I don't know. Probably not. He had many other responsibilities. And later on, we all heard that he'd married the most beautiful woman in all Britain."

"The most beautiful woman in all Britain? Mother, the most beautiful woman in all Britain . . . is the queen!"

"Yes, Lute, that is what they say."

"Mother . . . then the man you have been talking about—"

"Yes, Lute, the man I've been talking about is the man who's recently become your new friend in the city."

Lute sat in stunned silence. He was trying to take in what his mother had just told him.

Finally he said, "Mother . . . when I see him again, what do I *do?* Mother . . . what am I supposed to *tell* him?"

Lute's mother took a very deep breath. She just looked at her son and gave a small shrug of her shoulders.

CHAPTER 29

Tom came suddenly awake. Something was wrong. Was someone messing with the horses?

It was so early the birds hadn't begun chorusing. Only the faint light of pre-dawn shone in the forest. Tom glanced over at Merlyn. The strange old man was shrouded in his thick woolen cloak, twitching and snorting softly in his sleep.

Crawling on hands and knees, Tom moved to where he could view the horses. Nothing seemed amiss. As he peeped cautiously around a tree trunk, Raguel stared back at him, a reddish glint in his eye.

"Can't put nuthin' over on you, you old devil," Tom muttered beneath his breath.

Raguel stamped his foot impatiently. He was ready for his morning feed.

"All right, all right," Tom whispered, "don't get your small clothes in a bunch."

The lad crept beneath the overhanging branches and found the sack of oats. When he bent down to open it, that's when he sensed movement farther back in the woods.

Tom crouched and then froze. "Easy, Rags," he whispered. "We'd best find out what's doing. And we'd best not be discovered doing it."

From behind him came another sound. Tom craned his neck and saw, no more than twenty yards from him, a man slipping quickly through the thick woods. A tall man; and in the pre-dawn dimness, it Tom took a moment to realize who it was.

King Rience. What in the name of Hades was *he* up to? And then Tom knew—the blighter was making a dash for it.

"Bastard!" Tom muttered softly. The fellow had given Sir Gawain his parole—his sacred promise as a nobleman that he wouldn't attempt an escape. And on the assumption that he was a man of honor, he'd even been allowed to keep his sword and retain his mount.

So much for King Rience's honor! Even Tom, who at his young age was well-schooled in the ways of the world, took offense at the man's ignoble behavior. A little scamp like Tom stealing a chicken from a local farmer was one thing; a high-born nobleman like King Rience lying through his teeth and violating a sacred trust was quite another. Even to Tom it was despicable.

Tom stood still as a stone as King Rience moved stealthily through the woods. When he'd disappeared from view, Tom rose slowly and slid the bridle over Raguel's long head.

Tom heard soft noises from the direction King Rience had gone. King Rience, Tom guessed, had arranged a rendezvous with some of his confederates, fellows who were now out there awaiting him. The filthy lice-ridden shagger was like to get away!

Tom slid up onto the horse's back. There wasn't time to saddle the black, so Tom would have to ride bareback—for an able rider like Tom only a minor inconvenience.

But before he'd put the black into motion, Tom hesitated, for he realized that someone else was moving through the woods. This person was making no attempt at stealth. Tom could see that he was mounted and armed. Whoever he was, he was eagerly pursuing the escapee.

The unknown rider hurried on ahead and was soon clear

of the forest. Tom could hear the rapid patter of the horse's hooves as it picked up speed.

Tom dug his own heels into Raguel's sides. In a trice the black was gliding swiftly through the forest in the wake of the two men. Only a moment later, once Tom and the black had passed out from beneath the overhanging branches, the boy spotted dark shapes moving up the incline toward a cleft in the hills half a mile away.

The second man's horse, Tom could see, was closing the distance between him and the fellows ahead of him—men who weren't yet aware of him. Tom wondered at the man's audacity, for he was just one lone man in pursuit of several fully armed knights. Was the fellow in league with them? Either that, Tom thought, or he was the Great Fool of the World.

The lad gave Raguel his head, and the black shot forth with lightning speed. In only a minute or so he'd eaten up much of the distance between him and the riders ahead of him. Raguel was a wonder. Little Tom, riding bareback, must have felt like a feather on his back.

Now Tom saw that there were four men who were being pursued by the lone rider. And it was just then that they realized a rider was closing in on them; they halted their mounts and spun them about.

The sight of the riders awaiting him didn't seem to cause the solitary figure any alarm; all he did was spur his horse to an even greater pace. As he rushed right at them, he held his upraised blade high above his head. His fearsome blade glinted in the early morning light.

Tom, still a hundred yards away, could hear the man's blood-curdling shrieks as he made his final charge.

"That there's one crazy fool," Tom said to himself.

The rider's steed churned his powerful legs, his hooves sending dark clods flying behind him. The slight incline proved no hindrance for horse and rider.

The trio of riders who'd swung around to oppose the solitary rider spaced their mounts widely to give themselves room to maneuver, a strategy, as it turned out, that worked to the advantage of the lone man. The fourth man—King Rience— took up a position behind them.

As the attacker was nearly to them, his sure-footed charger swerved suddenly to the left. In an eye-blink, the man's blade entered and was extracted from the throat of the outside rider's horse. The beast shrieked and rose on its hind legs, then crashed down violently onto its right side, crushing the leg of its rider.

At virtually the same moment, the lone rider, his shield in his right hand, checked the lance thrust of the defender to his right. Then he and his mount moved behind them, circling to where he could set upon the figure on the farther side. The rider in the middle found himself spinning in circles, his ill-trained mount thoroughly confused by the flurry of activity surrounding him.

The frightened beast on the farther side reared up frantically; it tossed its rider like a sack of oats.

As Tom watched, the man rode roughshod over the downed man, crushing his body to lifelessness. The middle fellow regained control of his mount, but too slowly—for as he did, the lone rider's lance impaled him. His terrified horse bolted; it dashed on up the incline, its rider slumped backward in his saddle, the lance protruding from his torso.

But the matter wasn't settled just yet, for as this initial flurry of fighting was ending, King Rience, with upraised weapon, charged toward the exposed back of the lone rider. And as courageous and skilled as that fellow was, his demise was imminent. If not for Tom and Raguel, it would have been.

Acting upon his own instincts, the black swiftly interposed himself between the attacker and his intended victim. Rising on his powerful back legs, the black brought his forelegs crashing down upon both the horse and its rider.

The rider went sprawling, the horse tumbled onto its side. When the beast scrambled back to its feet, now riderless, it limped painfully away from the melee. With an audible groan, King Rience rose slowly to his feet.

The rider sat quietly on his mount, looking down at the man.

"I capitulate," King Rience muttered just above a whisper, "I capitulate."

Picking up the sword that had fallen from his hand, he held it out, hilt-first, to the lone rider. It was the sword Gawain had allowed him to keep after he'd given his parole.

"You *capitulate?*" the man said with a smirk. "Yes, I bet you do."

He nudged his mount closer, then reached down to take the proffered weapon. For a moment he held the sword in his left hand. He ran his eye over it appreciatively.

"A fine blade," he said, once more with a smirk, "a very fine blade. It is a blade perfectly suited to the killing of a king."

He plunged the blade into the chest of the startled man.

From only a few yards away, Tom and Raguel bore silent witness to this final event. When the man turned toward them, he gave them a cheery grin in the dim early light.

"We did well, didn't we? I'd like to think I didn't need your help, but I'm not certain of that. Anyway, your timely assistance was appreciated. So I really ought to offer you a token of my gratitude. Yes? So, what would you like it to be?"

"Sir," Tom replied, "we just done our duty. Done our duty 'gainst a very bad sorter feller. Glad to do it, sir. Me 'n the black, we don't be needin' no tokens o' gratitude. No sir, not no nuthin' a-tall."

"You are far too modest, laddie, far too modest. Oh yes, I think recompense is definitely required."

As he rode up closer to Tom and Raguel, he jingled a small leathern pouch attached by a thong to his belt. Tom eyed the pouch, paying no attention to the fact that the man was still clutching King Rience's sword in his other hand.

With snake-quick movement, the flat of his sword cracked hard against the side of Tom's head. Raguel, sensing the man's intentions, had begun an evasive maneuver; but for once the beast hadn't been quick enough, and the blow sent the lad flying. His small body came down hard in a thick clump of bracken.

"*There's* your well-earned recompense, laddie. Now then," the man said to the black, "what about you?"

Raguel stared at him, his eyes glowing. "You certainly are a beauty. You and I would make quite a dashing pair. But . . . taking you for my own, much as I'd like to, would be a colossal mistake. You, you gorgeous creature, surely belong to someone of note, someone who wouldn't take kindly to my possessing you. So, alas, I will have to leave you to your own devices." The black just snorted.

Wasting no further time, the lone man draped the lifeless body of King Rience over the back of the only remaining horse. Then he slid up onto his own mount, and, holding the reins of the other horse, he began the short trek back down to the British encampment.

As he rode, he couldn't help smiling, knowing that he had

just won for himself a substantial measure of glory. Henceforth he would be known as the man who'd taken down King Rience of the Outer Isles.

The old man couldn't understand Tom's absence. Where could the lad have gone? He surely wouldn't have scarpered. Was he off somewhere stealing another chicken? Not likely, since the boy's mount was still here.

Nor could the old man understand the sheen of sweat on Raguel's coat. The horse had been well exercised quite recently. Was that Tom's doing? Had the dratted creature thrown the boy off and then abandoned him? He supposed, given the black's devilish nature, that was a possibility.

Much activity now surrounded Merlyn, for the British army was in the process of breaking camp. They would soon begin the long, slow journey back to the city.

But as Merlyn watched them, he knew he wouldn't be going with them. Not just yet. Not until he'd solved the mystery of the missing boy. He'd begun to fear that the little urchin was lying dead somewhere. If so, he would search until he'd found the little fellow's body.

Merlyn looked the black square in the eye. "Will you help me?" he whispered. "Are you the one who did this? Are you the guilty party?" The horse stamped impatiently.

"Is that a 'no'? Then take me where we need to go. I need your help." Raguel snorted loudly and shook his magnificent head. He seemed to be inviting Merlyn to climb up on him.

"I'm not riding bareback," Merlyn grumped. "So you just keep your socks on till I get the accursed saddle on you, you brute." The horse snorted.

Giving the black his head, Merlyn and the now-saddled

horse passed out of the forest and began to ascend the incline toward the distant cleft in the hills.

Soon Merlyn could see the dark shapes of the carrion birds, many swirling, some settling, halfway up the hillside. As he neared, the birds emitted angry cries at those who disturbed their dining on the corpses of horses and men.

As the black carried him closer, Merlyn's heart sank. He dreaded seeing what he expected to see—and then there it was, lying half concealed in a thick clump of furze, the crumpled body of the boy.

Merlyn climbed down from the black. With little concern for his hands and arms, he groped amongst the thorny bushes. Slowly and gently he freed the boy's body from their persistent grasp.

Merlyn laid the lad out on a grassy spot and knelt down over him. The sight of the angry contusion on the side of the lad's head caused the old man's heart to clench. Merlyn didn't understand why he'd grown so fond of the little scamp, only that he had.

Holding his hand against a vein at the side of the boy's throat, he felt for a pulse. No, nothing. He pressed harder. Then he felt it. *Yes*, the small frail body still possessed a very faint spark of life! Merlyn breathed out the huge breath he'd been holding. He felt his confidence surge.

"Saints be praised," he mumbled. "If anyone can save this lad, I'm the one who can." Raguel just snorted.

The
RECOMPENCE

CHAPTER 30

On a late October morn, Lute rode through the small, closely guarded postern gate that led out from the city's highest level. He trotted across the small bridge, nodded a greeting to the sleepy-eyed guards, then rode out into the great meadow that extended for many miles to east of the city.

Lute hadn't ridden here for several months, not since the mid-summer morning when he'd come here on Merlyn's black stallion and found the king riding here as well. That was the day the king had extended to Lute the hand of friendship.

But today was quite different—a chilly autumnal morn on which the dawning came late. The rising sun barely shone through a gray and hazy sky. Wisps of morning mist hung heavy above the expanse of greenish-brown grass over which the lad and his mount now rode.

Lute put his heels into the sides of his stallion, a horse he now knew well and cherished. He was a powerful young stallion of superb quality, the equal to any of those ridden by the city's finest knights. And yet as good as he was, Lute knew he wasn't a patch on Merlyn's black, the horse on which he'd been mounted the day he'd met the king.

The gray, chilly weather suited the youth's mood. It was an anxious time for him, for he knew his life had reached a major turning point and that when he'd passed it, nothing would be the same again. On the one hand, he was on the brink of realizing his fondest hope: on All-Hallows Eve, after his two months of training, Lute and five other young men would keep vigil in the great minster; and then at the service of matins the following day, they would receive the accolade of knighthood.

And thus Lute's feelings of exultation. But at the same time, another matter was causing him real trepidation. For circulating through the city were rumors of the king's imminent and victorious return. Having provided the support King Ban and King Bors had needed in their wars—and having returned the great favor they'd once done for him—now the king and his army were coming home. And Lute knew that once the king was back in the city, he had to inform him—indeed, *confront* him—with the knowledge he possessed, the knowledge his mother had finally confided in him. Lute found the thought of doing that more than a little daunting. And he had no idea how best to do it.

Lute hadn't yet sought out his uncle's advice on the matter; in fact, he hadn't even revealed to his uncle what he now knew. Why was he dragging his feet? Maybe, Lute told himself, it wasn't his uncle's advice he wanted. What he wanted was *Merlyn's* advice. But where *was* Merlyn? When Gawain's army returned in triumph after their victory over King Rience and his rebels, the old man hadn't been with them.

Lute was worried about Merlyn. He felt a great need to see him. Although he hadn't known the old man for very long and couldn't claim to know him well, he'd developed a deep affection for him and had come to trust him completely. But where was Merlyn now? Two months was a long time to have heard nothing at all from the old duffer.

Anyway, on this gray and chilly morn, Lute had come here to exercise his warhorse. And so, shoving those thoughts out of his mind as best he could, he got down to the business of putting his steed through his paces.

Lute exercised the noble, good-natured creature for most of the morning, following a regimen of exercises now very familiar to both horse and rider. But as he did, he couldn't help thinking about the day he'd ridden here with the king; and he couldn't help imagining what he might say to the king, should the man turn up today unexpectedly.

But the king didn't turn up. And all morning long, Lute had the entire expanse of the meadow to himself. Frankly, he found that a relief. The meadow remained his private space, which suited his mood. He was happy to have no chance encounters with anyone—and especially none with the king.

Unbeknownst to Lute, however, he *hadn't* been the only person out there that morning. For overlooking the great expanse of lea from the cover of an alder copse, another man had been watching the youth. The man was standing beside his magnificent horse, well concealed from view. All the while he watched the lad, a broad smile graced his lips.

"Oh yes," he muttered to himself, "you are indeed an impressive young fellow. And I'm guessing it won't be long now before we find out just how impressive you truly are."

A little farther back behind him in the copse stood another small horse on whose back perched another small rider. That rider also watched Lute intently. That rider was a boy whose name was Tom.

Merlyn and Tom had returned.

As the long afternoon shadows slanted down from the high city walls, the old man and his grubby little companion rode their horses across the narrow bridge toward the postern gate leading into the city's highest level. The guards at both ends of the bridge, recognizing Merlyn as one of the king's most favored advisers, waved the two riders through without hesitation.

As the mismatched pair rode by—the strange old man on his magnificent black stallion and the weedy little waif on his sway-backed mare—the guards couldn't conceal their smiles of bemusement. Not eager to have his return widely known, Merlyn had intentionally delayed their entry until dusk approached, a time when few others were likely to pay the two riders much notice.

Once inside the city, the old man and the boy passed quickly down to the third level and into the now-darkened narrow byway that led to the back garden of Earl Thomas's demesne. En route, they'd greeted no one and no one had greeted them.

When Merlyn rapped loudly on the locked gate, it took some time before a sour-faced Gwilym finally came and opened it. He glared silently at the sight before him, his arms crossed upon his chest. "Humph," he finally said.

"And a warm and cheery hello to you too, Gwilym," Merlyn said. "Now step aside, sir, and allow two weary travelers to come in, hey?"

"Humph," repeated Gwilym, as he reluctantly stepped aside.

When Raguel snorted loudly, old Gwilym practically jumped out of his skin, eliciting a soft chortle from Tom. Old Gwilym glared scornfully at the little ragamuffin in the company of the dratted old wizard.

Thomas and Julianna's welcome was far warmer, and in only moments Julianna was attending to the immediate needs of the young lad—bath, fresh clothing, food, and some minor medical attention. Gwilym was reluctant even to touch the lad's stinking rags, but finally deigned to when Earl Thomas looked at him askance.

"Lute's down in the lower city," Thomas explained, "but

he'll be back by the time of our evening meal. While your lad is bathing, Merlyn, could I persuade you to share a jug of cool wine with us?"

"I believe you could, Thomas," the old man replied. "Yes, I believe you could."

But when Earl Thomas tried to pry out of Merlyn the story of where he'd been and why he had stayed away so long, he had little success eliciting it. Merlyn was being very tight-lipped indeed.

"Does your reticence have anything to do with this lad you've brought with you, Merlyn?" Thomas asked hopefully. "He's received a terrible head wound, hasn't he? Did that occur during the fighting with King Rience?"

When the old man still didn't answer, Thomas said, "Come now, Merlyn, you know you are among friends here. You know we would never violate your confidence."

Merlyn finally nodded and proceeded to give Thomas a very truncated explanation of who the boy was and why he was with him. He didn't, however, offer any commentary on what he suspected had caused Tom's head wound or who he suspected might have done the deed. As much as he trusted Thomas, those were things he didn't intend to reveal to anyone, at least not until he knew the truth with certainty. But once he did know the truth, someone would experience the wrath of Merlyn. And that someone, Merlyn suspected, was named Mordred.

When Lute returned at last with his purchases, he set them down and rushed over to the old man, whom he warmly embraced. And the old man, a person who rarely encouraged close physical contact with others, for once made an exception.

When Lute caught sight of the small boy who'd been sitting

quietly on a stool in a dark corner, fresh from the first real wash he'd had in a month of Sundays, he glanced at Merlyn questioningly.

"Tom," Merlyn said to the boy, "this is Lute, the youth I've been telling you about."

"Hello, Tom," Lute said. He went over and grasped the boy's small hand. Tom grinned shyly.

"Tom's been looking after the black for me, Lute," Merlyn said. "He's a wonder with horses, young Tom is."

"How fortunate, sir," Lute replied, "considering, umm, your own facility with horses."

Little Tom let out a belly laugh, causing Lute and Earl Thomas to laugh as well. Even the old wizard couldn't help grinning, even if their laughter was at his expense.

The evening that followed was one of the most pleasant any of them had spent in quite some time. Throughout the evening, young Tom never uttered a single word. He just sat there looking from one person to another, grinning the entire time. The little stray waif had never before experienced an evening quite like it.

CHAPTER 31

Mordred was secluded in his favorite spot. From here he had a clear view of the two large windows in the king's private palace that faced toward the practice grounds. Here, amidst a small cluster of trees and low shrubs, he could see and not be seen.

He came to this spot often, hoping to satisfy his fantasies with surreptitious glimpses of the queen. Now and then his wish was granted, though more often the woman he caught glimpses of was the queen's lady-in-waiting, quite worth it in itself, though not nearly so thrilling as the actual sight of the queen.

Thus far, in the several months since his arrival in the city, he had only met the queen face to face a single time. That was in the great hall of the castle during the grand celebration following Gawain's triumphant return from the battle with King Rience, when the queen, along with Sir Jordan and Sir Ulfin, had officially received and recognized Gawain and his brothers as the heroes they were.

When the queen had taken Mordred's hand in hers, their eyes briefly met; and though she didn't speak, she offered him a kindly smile. As she did, the young knight believed he saw a brief flicker of interest come into the queen's eyes. Perhaps he'd only imagined it; perhaps it was wishful thinking. And perhaps he only imagined that her fingers pressed his with just a little more pressure than he would have expected. Mordred sighed at the recollection.

A sudden movement now caught his eye, and he leaned hard against the tree behind which he stood. Yes, he was in luck, for this time it really was the queen. A golden-haired woman robed in a long dark gown of blue walked across his line of sight in one of the windows. When she reached the second window, she paused, turned, and looked out.

Stunned by her radiant beauty, the young man's eyes began to glaze over, his brain to swirl. The sight of the most beautiful woman in all of Britain was almost more than he could bear.

> *Wild seas crashed harshly 'gainst ravaged shores.*
> *Fierce men fought foemen on darkling plains.*
> *Ravening fires raged through doomed cities.*
> *Wild wolf packs ranged 'cross moors and mountains.*
> *Children cried, widows mourned:*
> *Multitudes fell; multitudes died.*

Mordred slowly returned to full awareness, not knowing how much time had passed. But the window he'd been staring at was now empty. It didn't matter. His sight of the woman, however brief, would sustain him for days.

Taking care to avoid being seen, the youth slipped away from his hiding place. Now he would go down to the market square on the city's lowest level. Perhaps he would run into the young woman called Gwendolyn. He would like that.

❖

"Don't go picking any purses, eh?" Merlyn said to the young boy, as he and Tom and Lute began their descent of the great central stairway that led down to the city's lower levels.

"What a thing to say!" Lute remonstrated.

"Oh, just having a little joke with young Tom, you know," the old man replied. "Me and the boy, we like having our jokes."

"Pick *purses?*" the boy said to Merlyn, seeming aghast. "*Me*, sir? Not on your life, sir. Oh no, sir, never *me*, sir!"

"No, no, of course you wouldn't," Merlyn said. But Lute couldn't help noticing the sly wink the old man shot the little urchin. And the big grin with which the little urchin replied.

They were far from alone, for a great number of others were also descending the wide set of stairsteps. And many of them seemed in a terrible hurry, as if they feared being late to an important event.

"A lot of these folks seem to know something we don't," Merlyn muttered.

"Mightn't it be the king?" Tom suggested.

"Ah, yes," Merlyn replied, pursing his lips, "now that I think about it, that's quite likely what it is."

As they descended the final few steps, they could see that a huge and motley crowd had already assembled in the large market square. Quite a few noble folks were scattered amongst the much greater number of commoners. For the moment, social distinctions were set aside as an air of anticipation united everyone crowding the square.

"Lute!" a voice sang out. "Come and join us, lad."

Lute recognized the voice of Mordred, who along with several others had commandeered a choice spot in front of the square's central fountain.

Lute shouldered his way through the bustling crowd and reached the other young knights. But when he swung about with the intention of introducing Merlyn and Tom, they hadn't followed him as he'd expected. Where had they gone? Lute shrugged, then turned back to Mordred, who stared at him intently.

"Lost somebody?"

"Yes, well, sort of. But never mind. I'm sure they'll turn up."

"Who was it you lost?"

"Oh, just the two friends I was with. Anyway, they are plenty capable of looking out for themselves."

"Well, now you've found yourself some different friends. Maybe even better ones, eh? Ones who won't just suddenly disappear on you."

In the very moment when Mordred called out to Lute, young Tom had snatched Merlyn's hand and pulled him back out of view behind the fountain.

"Tom, what is it? What have you seen?"

"It be him, sir. The bastard that went for me. The one a-talkin' ta Lute. Him's the bastard tried ta do for me, sir."

Merlyn, taller than most of the folks about them, tried to duck lower to keep his head from poking up above the others. Then he peeked cautiously around the edge of the fountain to get a glimpse of the fellow talking to Lute. He wasn't terribly surprised at what he saw. The sight confirmed his suspicions.

"Yes, I can see the bloke now, Tom. And I know who he is, too. Not such a nice fellow. And not someone we want seeing us, either. We'd best be careful to watch and not be watched, eh?"

"I'd like ta kill the shagger, that I would," muttered Tom. He ran his fingers over the sheathed knife on the belt beneath his cloak. Merlyn caught the lad's words and nodded grimly, understanding his sentiments.

"For now, let's just make sure the shagger, as you call him, doesn't kill us first."

"I'll be ready for 'im, sir. This time it's like ta be me offering that shagger 'recompense,' not the other way 'round."

"Recompense?"

"That be what he claimed ta be givin' me. Recompense for helpin' 'im do for King Rience."

"Some recompense."

Tom rubbed his hand against the side of his head where he'd been bashed by the flat of Mordred's sword—reminding himself of his recompense.

Through the city's great barbican and its inner set of gates marched six colorful fellows holding bright, shiny horns across their chests. Three stepped to one side and three to the other. In unison, they raised their horns and sounded a royal fanfare.

Then the huge crowd in the square parted as the six trumpeters advanced to the lowest steps of the broad central stairway. Again they raised their horns and sounded the fanfare. This time everyone in the square dropped down upon their knees. Silence prevailed.

The king himself walked slowly into the square.

He halted and surveyed the scene before him. Then he gestured with both arms for everyone to arise.

Smiling, he continued walking toward the central stairsteps. He climbed up a few steps, then stopped and turned to gaze back upon all those assembled in the square.

He paused for a long moment before shouting out, "It's wonderful to be home again!" En masse the people responded with a wild and raucous cheer. Then many individual voices shouted out more personally styled greetings.

As Mordred and Lute were taking all this in, each of them wrestled with emotions particular to him—Mordred's a mixture of envy and admiration, Lute's a mixture of adoration and trepidation.

As Tom took all this in, the little lad began to swell with pride; never before had he found himself part of a gathering of this magnitude. And never before had he imagined that he might find himself an accepted member of ordinary society. It was all very strange; and all very wonderful.

Merlyn's eyes darted this way and that—and in particular, to Mordred. He was trying to read the young fellow and finding it hard to do. Who *was* this Mordred, and what was he up to? Whatever it was, it wasn't anything good. Just as Merlyn had hated to see Lute riding on Raguel, he hated to see Lute in the company of this vile young man. It didn't augur well.

When Tom saw where Merlyn's eyes were focused, he found himself fingering the knife beneath his cloak. "Just you wait, ya shagger," he whispered.

The king remained standing there silently, surveying the scene before him. To Lute, his face looked somewhat haggard and careworn, and his body thinner than usual. But his eyes were bright and his smile broad. Indeed, whatever hardships the man had recently experienced, he was truly glad to be home once more.

"Thank you for your wonderful welcome!" the king shouted to the multitude. "I have missed you. And I have missed our beautiful city!"

Again the crowd erupted into a cheer that echoed, resounded, reverberated from the city's lowest cobblestones to the tip of its highest tower.

If the king was glad to be back home with his people, his

people were even gladder that he was. The denizens of Uther Pendragon's magnificent city greatly loved their noble king. They knew they were blessed to have such a king.

When the trumpets had initially sounded, Rafe and Gwendolyn were standing in front of the ironmonger's shop. Despite his hostility toward the noble classes, Rafe had always remained in awe of the king. So now, while he and Gwendolyn waited, he kept his eyes focused on the main city gateway, watching for the entrance of the royal party.

Gwendolyn's eyes took in a wider swath, moving freely back and forth over all the folks who'd congregated in the square. She'd noticed Lute and his companions as they'd descended the central stairsteps, and she'd watched as Lute had joined Mordred and his friends. She didn't like Lute associating with Mordred. She felt quite an aversion toward this vain young man who'd become so celebrated a figure since his heroics against King Rience.

She wondered, too, about Lute's rather mismatched pair of companions. Who was this tall old man and the little ragamuffin by his side?

The sound of the trumpeters' fanfares sent a thrill coursing through her, and, unconsciously, she put her arm through Rafe's. When the king passed through the square and all the citizens dropped to their knees, she and Rafe knelt side by side, their thighs touching. And when everyone rose back to their feet, her arm still remained threaded through Rafe's.

Like Gwendolyn, Mordred's roving eyes were always quick to take things in, and when he'd noticed Gwendolyn standing arm-in-arm with Rafe, it disgusted him. He'd been attracted to her since he first saw her, but her taste in men revolted him. How could she abide the presence of that imbecilic lout? And how could she prefer Lute to a man such as him? Such an undiscriminating young woman wasn't worth a second thought. Still, it galled him.

"He's a good king," Rafe muttered to Gwendolyn. "Not like some we had before. Or so folks say."

"Oh yes," she replied softly. "He's not at all like his father, King Uther Pendragon."

"Now 'n then the apple falls more 'n a few feet from the tree. Still 'n all, he's got some pretty vile fellas about 'im."

"Yes, sadly, he does." She knew who Rafe meant, for he was staring at Mordred.

And just at that moment Mordred's eyes met those of Rafe. Mordred lifted his hand in a greeting and gave Rafe a beaming smile.

But Mordred's gestures bore no relationship to his inner thoughts. "You, my friend," Mordred said to himself, "are not long for this world. For the life of me, I don't know why I should even bother with a worthless worm like you. But, I *will*. And when I do, it is going to give me a great deal of pleasure. Even if you aren't really worth the bother, a fellow always needs to keep his skills sharp."

Mordred chuckled to himself.

CHAPTER 32

Following the All-Hallows service in the minster, Queen Margause of Lothian wined and dined four of her five sons—Gawain, Gaheris, Agravaine, and Mordred—in her private chamber in the castle. Only Gareth, who was off pursuing adventures of his own, was absent.

Like most of the important British nobles, Queen Margause had come to participate in celebrating the king's return. But she was also there to acknowledge Mordred—the "boy who was lost"—as her fifth and youngest son. Indeed, no one who saw the two of them standing side by side could possibly doubt that they were mother and son.

Of the brothers, it was Agravaine who'd most quickly taken to Mordred. The pair of them appeared to have a natural affinity. Gareth, though, had instinctively shied away from his younger brother; Gawain and Gaheris, while outwardly welcoming and careful to observe all the social niceties, were reserving judgment until they knew Mordred better.

As the others were exiting the chamber, Mordred bid them adieu, then remained behind. The young knight was determined to have a private audience with his mother.

"I would like to be alone," she informed him brusquely.

"Soon, Mother; but not just yet."

"Did you not hear me? I wish to be alone."

"Oh yes, I heard you. And I promise to depart anon. But first, Mother, I need to talk with you and I need you to be honest with me. Do you think that's possible?"

"When have I not been honest with you?"

"Mother," Mordred said, fingering the ring his mother had left with him sixteen years ago, "on that day when we discovered our true relationship, you told me that my father was King Lot of Lothian." For the briefest moment the queen's composure wavered, providing Mordred all the proof he needed.

"Madam, I need to know about my father. I need to know the truth about my father."

Margause stared into Mordred's pale blue eyes, eyes that closely mirrored her own. He was certainly her son—in physical resemblance and in more than physical resemblance.

"The truth?" she said. She was unsure how to proceed. Should she actually tell him the truth? And if she did, what might it lead to?

"You and I, Mother, we are both consummate liars," Mordred said. "Did I inherit that from you? Or was my true father one also?" His remark brought a thin smile to Margause's lips.

"I suspect the credit for that belongs to me," she replied.

"What have I inherited from my real father? Anything at all?"

"That, Mordred, remains to be seen. Let us hope you have."

"So he is a person from whom one might inherit something good?"

"Oh yes, perhaps the very best things one *could* inherit."

"So tell me, who is this paragon from whom I might inherit sterling qualities. Clearly *not* King Lot of Lothian, from all I have heard about the fellow."

"Lot had his virtues, Mordred, we must give him his due. But no, Lot wasn't close to being the man your father is."

"*Is?* So my father still lives?"

"Mordred, do you really not know who your father is?"

"No, I do not know who he is."

Margause breathed out a deep breath. "Then perhaps you are more naive and innocent than I'd thought. Perhaps *that* is what you inherited from your father."

"I'm sorry, Mother, but I have no idea who you are talking about."

"I wonder if I should really tell you."

"Mother . . . you *must* tell me."

"What if I don't?"

"Then I should be forced to wring your beautiful neck." The look on his face told her that he was deadly serious.

Margause laughed. "I believe you really might do that."

Mordred sat there in silence, waiting. He knew she would tell him, that in her heart she was *longing* to tell him. All he had to do was wait. And he was right.

"I'm quite surprised, Mordred," she said, "that with all your acumen, you haven't already figured it out for yourself. Mordred, your father is . . . the king."

The young man's face froze into an unblinking mask. The *king?* That possibility had never crossed his mind. His own true father was the *king?* Could that possibly be true?

"It's true," she said, as if reading his thoughts. "And I will readily confess that my seduction of that innocent young man isn't a deed I'm proud of. But as it gave us you, I can't say that I regret it. No, looking back now, I would have to say it was worth it. In addition to the pleasure it gave me at the time."

Mordred was struggling to take it all in. He was trying to process the implications of this stunning revelation.

"Mother," he said haltingly, "does that mean that I might actually be heir to the throne? The king and the queen have no children—yet I am the son of the king. Mightn't that make me the heir apparent?"

The queen, her head tilted thoughtfully, offered no reply.

"Mother," the young man went on, "I was the little boy who disappeared. Was *that* the reason I disappeared? Because someone didn't wish me to be the heir apparent?"

The queen didn't immediately reply. But when she did, she sang a little jingle:

> *"When a star falls on Beltaine Eve,*
> *So the Sybil once did say,*
> *A leopard born of a lion,*
> *Will Albion lead astray."*

"They were *afraid* of me!" Mordred expostulated. "They were afraid of me, so they tried to kill me. Because I am a bastard? Because . . . I am a child of *incest*? Was that *my* fault?"

"It was no one's fault," Margause said softly. "We didn't know."

"Well, *somebody* knew. Why else would they try to kill me?" Mordred rubbed both of his hands back and forth quickly atop his thighs, his torso making small rocking motions.

"Afraid of me, were they?" he finally said. "Well, then, I shall *give* them something to be afraid of!"

Margause, startled and yet pleased by her son's great outburst, hesitated a moment before speaking. Then she said, "Together, Mordred. We shall do it together. For now, though, we must exercise every caution. Above all, we must be wary of Merlyn."

"*Him* again! Well yes, we shall be wary of him. And when the opportunity arises, we shall rid ourselves of him."

"It is essential that we do."

"A little while ago you said you wanted to be alone. Now I wish to be alone, too. So I shall leave you to your solitude."

The queen nodded her understanding. But as the young man was nearly out the chamber door she sang out, "Mordred? A few moments ago you said you might have to wring my lovely neck. Mordred, do I really have a lovely neck?"

Her laughter reached his ears as he was closing her chamber door.

CHAPTER 33

Lute, never very comfortable with pomp and circumstance, had managed to endure the ceremony. Now he was officially a knight. Just as he'd hoped, the king himself bestowed the accolade. Gawain attached his left spur and Earl Thomas buckled on his sword. Lute felt honored, humbled, and grateful. Yes, now he'd achieved the very thing he had always dreamed of achieving. And yet . . .

And yet, for Lute, what should have been a joyous and triumphant occasion had turned into a rather painful ordeal. He'd put the best face on it and suffered through it; but it really had been an ordeal. This experience which should have filled the lad with inexpressible joy hadn't. Why *hadn't* it?

At the end of it all, Lute felt drained and empty. Was it because he could no longer luxuriate in the joy of anticipation, having now achieved his goal? Or was it something more than that? Lute felt all at sea.

When the other young fellows went off to celebrate, Lute chose not to go with them. He needed time to himself, time to sort out his feelings, if he possibly could.

He wandered out to the athletic fields which, in the late afternoon, were entirely deserted. He sat down alone near the top of the viewing gallery and looked down upon the empty sward where he'd worked so hard to perfect his riding skills.

To his surprise, he found himself *not* recalling all that he'd done here but rather thinking of home—of his mother, of his friend Robin, and especially of Jill. The kinds of thoughts he'd been having about Jill recently were not exactly brotherly thoughts. He had dreamed of her the other night, an exciting and rather disturbing dream.

Lute felt quite drawn to Gwendolyn, a cheerful, attractive young woman with whom he'd formed a genuine bond of affection. But the thoughts he'd been having of Jill lately were of a different kind. All the while he'd focused on his preparations for knighthood, his childhood friend and what she meant to him must have been percolating beneath the surface of his consciousness. Lute found this realization quite perplexing.

But why, he wondered, wasn't he more excited about being a knight? And why were these strange new desires surging through him? And when would he work up the courage to confront the king about the matter of his paternity? Maybe he *shouldn't*. Maybe he should simply go home and leave all of these things behind him. Maybe he should prepare to become the Earl of Sanham and then do his very best for his people. Why shouldn't he? It would be a good life.

By the time the afternoon shadows had lengthened, Lute had resolved nothing. All these things which had previously brought him joy—the excitement of the city, the grandeur of the king's court, his growing friendship with Gwendolyn, his newly achieved knighthood—now none of them held much allure. What should he do?

"You've been sitting here for quite some time," said a voice Lute knew he should recognize. "I don't wish to intrude upon your privacy, but I'm concerned about you."

Lute gave his torso a half turn and found himself staring into the face of the king.

"Oh, Sire," he said, dipping to one knee. "Yes, I suppose I've been here a while. Did the last bell sound the hour of five?"

"I don't know myself," the king said with a laugh. "I, too, have been rather pensive today. But if I am remembering correctly, you are Lute, the nephew of Earl Thomas. I know that we knighted you this morning, and it seems to me that we once rode together back before events took us to different places. Isn't that so?"

"Sire, dare I ask why *you* are pensive today?"

"You may, but I won't be able to tell you. It just happens sometimes. Sometimes a sadness comes upon me that I can't explain. It never lasts for long. And, given my responsibilities, I rarely have time to reflect upon it. Too many things intrude. But Lute, dare I ask you what sorts of things have been weighing upon *your* mind?"

Lute hadn't expected this opportunity for a private conversation with the king. As hesitant as he was, he knew he had to take this chance to confront the king.

"Sire," Lute said, the words almost sticking in his throat, "do you remember a young woman named Lyonore?"

The king's eyebrows lifted. His lips parted slightly and he stared wide-eyed at Lute. He was stunned by Lute's question.

"Lyonore?" the king said softly, hardly above a whisper.

"Yes, my liege," Lute replied just as softly. Nervously he pressed his teeth into his upper lip, waiting for the king to speak further.

"Why do you ask?" the king finally said. "Do you know of her?"

"Yes, Sire, I know of her. She is my mother."

The king continued to stare at the young man. Finally he expelled his breath through rounded lips. Then he nodded his head slowly.

"Lute," he said, "since the first time I saw you, I'd been wondering who it was you reminded me of, or why I thought I'd seen you before. Now I understand."

The two of them stood there in silence, each staring into the other's face.

"So yes, Lute," the king finally said, "I did once know your mother. I hope she and your father are well."

"Sire . . . I have never had a father. It has just been me and my mother."

The king reflected on Lute's words.

"Where is your mother now?"

"She's where we've always been, Sire."

"In Sanham? I sent messengers to look for her there. They were told she was no longer there and that no one knew where she'd gone or what had become of her."

"That's right, my liege, she didn't stay long in Sanham. Sanham isn't where we live."

"But why did she leave? Why couldn't she have left word where she could be found?"

"Sire, when my mother discovered she was with child, she chose to leave. In the condition she found herself, she was too ashamed to stay in Sanham."

"She was with child?"

"Yes, my liege. With me."

Neither man spoke. They just stared at each other. Finally the king said softly, "If Lyonore is your mother—and I don't doubt that she is—then tell me, Lute, who is your father?"

"Sire, as I said before, I have never had a father."

"What I mean is . . . Lute . . . you know what I mean."

"I do, Sire. And since my mother says she never had physical dealings with any other man . . . you, my liege, must have sired me."

The two of them stood without speaking for what must have been a full minute.

At last the king reached out and placed his hand on Lute's shoulder. He squeezed it gently and smiled a tight-lipped smile.

"Lute," he said softly, "it was no fleeting fancy. I hope you will believe that. I'll admit that I only knew your mother for a very few days. They were wondrous days, and during them she came to mean a great deal to me.

"She'd been gone from the city for perhaps a week before I realized she was gone. During that time I'd been caught up in the press of business. We had won a great battle, but there were other rebel forces that needed contending with.

"As soon as I could, Lute—it was a month or two later—I sent messengers to Sanham in search of her. They returned empty-handed, saying she wasn't there, and no one could say where she'd gone. So it seemed that she didn't want me to find her. I could only assume she no longer felt about me the way I still felt about her. Lute, I had to respect her wishes."

The king, looking a bit embarrassed by his self-justification, stopped and waited for Lute's response. Lute had none to give.

"Where did she go, Lute? Where have you and your mother lived during all this time?"

Lute shrugged. "Nowhere, really. Just in a small hamlet. The relative of a friend lived there. She kindly made a place for us in her small cottage."

"Lute, did your mother tell you about me? Was it she who sent you here?"

"No, Sire, she never told me about you. Not for sixteen years, not until a few months ago. Nor did she send me here. Indeed, she didn't want me to come. No, it was Merlyn who first told me I must come here. He told me that here was where my destiny lay.

"Right at this moment, though, I'm not so sure that he was right. I've been thinking lately that my destiny doesn't really lie here. It lies somewhere else. Perhaps in Sanham."

"Lute," the king said softly, "come here." He reached out and pulled the young man to him, hugging him tightly.

"You are my own flesh and blood. And the flesh and blood of someone I cared for very much. Lute, I hope Merlyn was right. I hope your destiny lies here."

"I don't know, Sire. I truly don't know."

CHAPTER 34

The storm broke upon the city out of a dark and ominous sky. Off to the west, the sky had filled with black clouds before the wind-driven rain arrived in gusty sheets. People scurried for cover. Flashes of lightning illuminated the highest tower in the citadel and the pinnacles of the great minster.

The storm grew ever fiercer. Streams of water gouted from gargoyles and rushed noisily into the city's stone-lined drains. A river of water poured down the great central stairsteps, emptying into the market square before finding its way to small channels that carried it toward the city's encircling river.

As the thunder and lightning crackled outside of Earl Thomas's stout dwelling, Merlyn and Lute, both concentrating deeply, were huddled over a chessboard, their heads nearly touching. Thomas and Julianna and Tom sat closer to the glowing coals in the fireplace.

"Check!" Lute suddenly declared, moving his knight to a square from which he threatened both Merlyn's king and his sole remaining rook.

"You rascal!" Merlyn shot back. "What devilish fellow taught you all those sly moves of yours, eh? Well, no point in going on now, Lute. The match is yours."

"Bested ya again, eh sir?" Tom proffered mirthfully, bringing chuckles from the others in the room.

"Helps to have a young brain, Tom. Speaking of which, today is just the day to begin teaching you to read and write."

"Read 'n write? What be the good o' that, sir?"

"Might well serve to keep you from a life of crime, Tom."

"A life o' crime? Bit late for that, innit sir?"

"One can always hope," Merlyn muttered, "though, sadly, I have a long and inglorious history of pursuing lost causes."

"Tom is no lost cause," Julianna declared adamantly.

"Mistress," Tom said, grinning, "you be one nice lady."

Merlyn did begin teaching the lad about the making of letters and the sounds they stood for. But after an hour of brain-racking studiousness, Tom begged to be allowed to go out and roam about in the city. The rain had slackened somewhat, though a chill wind still howled out of the darkened sky.

"Needin' ta clear me brain a bit, sir. And I can promise ya, sir, I won't go pickin' no purses—not now you've gone 'n saved me from a life o' crime."

"And don't go stealing any chickens, either," Merlyn grumped.

"Now you mention it," Lute said with a wink, "a thick and savory chicken stew might be just the thing for our evening meal."

"Don't be encouraging the lad, Lute. Not when we've got him on the straight and narrow at last."

"Bundle up good, Tom," Julianna said. "Don't want you catching a chill."

"Yes, mistress. Thank you, mistress," he replied.

❖

Mordred wasn't daunted by the storm. In fact, he believed it suited his purposes well, masking the actions he intended.

He would start simple. Rafe would be his first victim. All the others on his list were far more important than the ironmonger's apprentice, but each of them presented unique and difficult challenges. Not too difficult, of course, not for one so proficient as Mordred. And some of them could wait. Like Lamorak, the young knight who'd publicly humiliated Mordred by besting him in swordsmanship. His turn would certainly come, but for him there was no urgency.

Merlyn, though, was quite another matter. He had to be dealt with, and soon. Lute was high on Mordred's list, but it was Merlyn who posed the gravest threat. Mordred would need to formulate his plan for Merlyn and carry it out soon. His mother had some suggestions pertaining to Merlyn's demise, and to Mordred's thinking, they were definitely worth considering.

Eschewing the central stairsteps, Mordred moved quickly through a dark and circuitous little back lane as he made his way down to the city's market square. It was a devious route, well-suited to his devious purposes.

At the end of the dark lane he paused to take in the square. It appeared to be totally deserted. The wind and rain *whooshed* across the empty square, rippling the water in the central fountain. Feeling sure that no one was watching, Mordred began to slink around the edge of the square in the darknesses created by the overhanging upper stories of the buildings.

He quickly reached his goal, the doorway to the ironmonger's workshop. Positioning himself outside, he patiently awaited the moment he sought. He didn't have to wait for long.

Tom fingered the sheathed knife beneath all the layers of protective clothing Julianna had insisted he wear.

His timing had been impeccable. For just as he'd entered the tree-lined square on the city's second level, he saw a furtive figure ducking into a dark alleyway. It was Mordred. Tom had been prepared for a long, wet wait before catching sight of the young knight, if he caught sight of him at all. Today, good fortune was with him. At least to begin with.

Tom ducked into the dark little lane, being careful to stay well behind his prey. Mordred was moving rapidly; he seemed to have a specific goal in mind, though Tom had no idea what it might be. Clearly, though, the shagger was up to no good.

At the end of the lane, Tom halted just inside of its dark opening and watched as Mordred slunk on around the square. Tom watched as the young knight stopped outside a doorway and positioned himself against the wall right outside it.

"Now we'll be a-seein' 'xactly what the bastard is up to," Tom muttered to himself.

After a wait of no more than ten minutes, the door of the ironmonger's shop opened and Rafe stepped out. Mordred snatched the fellow's cloak, pulled him up close; he slashed his throat with the speed of a stinging viper. His startled victim had no chance; he died almost soundlessly.

Clutching the body of the ironmonger's apprentice tightly to him, Mordred glanced quickly about the square once more. Nary a soul in sight. Hoisting the body over his shoulder, he staggered across the square to the central fountain and lowered it in. Mordred spun about and studied the square a final time. He saw nothing but the driving rain as it washed away the thin trail of blood left on the cobbles of the square.

As a final precaution, Mordred moved over beneath the sign marking the entrance to the Fox & Grapes. He remained in the gloom of the doorway for a full five minutes; no one entered the square. Rain beat down mercilessly upon the body floating in the fountain. Blood from the gaping neck wound created a pinkish froth on the surface of the water.

Feeling secure, Mordred once more slunk around the outer edge of the square, passed across the bottom of the central stairsteps, and darted up a different small lane.

Tom glanced about also, then followed him. Mordred's lead was too great for the boy; within a few minutes he'd lost sight of his prey. Where had he gone?

Realizing that he might have been seen and that Mordred might now be lying in wait for him, Tom turned back and quickly retraced his steps. He made his way cautiously back up to the city's third level.

Once there, he secreted himself in a wall niche behind some hanging vines and waited patiently. After a quarter of an hour, Mordred hadn't appeared. Tom concluded that for now he was safe and that Mordred hadn't known his activities had been observed. Tom's own desires had been thwarted, though, so for now his vengeance—his recompense—would have to wait. Swallowing his disappointment, he headed for shelter.

Tom passed through the back entranceway to Earl Thomas's demesne, threaded his way through the sodden garden, and slipped quietly into the kitchen.

"Now just look at ye," the voice of Gwilym grumped, "just a-drippin' all over my clean 'n tidy floor. Someone'll hafta be moppin' up all o' that mess you're a-makin'."

"Had yourself a nice little outing, Tom?" Julianna asked, stepping quickly to the kitchen and frowning at Gwilym. "I hope you got all the fresh air you were wanting and didn't catch a chill."

"Chill, mistress? Nah, didn't catch no chill. Went out 'n got me blood circulatin' real good, mistress. It were quite a thrillin' experience. Eye-openin' as well."

"What do you mean by *that*, Tom?" said Merlyn, who'd just come into the room. "What do you mean, thrilling and eye-opening?"

"Just a manner o' speakin', sir, just a manner o' speakin'."

Merlyn gave Tom a piercing look. The little urchin shrugged his narrow shoulders and stared at his feet.

Merlyn's eyes, narrowed to a squint, remained on him.

❖

"My liege," said the guardsman as respectfully as he could, "it's really not a good idea for you to be up here. You could easily be struck by lightning, Sire."

"I've been struck by lightning once this week already," the king replied. "Lightning surely won't strike me twice."

"Please, Sire, it's really not such a good idea."

"Of course you are right, Yonec. I promise you that I will be down shortly. I thank you for your concern."

The guardsman, knowing he'd been politely dismissed, retreated back down the steps. In fact, it wasn't thundering any longer, though the wind and rain remained as fierce as ever.

The sodden king now stood alone atop the highest tower of the citadel; it was his favorite place for contemplation. Over the years he had stood here a great many times, and he'd experienced every kind of weather imaginable. He loved looking down and seeing his father's city displayed in all its myriad conditions. Fog and snow were among his favorites. Today's brutal rain storm wasn't far behind.

But he wasn't here to think about his father; he was here to think about his son. The son he hadn't known he had.

And he was also here to think about his son's mother. Why, oh why, hadn't he tried harder to find her? Why had he allowed her simply to slip away? Surely she had meant more to him than that. Now that all those events had been brought back to him, he couldn't escape believing that he had treated her shabbily. Yes, he *had*. There was no escaping that fact. And yet there really didn't seem to be much he could do to make up for it.

If he couldn't do right by Lyonore, he could at least do all he could to do right by her son. Who was also *his* son. He *had* to. But how? And shouldn't he also take the lad's own desires into consideration? He couldn't just impose his own will upon the boy. What if Lute didn't wish to be acknowledged as the king's son? What if he didn't wish to be drawn into all the machinations and complexities of life at court?

He believed that Lute was truly a fine young man, a young man to make any father proud. The king's own desire was to make the truth known; he would relish claiming the lad as his own.

But if he did, what would be the ramifications? And, how

fair would it be to the queen? It was still possible, after all, that he and the queen could have a son of their own—though at this point that possibility was growing remote. Even so, how hurt would she be to discover that the king had fathered a son by another woman, even if it had happened long before they'd been married, long before they'd even met? Perhaps she would be understanding. And then again, perhaps she wouldn't.

The king looked down upon the rain-lashed city, a place that he loved. It was this city that linked him most closely to his father, a man he hadn't really known. The one real link between the king and his father was Merlyn. Merlyn, so the stories went, had played a vital role in the king's own birthing. Just as he had also played a role in the begetting of this young man named Lute. *Merlyn.* With a grim smile, the thought crossed the king's mind that Merlyn had quite a lot to answer for. The king knew he was in the city, though he hadn't yet seen him.

The time had come to seek out Merlyn.

A powerful gust of wind suddenly whipped the king's thin woolen cowl right off his head. Holding firmly to the wall before him, he watched the garment as it whirled and twisted out over the rooftops of the city. He watched it blow all the way out beyond the distant wall where it finally disappeared in the grayness beyond.

"Sire?" came a worried voice from down below.

"You can put your mind at ease, Yonec. I'm on my way down right this moment."

CHAPTER 35

"You were not the only one, Mordred," said Queen Margause. "*All* the male children born on that day were taken away."

"Bastards!" Mordred replied viciously.

"It caused a great deal of ill-will, as you might imagine. But all the authorities, civil and ecclesiastical, were united in claiming it was necessary. In time, most folks learned to live with it. King Lot, to his credit, never did. He held it against the king until the day he died."

"What happened to all the other children?"

"Out of the dozens who were spirited away, you are the only one who has ever turned up."

Mordred fingered the ring. *He* was the one who was protected, the *only* one. Didn't that *prove* something? Didn't it mean that his was a destiny like none other?

"Mother, did the king know that, in trying to do away with all those children, he was trying to kill his very own son?"

"I can't say for certain, but I honestly don't think he had anything to do with it. If he had known about it, I don't think he would have allowed it to happen. No, but the one who *certainly* knew about it was Merlyn. I even wondered if he hadn't had something to do with 'the star falling on Beltaine eve.' "

"Truly?"

"He has strange and unusual knowledge, does Merlyn. I can't say if he actually hatched the thing himself, but I wouldn't put it past him. He knew what the king and I had done. And he knew it was the king who'd fathered you. Even King Lot didn't know that."

"Why would Merlyn have anything against me?"

"Mordred, don't pretend you don't realize what you are."

"I am *flesh and blood*, mother."

"Mordred, you are a bastard. Not only that, you are a bastard begotten of incest. Mordred, you are *doubly* a bastard."

Mordred flinched at his mother's harsh words.

"Mother, I am merely flesh and blood."

"Yes. You share none of the blame, none of the responsibility, for the misdeeds of others. You were a beautiful baby boy who would have grown up to be a beautiful young man— just as you have done. You have been wronged terribly. Now those who wronged you must pay."

"Including you?"

"No, not including me. Because in helping you pay back the others, I will atone for my part in things."

"Fair enough, Mother. So, shall we begin with Merlyn?"

"Yes. And here is how I suggest we go about it."

❖

The city was burning. Huge and ravenous flames were leaping upward from the lower levels. Towering plumes of smoke filled the sky. The fire moved onward and upward with nothing to blunt its rage. On the city's second level, the leaden roof of the minster collapsed in the intense heat, crushing everything beneath it. On the highest level, the towers of the great citadel swayed, buckled, and fell. The royal palace itself fell prey to the great conflagration.

Merlyn awoke in a sweat. It was that dream again! What could it portend? This was the third time he'd had it, and it defied comprehension. Was the city actually going to be destroyed? Or was this dream a premonition of something else? Sometimes the spirit that spoke to Merlyn in his sleep was far more opaque than Merlyn would wish it to be.

Were things coming to some sort of a head? It appeared that they were. He just wished he had a clearer sense of things. But his brain, normally crystal clear, had become muzzy of late. There were forces at work, apparently, that were determined to interfere with Merlyn's designs, forces determined to undermine all he had been trying to accomplish.

Mordred, he thought. It must have something to do with that dastardly fellow named Mordred.

❖

In the chamber shared by several of the newest knights, Colgrevaunce and Mordred were dressing themselves for the great banquet.

"You, young sir, look resplendent," remarked Colgrevaunce to Mordred with a smirk. "One might think you'll be sitting at the high table right next to the king."

"No, not quite next to the king. But not so far away either, my friend, not so far away."

"Mordred, have you heard the big rumor?"

"What big rumor?"

"So you haven't heard. Well, listen to this. The word that's going around is that the king has a grown son! So what do you think of *that*?"

Mordred stood stock still, his facial features frozen. "A son?" he finally murmured. "A grown son?"

"Isn't that truly amazing? No one's quite certain who it could be."

To Mordred, this seemed as good a time as any to tell his friend the truth. "Well, Cole, what you may find truly amazing is that—"

"And what some folks think," Colgrevaunce interrupted, "is that it's that young fellow we've befriended named Lute."

Mordred was left with his mouth hanging open.

"What did you say?"

"That innocent child Lute. He's the one that some folks suspect."

"Lute? The son of the king? That hardly seems likely," Mordred said.

"That's what I say also. Why in the world would anyone think that Lute could be the son of the king? It's just as likely that I would be the son of the king as Lute," Cole proclaimed. "My mother says that I'm not—though she wishes I was." Cole chuckled at his own remark.

"Maybe it *is* you, Cole," Mordred said.

"Yes. And maybe it's you." At that, they both laughed.

❖

Colorful banners bedecked the walls and pillars of the great hall. Fires blazed in the huge fireplaces and bright torches flamed in the wall sconces. Positioned about the hall were many pairs of royal guardsmen standing rigidly at attention, their green tunics emblazoned with red dragons, their pikes and halberds standing upright by their sides.

Seated at the two long side tables according to hierarchy were a great many young knights. Lute and the other new knights occupied the seats farthest from the dais, a dais which remained empty.

Now beginning to process into the hall came all the greatest nobles. First the lesser kings and their wives, then the dukes, then the earls. One of the last was Earl Thomas; he was walking with a cane, with Julianna holding his arm at his other side.

Of all the highest-ranking nobles, only one came in unaccompanied: Queen Margause. The last of the nobles, she walked slowly to her seat near the dais, confident that all eyes were on her.

Following a short pause, Bishop Baldwin also entered the hall. Not far behind him came the king's nephews: Gawain, Gaheris, Agravaine, and Mordred. They would be sitting at the high table, with Mordred occupying the seat at the far left end. Four seats remained empty in the center of the dais.

Then the royal trumpeters entered the hall. Four formed up on the right and four on the left, before turning to face each other. Lifting their horns, they sounded the royal fanfare. Everyone rose to their feet. When the fanfare sounded a second time, everyone went down upon one knee.

A hush fell over the room as the king and queen entered. Walking arm in arm they processed slowly across the red-and-green tiled floor between the two long side tables. Reaching the dais, they turned about to face the room. The king motioned for everyone to rise and be seated.

As everyone was settling into their seats, two final figures entered the room: Kay, the royal seneschal and the king's own brother; and Merlyn, the king's personal sage and counsellor. They strode quickly toward the high table. They reached their seats just as the king and queen did also.

When the four of them were seated, Bishop Baldwin rose to his feet. Speaking in Latin, he intoned a brief blessing. He ended by saying: "We offer our heartfelt thanks to the Lord Jesu Crist, his blissful Mother, and all the Saints of Heaven, beseeching them that henceforth till our lives end they may grant us their grace." His final "Amen" was echoed by many others throughout the hall.

As the meal progressed, Mordred carefully surveyed all the assembled knights and nobles. Several times he and his mother caught each other's eye. And a few times he caught Lute's eye. He also noticed Merlyn glancing his way once or twice. One of those times he smiled and nodded at the old fool, who seemed to return his nod grudgingly.

"Merlyn," Mordred thought, "your time is about to end, you meddling old fool."

But then he looked down the long room at Lute. "As for you," he said to himself, "if what Colgrevaunce says is true, your time must end *today*."

❖

Lute had to admit that he was enjoying himself. It was truly a splendid affair. There he was, sitting in the great hall of the king's majestic citadel, a brother-in-arms with the king's own knights, including the Knights of the Round Table. It was what he had wanted for as long as he could remember.

Lute luxuriated in the sights and sounds, in the joyous atmosphere, in the heartfelt comaraderie. *He* was one of them. *He* had been tested, and *he* had proved himself worthy. Now he was one of them.

He ran his eyes over the people seated at the high table. The king and his golden-haired queen. Lute's own enigmatic friend Merlyn, the man who was responsible for his being here now. The king's clutch of nephews, young men he'd now come to realize were also his cousins. His eye paused for a moment on Mordred, the one person in the room who made Lute uncomfortable. He was a strange young man, at times a scary young man, and Lute hadn't been able to make much sense of him.

It suddenly came to Lute that despite the presence of just about every important person one could think of, there was still one person who was absent. That person was Gareth, the young knight called "Beaumains" by all the young working lads in the city. Gareth wasn't there because he was off somewhere on adventures of his own. Or perhaps he wasn't there because he, like Lute, wasn't fond of pomp and ceremony. Gareth was a fellow who'd willingly humbled himself and spent a whole year working as a scullery knave in the kitchens, a year in which he'd endeared himself to the ordinary folks and become their beloved hero. They had embraced him as one of their own.

Lute remembered back to that first day as he approached the city, when the young men were chanting "Beau-mains, Beau-mains," and a tall young fellow had looked over and seen Lute and nodded a greeting to him. At that moment Lute had felt him a kindred spirit. Now, as he reflected upon this absent young man, he wondered if he wasn't still a kindred spirit.

Lute couldn't help admiring the young man's independent-mindedness and his penchant for going his own way. When he was needed, such as in the final battle with King Rience, Gareth had been there. Indeed, he had been the one who had initially taken down the rebel king. But he'd modestly shrugged off any attempts to bestow special honors upon him. Such things had little importance to him.

Lute wished he knew him better. Maybe in time he would. Perhaps it was Gareth's example Lute should emulate. Yes, Lute was enjoying himself on this very special occasion. But he found himself admiring Gareth for *not* being here.

The king was also enjoying himself. He was delighted to see Merlyn again. He was delighted that nearly every important nobleman in the land was here, and that nearly every one of his important knights was here. And he was hugely delighted to see Lute down at the far end of the table enjoying himself.

He was tempted, sorely tempted, to take advantage of the situation and announce to this august gathering that his own son was present here with them today. At one point he rose to his feet and was about to speak when he felt Merlyn's gentle tug on his sleeve. When his eyes met Merlyn's, his wise old advisor almost imperceptibly shook his head no. Had Merlyn known what he was about to do?

If so, he was right. He hadn't yet discussed matters with Lute and didn't know the young man's feelings. And he hadn't discussed them with the queen. It would be hugely unfair to both of them to spring it on them here in this fashion. He so greatly wanted to, he truly did. But he knew he couldn't.

But with all eyes now on him, he had to do something.

"Let us drink to the ladies!" the king cried out, raising his goblet, "to all the lovely ladies!"

"Hear him, hear him!" many voices rang out in reply.

Queen Margause's eyes met the king's, and she gave him a very bright smile—before she modestly dipped her head in reply to his toast.

CHAPTER 36

In the end, Lute concluded he *didn't* need Merlyn to tell him what he should do. Gareth decided things for himself and so could he. He knew he had proved himself and earned a place here through his own efforts. The king might be his father, but the king hadn't had anything to do with what he, Lute, had achieved at court. Lute had done it on his own.

It pleased him to realize that he was now free—free to stay and follow the expected path of endeavoring to become a knight of the Round Table; or free to do something entirely different. It was his own choice.

"Uncle," Lute said to the old earl when they were alone together in the earl's sitting room, "I plan to leave the city again quite soon. That is, if you have no objection."

"Oh? What is it you're thinking of doing, Lute?"

"Sir, a few months ago you said it would please you if I would agree to being your heir, that you hoped I would succeed you as the Earl of Sanham."

"I did, Lute. There's nothing would please me more."

"Sir, I would like to go to Sanham now. I know that the man who's been filling in there has been managing things quite well; I would like to go and learn from him, and also from old Wat. Perhaps in time, sir, I could learn to be a proper overlord."

"Lute, you are a natural. You have the intelligence, the

energy, the personal skills—and most of all, you have the right heart—to do splendidly. You have my whole-hearted blessing."

For a moment, Lute had to fight back tears. "Sir, that means the world to me. If you don't mind, I would like to set off immediately. I may not have a chance to see Merlyn before I leave. Could you let him know what I've decided to do?"

"Of course, Lute, of course."

"You be *leavin'* us, young master?" said Gwilym, who as usual had been eavesdropping.

"Yes, Gwilym, I shall be out of your hair within the hour."

"Oh, young sir, I'll surely be a-missin' ya. Won't be the same 'round here without ya. Kinda got used to havin' ya here."

Lute gave the grumpy old fellow a hug. "Thank you for those kind words, Gwilym. I shall I miss you, too. Shall I carry your warm greetings to old Wat?"

Gwilym pondered the idea for a moment. "Well, young master," giving Lute the tiniest nod, "I s'pose ya could."

Gwilym hadn't been the only one eavesdropping. So had young Tom. He'd been getting himself ready to give Raguel his evening exercise. Perhaps he would alter that plan just slightly by trailing along behind Lute for a few miles as he headed on his way. He could give that great black beast all the exercise he needed while practicing his skills in secret pursuit.

His shadowing of Mordred had continued over the last few days, but he hadn't had any opportunity to exact his vengeance. Perhaps he would try again tonight after exercising Raguel. As he thought about that, the fingers of his right hand unconsciously moved up and down on the knife sheathed beneath his cloak.

❖

After the banquet, Mordred re-garbed himself. He slipped a lightweight coat of mail over a padded undergarment and pulled a jet-black tunic over it. The tunic was emblazoned with a silver falcon whose flaring talons flashed against a field of black. Black—Mordred's favorite color. Just the right color for a black-hearted villain who'd dispatched the ironmonger's apprentice and who would soon give Merlyn his just deserts. Tonight, this black-hearted villain would kill the naive young man named Lute, a young fellow some folks believed was the king's own son. If that was so, then it would be one son killing another—a story as old as time.

Mordred took up a position from which he had a clear view of the back entrance to the old earl's demesne. After waiting for just over an hour his wish was granted. There came Lute, riding one of his horses and leading the other. The lad was setting out on a journey. So much the better. Mordred could follow Lute at a distance, and when he was well away from the city, he could remove the lad from his list.

Mordred trailed well behind Lute as he and his horses trotted toward the little postern gate on the city's highest level. Mordred gave him an ample head start before he too passed through the gate. The guards, recognizing him as the young knight who had taken down the rebel King Rience, nodded to him respectfully.

Mordred rode across the river bridge, waved a friendly greeting to the guards on that side, and spurred his horse on out into the great meadow. Lute and his horses were now dark specks a mile or so ahead of him. Mordred smiled to himself. He planned to enjoy every second of the next few hours.

❖

Tom had given Lute a fifteen-minute head start. With the encumbrance of an extra horse and his travel bags, Lute wouldn't be moving at a very quick pace, and anyway, Raguel could easily catch him up. But Tom didn't want to catch him up, just shadow him closely, and then, at some point, startle Lute by turning up out of the blue. He would enjoy that.

By now the gate guards were familiar with Merlyn's stray waif; whenever he rode past them when exercising the black, they hurled good-natured abuse at the little lad, who grinned back at them and called them shaggers beneath his breath.

The black snorted as Tom gave him his head. Raguel was eager to run and Tom was quite willing to let him to take the edge off all his pent-up energies. As the powerful horse stretched out his long legs and found his perfect stride, the chilly wind rushed against Tom's cheeks and whipped his long, shaggy locks behind him. Tom crouched in the saddle like a jockey; horse and rider moved with a oneness across the greensward.

But they hadn't gone a very great distance before Tom sensed that something was bothering Raguel. Tom could read the old devil far better than he could read the letters Merlyn was wanting him to learn. And he quickly picked up on the fact that Raguel was fretting about something. What bee did the old devil have in his bonnet now?

Tom brought his restive mount to a halt so he could try to assess the situation. Tom scanned the long meadow before him. Then he saw it. Maybe a mile or so ahead of him rode a lone rider; and this lone rider wasn't leading a second horse. It wasn't Lute. From such a distance Tom couldn't be sure, but this lone rider looked like an armed knight.

Tom patted Raguel's neck. "Is that it, Rags? Is that what's a-stirrin' up your wicked old bones?" Raguel snorted.

❖

Mordred was gradually closing the distance between himself and his prey. He was easily five miles from the city now, and by the time he caught up with Lute, it would be more like seven—plenty far enough to suit his purposes. Bringing his horse to a walk, he reached back casually into the small bag behind his saddle and groped about for an apple. He would eat one now to keep his energy up; and, when all was said and done, he would reward his noble steed with an apple also.

Lute, meanwhile, was lost in his swirling thoughts. He hoped he was doing the right thing. He felt a bit guilty about leaving the city without having spoken to either Merlyn or the king; and he knew it had been crass of him to leave without finding Gwendolyn and telling her what he planned to do. Lute hated goodbyes, though, and he tried to persuade himself that his absence from the city might be a temporary one—though his heart told him otherwise.

Despite those twinges of regret, he was excited about the challenges and new responsibilities he'd encounter in Sanham. The first thing he'd do when he got there was track down old Wat and his dogs. He smiled at the thought of them.

Also pleasing were his thoughts about Jill, thoughts that insisted upon popping up inside his head. His mind returned to that delightful day they'd spent picnicking up on Barham Edge, the day he'd proudly pointed out to her the direction in which Sanham lay. He remembered the sparkle in Jill's eyes as he told her about the little earldom to which he was heir.

Tom was frightened. He felt certain the armed knight ahead of him was trailing Lute. And though he couldn't be absolutely sure, he feared the pursuer was Mordred. Tom believed that had he been able to come up against Mordred in some dark alley, he'd stand quite a good chance against the shagger. But out here in the open meadow on horseback, his chances against a skilled and fully armed knight were nil. If that rider really was Mordred, and if he did take Lute unawares . . . well, that was something Tom couldn't let happen. He had to figure out a way to warn Lute.

All he could think of was to take himself out of sight beyond the crest of hills that bordered the lea and then ride like blazes in hopes of getting ahead of the black knight. It was a long shot, but it might be possible, depending on the pace the black knight maintained.

Tom turned Raguel's head and spurred him to a canter. They threaded their way up a narrow combe and found a firm trail on the other side of the crest of the hills. It was an old drover's trail. The rough surface wasn't conducive to speed like the soft grass of the meadow, but they didn't have a choice.

Mordred stepped up his pace. He'd drawn to within a quarter mile of Lute, who remained unaware of his pursuer. There was a good chance he would be on top of the young man before Lute even knew it. He could see that Lute was dressed in ordinary riding attire and wasn't even wearing his sword. It was *not* going to be a fair fight. In fact, Mordred thought, it wasn't going to be a fight at all. It was going to be an *execution*.

Lute planned to ride a few more hours and break his journey in the little village of Brinstow. From there, it should take him just two days to reach Sanham. When he got to Sanham, he would head straight for Old Wat's cottage. In his mind he pictured the rollicking welcome he'd receive from Shep and Em,

Wat's pair of rambunctious dogs.

Suddenly, Lute was jolted from his reverie by the sound of hoofbeats; they were rapidly approaching from behind him. He dropped the lead-line of his other horse and swung his mount sideways. At that very moment, an armed rider was upon him.

Spotting a small cutback that headed toward the lea, Tom pushed Raguel into it, and the great black beast, fully aware of his rider's sense of urgency, responded with alacrity.

As they topped the crest of the ridgeline, Tom saw an appalling scene a hundred yards away: a mounted rider, garbed in black, was riding roughshod upon a man who lay crumpled on the grass. The downed man was Lute. Tom and Raguel were too late.

CHAPTER 37

Mordred leapt down from his mount and unsheathed his sword. Lute lay curled up on the greensward, his arms clutching his torso, his eyes shut tight against the pain.

Mordred stood over him and looked down. "Lute?" he said. "I think you have a visitor, Lute."

Lute forced his eyes open and looked up. "Mordred?"

"Hello, brother," Mordred said.

"Brother?" Lute gasped, the effort of speaking hurting his ribs.

"Yes, Lute, that's what I've been told. That king of ours—your father and mine—must've been quite the lad there for a spell. First begetting you on one woman, then me on another. To look at him now, you would never have thought so."

"He's not that kind of man," Lute managed to say, wincing against the pain.

"*I* certainly don't mean to judge him. Given the kind of man *I* am."

"Mordred, what kind of man is that?"

"Brother, you are about to find out."

A hundred yards away, Raguel stood stock still. There was no telling what thoughts ran through that black demon's head.

Tom could see Mordred standing over Lute. The bastard was staring down at him and speaking to him. Tom couldn't hear what he was saying, but then he heard quite clearly Mordred's high cackling laughter.

The tip end of Mordred's sword was now resting on Lute's chest. Mordred seemed to be fiddling with it. Was he making tiny incisions on his victim's torso? Tom loathed the shagger for what he was doing to Lute.

As Lute lay there in an agony of pain, Mordred kept on inscribing tiny cut marks on his exposed chest. Was he writing something in Lute's flesh?

"Well," Mordred finally said, breathing a big sigh, "enough is enough. This little adventure has given me real pleasure, brother, but now it's becoming tiresome. Time to bring it to an end. Any parting words before you say 'good night'?"

"Mordred," Lute said barely above a whisper, "I really don't want the kiongdom. I never have."

Mordred laughed loudly. "No? Well, I really *do* want it. So for me, it wouldn't be such a good idea to have an older brother hanging about. Who knows? One day you might have a change of heart and become just as greedy a bastard as I am. So, with heartfelt apologies, I must now say au revoir!"

But Mordred, being the total bastard he was, couldn't bring himself to end his taunting. In a final gesture, he leaned down and placed his sword flat across Lute's neck. Leaving it there, he straightened up above Lute and looked down at him. Blood was oozing from the series of little cuts he'd made on Lute's chest. He could just make out what he'd inscribed there, and it brought a thin-lipped smile to his face.

"Lute," he said, "if you're quick enough, you might beat me to it. Let it never be said I didn't give you a fighting chance."

That was the moment when the entire meadow reverberated with a spine-chilling scream.

"*What the . . . ?*" Mordred cried out, involuntarily jerking his head in the direction from which the sound was coming. His eyes took in the sight of a great black stallion rearing up on his powerful hind legs.

In that very brief moment when Mordred had turned his eyes toward the screaming beast, Lute snatched at the sword. He managed to grasp it with his right hand and lift it up.

Realizing what was happening, Mordred bent down and thrust out his hands to grip the naked blade that threatened him. Ignoring the pain, he squeezed the blade as tightly as he could. But the blood-slicked sword kept on moving toward his abdomen. And then it slid straight on into his body.

As the weapon impaled him, Mordred's mouth formed a silent oh. His eyes looked down into Lute's. It seemed to Mordred there was a sadness in Lute's eyes, a sadness Mordred didn't understand.

Then Mordred's grip on the weapon loosened. His body fell sideways and tumbled down on the grass, twitching.

Raguel's scream had caught young Tom unawares, nearly causing him to tumble from the saddle. By the time he got his shattered nerves under control, he saw that things out on the lea had changed. Mordred was now the one who was down, while Lute was struggling to right himself.

Tom spurred Raguel across the short distance to where Lute, now up on one knee, swayed unsteadily. Tom flew down off the horse and clutched his friend, steadying him and then helping him to his feet.

"Water?" Lute whispered.

Tom snatched his own water pouch from behind Raguel's saddle and handed it to Lute. Lute was now leaning back against his own horse for support.

Lute gulped down several large swallows, then he dashed some of the cool water against his face and chest.

"Goodness," he said in hardly more than a whisper. "That feels so good."

"How does ya, sir?" Tom asked softly.

Lute shook his head. "Not so good. More than likely there's some cracked ribs in there. Don't know what else might've been busted up when Mordred rode over me. Anyway, nothing too serious, I hope. At least the cuts on my chest don't look so deep. Old Wat will surely know how to fix me up."

"Old Wat?"

"The fellow I'm on my way to see."

"Oh, sir, ya can't be a-goin' on now. I'll help ya get back ta the city. Merlyn's the one you be needin' now."

"I'm sure you're right, Tom, but I'm not going back. I'm going on."

"Truly, sir, that don't sound so wise ta me. But if'n ya really mean ta do that, p'haps I oughter come along with ya."

"No, Tom, what you ought to do is go back and tell my uncle and Merlyn what's happened. Merlyn, especially, needs to know about Mordred." Tom nodded glumly in agreement.

It took half an hour for Lute to steady himself, physically and emotionally, and prepare to set out.

"Tom, tell Merlyn I hope to see him soon in Sanham."

"I shall, sir. And sir? Could I ask ya a favor?"

"Of course you can."

"Would ya mind, sir, if I was ta come along with 'im?"

Lute ruffled the lad's hair. "You darn well better, Tom." Tom grinned.

Wincing, Lute climbed back up on his riding horse, his warhorse trailing behind him once again on a long lead.

"Take care, sir! Hope ta see ya soon!" Tom shouted after him. Lute gave him a wave of acknowledgment.

Tom stood beside Raguel and watched as Lute rode off on his way. He and the black remained watching until Lute and his two steeds were mere specks on the horizon.

Mordred's horse was grazing a few yards away. It was a beautiful mount and Tom wondered what he should do with it. But, being wise in the ways of the world, he quickly knew he must leave it right where it was. He'd best get himself away from here as soon as possible. If anyone found out he'd had anything to do with the death of Mordred, it would surely bring some serious troubles down upon him.

Tom looked down one last time at Mordred. There he lay, this stinking pile of horse manure against whom Tom so badly had wanted his revenge. But Lute had beaten him to it.

Still, Tom was determined to have a part in it. Unsheathing his knife, he leaned over Mordred. For some time, he'd wanted to slit the bastard's throat, and now that time had come. Tom positioned the naked blade just beneath the man's chin. He jabbed with it and felt it prick the slimy bastard's skin.

Suddenly, Tom had second thoughts. What was he *doing*? Was it right and proper to mutilate a dead body? *No.* That was the act of a cowardly cur.

"Bloody hell," Tom muttered. Reluctantly, he re-sheathed his knife. But when he looked down at Mordred once more, something caught his eye. On the smallest finger of the man's right hand Tom saw a golden ring. He stooped down and ran his fingers over it. It was on pretty snug. But if he worked at it, he could surely pull it off.

Then the thought of Merlyn entered the lad's head once more. Merlyn wouldn't approve of what he was about to do.

Tom was torn. He wanted the ring. But, his conscience getting the better of him, he let go of the hand and watched it flop back onto the grass.

Tom sighed again. That old geezer's gone and got me on the straight and narrow, he thought, just like he wanted. Well, drat it!

Was there anything else he should do? Tom decided there wasn't. As for Mordred, Tom would leave the shagger to the crows—a fit ending for such an evil bastard.

Tom climbed up onto the back of Raguel. Without a backward glance, he set off for the City.

CHAPTER 38

Mordred lay still. Blood oozed from the wound in his abdomen. It was a deep wound, though not nearly so deep as it would have been had he not thought to wear the mail shirt beneath his habergeon.

As the darkness of evening descended, the fingers on Mordred's left hand suddenly twitched. They scrabbled at a nearby clump of grass.

Consciousness began returning to his brain. Mordred was alive. Just barely, but alive. He lay there unmoving for a long time as the senses in his body slowly stirred.

As he lay there only half alive, a thought stole silently into his awakening brain. Mordred's thin lips smiled and his mouth formed silent words: "Mordred, the little boy who disappeared. Mordred, the little boy destined to become king."

On his little finger, Mordred could feel the ring. Once it had been hung about his neck in an attempt to protect him. And it had worked. Mordred's ring was his magic talisman.

"Mother," Mordred whispered softly to the empty air, "it seems that we are still here. And mother, it seems that we still have things to do."

Mordred envisioned his beautiful mother, sitting alone in her private chamber. She was sipping a glass of sparkling red wine. She smiled at him.

"Oh yes, Mordred," he imagined her saying to him. "We still have things to do."

❖ ❖ ❖